The Night Porter

Mark Barry

The Night Porter
Published by Green Wizard 2014
© Green Wizard 2014

This book is sold subject to the condition that it shall not by way of trade or otherwise, be lent, resold, hired out, or otherwise circulated without Green Wizard's prior permission and consent in any form of e-transaction, format, binding or cover other than that in which it is published and without a similar condition, including this condition, being imposed on the subsequent purchaser.

First published in 2014 by Green Wizard
Green Wizard, Southwell, Nottinghamshire
Greenwizard62@blogspot.com

Cover design by Dark Dawn Creations

This is a work of fiction. Any resemblance of characters to actual persons, living or dead, is purely coincidental.

ISBN-13: 978-1495495380
ISBN-10: 1495495388

Acknowledgements

My gratitude is unbounded when it comes to my (long-suffering) editor, Mary Ann Bernal.

I wouldn't like to work with me, but she's worked on every novel I have produced, and she does it with a wry smile and only the occasional explosion.

When you see what I've attempted in this novel, you will understand why her patience may have been stretched and pulled to its very limit.

It's not often a New Yorker displays the patience Mary Ann does so, as scant reward for all the work she has done for Green Wizard in the past two years, and until we become household names (ha), someone *very like her* gets in the novel.

I'd also like to thank Tony Barry for supporting the covers, which Dark Dawn Creations design and create.

Thank you also to the software genius that is Stephanie Matulich for solving some serious manuscript errors, which were entirely of my own making.

And thanks to the wonderful Ngaire Elder and Mary Quallo for their beta reading, unyielding support, advice, and cheerleading.

And occasional jokes.

Most of all, I would like to dedicate this novel, which is possibly my best so far – and possibly one I will never surpass on so many levels – to my dear friend, author and Indie Radio DJ, Mackenzie Knight who passed away recently at a still youthful age. She was one of the good guys.

Her beautiful voice is still in my head and always will be.

The Ceremony for the Arkwright Literary Fiction Award

Is held every second November at the Arkwright Memorial Theatre in Wheatley Fields, a prosperous town in the Midlands of the United Kingdom.

The ceremony is a glittering occasion, and the award for each category – colloquially known as an **"Alf"** – is highly prestigious and potentially lucrative for an author.

Many shrewd literary pundits consider the Arkwright Ceremony to be the world's fourth most important literary awards ceremony, after the Booker, the Gamora and the Whitbread. Category winners can expect to earn substantial advances, commissions, and royalties from their work for many years to come.

The grand prize is the Gold Award for Best Writer – a highly sought after accolade. Following the award, winners can write their own royalty cheques and publishing contracts. Authors are nominated over the internet, subjected to an online vote, and judged by established writers, scribes, authors, critics, commentators, TV analysts, readers and academics as part of a final panel. The awards are restricted to current residents of Great Britain and the USA. The 2013 award is, for the first time, being televised live on cult satellite culture and literature show, *Brilliant Books* and a half hour highlights show on the BBC.

This year, due to changes in the demographics, and the rapid increase in the popularity of e-books, interested readers were encouraged to vote for **Independent Publishers and Authors.** This category includes self-publishers and those who produce e-books exclusively for organisations like *Banks and Nesbit, KoKo, ProsperoReader, Splat!words* and the ubiquitous market leader, *Tarzan*, with their invention, the **Spark**, a dominant e-reading device. The inclusion of 'Indies' has led to vehement, inflammatory, tub-thumping protests from traditional publishers and traditionally published authors, leading to severe, often violently expressed internet debate, a veritable barrage of letters to the *Times*

Literary Supplement and two resignations from the Judges Committee.

However, due to the overwhelming generosity of the sponsors, the Arkwright Family and Heirs, a benevolent family trust based in Wheatley Fields since 1860, protestors who objected to the Indies on some principle or other, would miss out considerably.

There is the TV coverage to consider. The media interviews. The literary supplements. The internet and social networking coverage. Authors – and judges – are interviewed in a series of managed press conferences. There is the social dimension to consider: the chance to meet with friends and authors. There is also the money.

The winner of the Gold Award – the Best Writer Grand Prize[1] – collects £1m.

The trophy itself, a sculpted hand holding a fountain pen chiselled in gold and amber, is highly sought after. Furthermore, the author keeps the trophy in-perpetuity. Each of the categories attracts a bursary prize of £100,000, plus a solid silver version of the above trophy.

Also, at a time when the average author struggles to make any sort of living, the Committee pays expenses for *each* nominee – forty of them this year. There is the two weeks, all expenses paid stay in a top quality hotel. The lavish hospitality at the Ceremony itself – and some of the post-ceremony parties – is legendary in the literary community.

Considering all this, after thinking about it, comparing the strength of their convictions, with all this added value, the two resignators (once best selling contemporary fiction authors who had seen their income

---

[1] Winners of this tend to be household names and because of the desire of the Trust to spread their influence and reputation, populist writing is encouraged, which eliminates the slightly elitist agenda of the other award ceremonies.

halved since Tarzan launched the Spark and who had been writing professionally for an average of a hundred and seven years between them), reconsidered their position and asked for their resignations to be ignored, which happened.

Some of the authors are allowed to stay at the best hotel in Wheatley Fields. This is **The Saladin Inn** at the junction of Eastgate and the Charlestown Road, nearest the High Street. First built in the 13th Century, there are still original timber beams and several cornices and etchings, which date back to that time. It is steeped in history and from its vantage point at the coaching crossroads, its welcoming edifice had witnessed the history of England.

From the latter years of the savage Normans, the power–crazed Plantagenets; the wise Saracen himself, the Magna Carta, Poitiers, Agincourt, the Field of the Cloth of Gold; the Armada, the Plague, the English Civil War, Blenheim, the Madness of King George, the butchery of Waterloo, the Dark Satanic Mills, and the senseless slaughter at the Somme.

Famously, it was the last resting place of Charles I before he was handed over to the marauding Scots in the town named after him at the conclusion of the English Civil War. The room where he stayed is now known – perhaps predictably – as the Charles the First Suite. There are twenty four rooms including the King's Suite, the Queen's Suite and the King and Queen's Suite. If you have to ask the price of the latter room, you cannot afford it. It is never displayed, and it is never discussed by those who stay there. The hotel is an avowedly full service hotel with a full complement of staff, and it is almost always fully booked.

Four authors are staying there this year; two UK and two from the USA. No nominated author in the forty eight years of the award has ever turned down the chance to stay there, and none are expected to do so in the future.

Part 1

How I Became A Night Porter (and Other Stories)

I am a night porter.

I am *the* night porter.

I have always been a night porter. I have had no other position, even as a young man. I will make a prediction and say I shall always be a night porter. I am a hard worker and thus, have no dreams of retirement: I like work. I am sure that many of you reading this picture a night porter as an elderly gentleman (perhaps a slightly raffish figure, or a greying chap with spectacles, squinting over his register; or an immaculately dressed ex-Batman from the war, or perhaps, a brilliantine-groomed ex-butler retiring from service in the Shires), and while you would be mistaken in my case, there is clearly nothing stopping a professional night porter from continuing to port well past retirement age.

I am a young man, not an old one. I am middle aged, actually, in terms I grew up with, but now, there is no such thing. Erikson is dead. You know, the fellow who talked about the Seven Stages of a Man's Life (in those sexist days of the forties and fifties).

Nowadays, you are young, or you are old: There is no in-between. I consider myself young, though there are many people of my chronological age who have taken shelter in the other camp and are more than happy there.

Biography leaves me cold (and lucky for you, so does autobiography), but it is important to mention that I became an apprentice night porter as a student in a hotel in Plymouth called the Continental when I was nineteen. That's sixteen years ago, if you must know. I was a student in Devon and was working part time in the kitchens at night while I studied something dull and pointless in the day.

I would like to say I had a plan, a structured approach to eventual night porterdom, but I started out on my journey with a moment of fortune, even if it resulted from the misfortune of another.

Early one evening, the hotel's incumbent night porter – an urbane fellow in his fifties called Neil – came to work as usual, offered his colleagues a pleasant greeting, changed into his uniform, let himself into one of the hotel's three hundred rooms and blew the back of his head off.

To do this, he used his grandfather's old service revolver (which had seen service at Tobruk), and because Neil made a terrible mess of the wallpaper, the room had to be taken out of commission for a good three months.

It was one of the best rooms in the hotel and had been freshly decorated. Management was furious (hotel management being a brutally unsentimental and occasionally, clinically psychopathic state of mind), and the Continental's higher echelon believed that Neil did it on purpose. As a protest. As an industrial thing.

I will never forget Marie O'Gorman, the top woman there, a real shoulder pads and high heels type, lamenting his decision to come to work to shoot himself, as if it was the most selfish thing that a man could do. Not once did she offer condolences to his friends in the hotel. Not once did she express sympathy. She openly described Neil as a man whose selfishness had cost her around ten thousand pounds, which meant she would have to spend good management time creating an Emergency Financial Plan for presentation to the Directors in Chicago. I remember being shocked at how harsh she was, but nowadays, older, wiser, I wouldn't bat an eyelid. I've met hotel managers who make Marie O'Gorman look like Mother Teresa. They all do it for effect, I'm sure. The higher you go, the harder these people perceive they need to be. I suspect (with the exception of the clinical psychopaths among them, who have no feelings one way or another) that they are much softer at home, and much of their callousness is an act.

Anyway, I digress. The unfortunate business of Neil's suicide left the hotel without a night porter, and when Bill Dixon, the night manager, was beating himself around the head wondering what to do, as he was a busy man and couldn't spend his entire night sitting behind the reception desk, I seized my chance. I happened to be in his office listening to his endless mutterings as he sorted out some wage underpayment issue or other. Seizing the moment, I volunteered for the post. It was one of those moments I instinctively knew I would regret forever if I missed it, and so I went in for the kill.

Dixon looked at me askance. With a patronising tone, he asked me whether I had experience. I said no. I didn't have much experience in anything, I said. I was young, enthusiastic and full of potential and best of all, I liked working in the darkness, I liked being up late at night, and I liked listening to people's stories. That doesn't make you a night porter, Dixon said to me dismissively, and I replied firmly, yes, it does, that's *exactly* what being a night porter is all about. That is the core of it. That is the essence of it. You can train me to do the rest, I concluded, which surprised me, as I was not – and am not – particularly strident or assertive.

I must have been convincing because without much fuss, he told me to take off my KP whites and get upstairs to the changing room. In there, was a spare uniform, which fitted. A pressed white shirt. The hotel livery on a pale lemon-striped vest waistcoat, grey trousers (slightly big for me, but I was wearing a belt on my jeans, and I got away with it), and incredibly shiny black shoes.

Dixon gave me an hour's training, and then went off with Forensics, and to calm down the shaken elderly couple unfortunate enough to be next door to 247 when Neil's gun went off. I would have been shaken, too, the sound of the gunshot. The metal crushing bone as it escaped the skull, the shriek of the dead. Not what you expect at an expensive, full service hotel – though now, after sixteen years, after all my experiences as a professional night porter, I can tell them that suicide and death are the twin subtexts of the narrative behind every hotel, though you never see that discussed in the brochures.

You would never see that as an agenda item at a Chicago Board meeting.

I continued to study for a while, but at the end of the second year, I made the decision to make being a night porter my career and left Uni. A delighted Bill Dixon gave me unlimited overtime as a reward, which worked out at five twelve hour nights plus any two, and it was a much more interesting prospect than my course. I had never particularly got on with the students there, who were a dull bunch. I certainly didn't enjoy my subject, and the lecturers were dry and out of date. No, it was an easy decision to specialise.

However, my father, with whom I had experienced a strained relationship, was livid – apoplectic, even – and because of the decision, my father and I no longer have a strained relationship, or any relationship at all (my mother is dead).

This was sixteen years ago. I understand he married again, to Britney, a much younger woman from Basingstoke whom he met at work, and as a consequence, I have a half-brother and a half-sister whom I shall never meet. He wanted me to be something, I know he did. An architect, a solicitor, a chartered accountant, a managing director. When I told him that I was going to *be* something, a *night porter,* his face was incandescent. A contorted look of frustration and rage.

That was the last expression I ever saw on his face.

A pity, really.

Everyone should have a dad, and I think of him on occasion, even though he wasn't the best dad in the world. I miss him in the sense I would miss a car, a bank account, or the ability to listen to music. Things you take for granted. It left a hole in my life, which took a while to fill, but fill it did as I became more and more skilled in my profession. To me, there's nothing more professional than being a night porter, and I carry out my duties to the best of my ability. There isn't a surveyor, or a lecturer, or a psychologist who is more dedicated to their role than I.

I port with zeal.

The Saladin

A night porter needs a hotel in which to port: And here I am, behind the mahogany reception of The Saladin Inn full service hotel in Wheatley Fields. As it is quiet (and has been for a week or so), I walk across the carpet to the front door and look out onto the High Street. The streetlights penetrate the darkness, coating the concrete in a pale, obtrusive tangerine. I haven't heard a car pass in an hour, and all is silent, except for the groan of the wind. It has been raining, and the pavement glistens. Puddles punctuate concrete heading in both directions.

I look over at Dorothy's, the upmarket ladies boutique, on the corner for decades, if not eons. Not three months ago, the area was flooded in a flash flood, the likes of which had even elderly residents scratching away the topsoil of their memories.

Twenty millimetres fell in about an hour and a half and the segment of the High Street on which I gaze right now, that night resembled rapids.

Seriously.

Rapids.

Houses down on Steeple Street flooded, and if there was such a thing as a state of emergency in the prosperous town in which you live and I work, it would have been declared, the sirens sounding over the town.[2]

---

[2] I'm being facetious here. Sirens are banned in Wheatley Fields. Even Police sirens. It is incumbent upon them to race down Eastgate in emergencies with a Constable waving a bright yellow-chequered flag out of the passenger side window

The Bramwell pub – the second most vulnerable to closure of the nine Wheatley Field's hostelries and situated in a hollow, which acted as a repository for the water flow – was soaked to the rafters. It will take it six months to re-open, and local gossip indicates it might never re-open at all.

I've enjoyed a pint of Bishop's Mitre in there, and closing would be a shame. The chap who runs it is an ex-serviceman called Michael, and he deserves success, I think, and even if he were a horrible man (and there are two hostelries in the town run by such), I still wouldn't wish the pub to close. You can judge the health and vitality of a town like The Fields by the number of pubs it contains, or, as a friend of mine puts it, the number of a town's *convivariums:* places where people meet, encounter, congregate, laugh, whisper, plot, and scheme.

The wind at night is different from its daytime counterpart, and there's something refreshing about it. Something brisk. I let the wind embrace my face, and I close my eyes. I wonder, on occasion. Had Neil appreciated these little night time things, he might still be here. Sixteen years older and sixteen years less dead.

Six weeks ago, I heard about the coming authors from Cat, the manager. She spoke to me directly and also backed that up with a memo. The night I heard, Cat was waiting for me when I arrived at work.[3] As I walked to

---

and shouting a lot. Parish Council ordnance: Emergencies are declared by word of mouth so not to jar the prosperous locals, entitled, as they are, to their peace and quiet.

[3] Which in itself, was a worry. I'm not a fan of management, and one of the great advantages of being a night porter is that we work in different time zones, by and large. They do their thing – a good night porter does his. The Saladin does not have a night manager, though many of the big

the desk, unbuttoning my raincoat, she leaned against the reception desk and studied some papers.

Catriona Brahms (who likes to be called Cat), is at least six years younger than me and, rumour has it, has her eye on a big job in the City, one of the chains. She is cocksure and ambitious. Attractive, though I seldom indulge at work. Far too dangerous.[4] Ash blonde, which she occasionally lightens, with a tightly wound figure topped with curves. I like her long legs, which, in the summer, she shows off on occasion, wrapped in a suitably staid pair of tan tights for the sake of professionalism.

More than one man – and memorably, following crossed-wires of considerable proportion, a woman – has chanced their arm on asking Cat for a night out, but she has never said yes, and people have lost their jobs and room bookings because of it.

Generally, I avoid her. It is not that I dislike her any more than any other manager I've worked for. Not *in*

---

business hotels do, and I have worked in a few, but one of the attractions of The Saladin is that I don't have to be micro-managed. In effect, I am the manager as well as the night porter. Yes, I like that feeling. I enjoy the responsibility and the opportunity to strut my stuff managementwise, so to speak.

[4] I know several people who have had to leave good, solid, well paid jobs they enjoy because of relationship breakups with work colleagues. Especially the bad ones. One fellow, the night manager at a hotel I worked down in Hemel Hempstead, walked in on his long-term girlfriend, the Head Receptionist, administering, er, oral comfort to a guest in the linen cupboards. He suffered a nervous breakdown in the end and had to leave, though, I am pleased to report, he pulled himself together and is now working as a Bar Manager at a golf resort on the west coast of Scotland. His girlfriend? Don't know – I hardly ever spoke to her: She worked in the daytime. How could they work together after that? I am sure that YOU know similar stories. Workplace relationships? Just say no…

particular. On the contrary, actually: She's quite nice, for the profession. It's just that she likes to think of herself as the ultimate professional, and so do I, so it's not good for the two of us to occupy the same space. It defies immutable laws of physics. Already I was feeling uncomfortable, as if our co-existence might cause a rift in the space-time continuum leading to the formation of a matter-vacuuming black hole. And no one wants that.

Gingerly, I took up my position behind the reception desk and logged onto the PC.

'Hello, Cat, how are you.'

'I'm fine, mate. How are you?' Cat calls everyone mate, like some rugby player at club night. To my knowledge, she has never used my given name. I put this down as a generational thing – the young don't bother with names all that much – and I am not offended by it.

'I'm fine. What brings you to these parts in the dark?

'Have you heard of the Arkwright Author Awards?'

'I can't say that I have, no, Cat.'

'It's like the Oscars, except they call it the Alfs.'

'The Alfs?'

'Arkwright Literary Fiction Awards. Based here.'

'In The Saladin?' I replied.

'No, in the town. Down at the Memorial Theatre. Our hotel is involved, though. Exciting stuff.'

'Is it? How so?'

'We're taking four shortlisted authors as guests for a fortnight in November. And I'm telling everyone here that they are to be treated like rock stars. Whatever they want, they get. It's quite an honour for our hotel to be involved. There will be press, TV, bloggers...'

I noted that Cat had her hair in a bun, which pulled back the lines around her eyes. Alongside her formal grey suit, she resembled a librarian about to retire. She looked much better with it down, but I valued my role at The Saladin, so I filed that mental note in the cabinet labelled Observation rather than the one labelled Well-

Meaning Advice. I limited myself to something bland instead.

'That's good news, Cat.'

'Mate, the Awards Committee is spending an absolute fortune with us. They are hiring the four best rooms. Three meals a day. An open bar...'

'...an open bar?' I could see carnage on the horizon.

'Deffo, and it will be up to you and Martin to see that isn't abused by the other guests here at the same time. They have booked another five rooms for delegates, and judges, and VIP's who will be coming and going throughout November and not only that, they have booked double rooms in the hotel for the week immediately prior to the ceremony – just in case.'

'That's a nice bit of business.'

'You're not kidding. And that's not all. A press conference is planned for the hotel. Can you imagine the bar bill and the catering? The extra room bookings?'

'Woosh.'

Cat leaned over, her polo neck jumper, the colour of fresh fallen snow, the brightest thing in the ancient hotel – so bright, I nearly flinched. 'You are going to be fundamental to the day-to-day enjoyment of their stay at The Saladin. Whatever these four want, they get.'

'I'd do that for any of our guests,' I reply defensively, and unnecessarily.

'I know you would. You come highly recommended, seriously. I am not having a pop: I'm telling you how important this is going to be.'

Anyone complimenting me on my professionalism immediately finds themselves in my good books. 'Thank you, Cat.'

'If they want beer from the One Stop, find some. If they want cat food, hair grips, shoes, CD's, books, find some or send Martin Sixsmith and take over the bar.'

'Will do, Cat.'

'The Alpine Hotel on the other side of Wheatley were lobbying like mad for this deal, and though they got a piece, it wasn't a chunk like this. This could see us through the winter. You weren't here last year, and we struggled. We lost money. If everything goes well, we'll make the Board happy. Don't forget the Dick Whittington Chain.'

The Dick Whittington Inn is a chain of cheap walk-in motels, which run with a receptionist and six cleaners. Food in the reception dispenser. No night porter. No site manager. No bar. No food. Bed and out. They had changed the face of hotels in Britain and everyone in my profession feared them because they kill jobs faster than a speeding bullet and make any notion of professionalism in the hotel world redundant.

'What about them?'

'Kevin told me that they've been having a look at the books. Head office said if we have a bad winter – '

'Say no more. I'll be on the alert.'

'And keep an eye on Kerry, Gavin and Sixsmith. They're all local.'

I noted her comment with a simple nod, and she continued. 'We're lucky that Joshua Arkwright lived here. Victorian Philanthropist. Colossal amount of money. Usual stuff. Textiles. Mining in Africa. All that King Solomon's Mines Empire thingy.'

'And his Trust owns the theatre?'

'Plus several of the Prebends and that gorgeous old summerhouse behind the clinic opposite The Three Steeples. Lot of fuss there last year. A fire and an explosion with several dead.'

I nodded enthusiastically. 'Yes, I heard about that.'

'No one ever got to the bottom of that. They own thousands of acres of farmland and the Articles of Association of the Trust means that they can spend money around the world, but 51% of it must always be spent in Wheatley Fields. Mary Beth, the lady who organised the booking, was very informative. Please her, and we'll keep the parasites away,' Cat said, revealing a layer of passion I didn't know existed. I always thought she wanted out, a bigger job. I might have been wrong.

'You must like it here, Cat.'

She picked up her papers and smiled for the first time.

'I do, yes. I'm going to make it secure before I go if it kills me. But that's later. I'm off. Been a tough one. Mrs Purefoy in eight has been a pain. Says she's lost loads of cash and that Magda has taken it. Pure racism if you ask me, but don't get involved, okay? Refer her to me, yeh?'

'I won't. And I will.'

'Laters, mate.'

'Sleep tight.'

I still read newspapers, and I follow the arts, but I don't read books. Or write. I've never written anything outside work, a memo, a note. Had I sufficient ability, I would have liked to paint still life paintings. The Saladin has many on its ancient walls, and I can stare at them for hours. However, I can barely hold a brush to gloss the skirting in my flat, so art was out as a career option.

Is writing art?

I settled back with my chocolate muffin and poured a cup of black coffee from my flask.[5] I thought about what it meant to be an artist, for no other reason than I could.

Cat came to see me one night shortly after, and she handed me a note in a thick brown envelope.

'Got the four names.'

'Of the scribes?'

'That's right. I wrote this the other night,' she says, pointing to the envelope. 'I got a bit inspired! It's about

---

[5] Hot drinks are free here, of course, they are, just boil the kettle, but I prefer to take a special brand of coffee that I buy in a half-pound bag from The San Salvador Coffee House – rich, and dark, and black as the eyes of the devil, as my mum used to say, bless her.

them, a bit of a sketch on each. Okay? Have a butchers so you get to know something about them. In advance.'

'Fine, Cat. I shall do.'

'I know you will. Brilliant, brilliant. I'll be setting a test later,' she said, winking at me.

My manager, that day, was in a fine mood. Bookings were up year-on-year, and she had just been complimented by the Board for the work she was doing. In fact, everyone in the hotel was buoyant because she had also mentioned the possibility of a bonus for everyone, something which hadn't happened for several years. Two thousand and seven to be exact. Nothing like the thought of folding to motivate staff to offer excellent customer service. As a professional night porter, I had received a few bonuses in my time, and I could do with one[6] quickly as I had a few expenses coming.

I put the notes aside and carried on with my work. It was next day before I finally got the chance to read Cat's jottings.

I separated the top of the envelope with a butter knife[7] and removed the A4 sheet.

---

[6] I don't want to give you the impression I am a poor man in need of cash. I manage my finances correctly, and I didn't *need* a bonus. I certainly wasn't *relying* on a bonus – unlike young Gavin, whose addiction to the hypnotic machines in the Charlestown bookies was a stick, which others used to beat him with. Not me, of course. It never pays to be bitchy as a night porter – a lesson I learned when I was much younger. I don't want you to consider me profligate in any way. I am a firm believer in Dickens' doctrine – earn a pound and spend a penny more – misery; earn a pound and spend a penny less – happiness.

[7] A clean one.

Dear Team,

I am sending you this memo in preparation for the arrival of the authors in November. I have allocated their rooms on the computer. They are here for two weeks all expenses paid by the Arkwright Trust, whom some of you know. They are to be treated as VIP guests. Remember the time we had the Qatari royalty to stay? It is that level of service I expect here. I explained why in last week's staff meeting.

This is an honour for the hotel, and I would like the Arkwright Trust to return in two years' time. I have researched the authors on the internet and have combined it with information I received from Mary Beth Burnell of the Awards Committee to produce a factsheet on each. It is not exhaustive, but it will give you some idea of the people who are coming to stay with us. Please do not leave this lying about. THIS INFORMATION IS CONFIDENTIAL. Please return to me after reading if in doubt.

1. <u>Mrs Amy Cook</u>

One of the biggest selling authors in the world. Lives in Egham in Surrey. Wife of Major Archie Benson of the Royal Marines. English. Age indeterminate (she hides it jealously, though 53 has been leaked online by school friends). Bestselling romance novelist who writes under the name **Madeline France**. Published Author of eighteen novels including the massive best sellers *'Sisters', 'Behind the Lace', 'Blood Red Roses'* and *'Love in Vegas'*. The third of those was the biggest seller of 2004 and made her for life. Nine of her books have been turned into films – none especially successful. She's a winner of nine literary awards, including the *Golden Rose of Romance, American Romance Author's Award, Romance Author's Author of the Year, le Palme'd'Amour* and is the current Arkwright holder for *Best Romance*.

She is a leading contender for the Gold Award for Best Writer. Her book, *'Amelia'* is a radical departure from her usual romantic fare and has been applauded for its literary nature.

Amy is a prodigious smoker and smokes in her room regardless of health and safety. I shall speak to you all about this. Writes a regular comment for *The Guardian* on feminism. Highly intelligent and charming, but can be extremely demanding. She has been known to walk out of hotels without paying because of poor customer service, leaving thousands of pounds of debt.

2. Jo Marron-Saint

Writes Young Adult and New Adult fiction. She is single, 21, and from Orange County in California. Popular in the US. Largely unknown in mainstream UK fiction, though this will change.

Writes a series about a scatty Succubus who, despite her indoctrination, falls in love with the humans she meets rather than vacuuming their souls to hell. Along with a teenage Werebear, she fights supernatural villains and is wanted by both heaven and hell for many misdemeanours, both intended and unintended. The series – *Heart and Soul* – is a big seller in the US. Arkwright-nominated for Best YA novel for her latest segment, "*Bloodshot*". She is known for writing in a "street" vernacular – with plenty of OMG's and Stuffs and what are known as irrelevant connectors – e.g. er, like. This has attracted attacks from critics who accuse her of being childish. This is her first award ceremony, and her visit will be the first time she has left the US. Not much else is known about her except she has the reputation for being very nice.

3. Frank Duke

Is a 56 year old author of thrillers, pure and simple. His books sell by the truckload, and they involve lashings of sex, violence, murder, torture, gunplay, political intrigue, apocalyptic predictions and double crosses. What he lacks in writing ability, he makes up for in explosions. His hero, Mungo Hall, is a black ex-CIA agent whose mission is to fight corruption. Based heavily on James Bond, he travels the world, shoots people, cracks jokes, sleeps with beautiful women and escapes from seemingly impossible situations. He is from Chicago and is married (to Harty, who stays in the background). Came to prominence playing lead guitar in a late seventies jazz / funk / rock band who had one hit. He served briefly in Vietnam before that. Frank is tall; six foot seven. A diehard Republican, who distrusts foreigners (this is his first visit to England), and he can be unkind to domestic staff. Like Jo, this is his first nomination for any award, Best Thriller, for the book "*Shakedown in Chicago*".

4. Julian Green

Julian, 36, is the first self-published author to be nominated for an Arkwright. He has no established profile, no audience, no distribution deal or any reputation. You will not find his books in shops (as yet). Online only. The reason for the nomination – in the Best Contemporary Fiction category – is that he has written a book, which the critics have compared to the greats. A fan sent it to *The Guardian*, who loved it; his book has been touted in all the best supplements and literary journals. However, the Independent Community don't like the book – one reader said his book is the most depressing book ever written. He is thirty six and '*Notes and Fears of a Middle Aged Man*' is his sixth novel. Compared to the other authors staying here, he writes like Shakespeare, but their earnings dwarf his. It was rumoured on a website that he claims government benefits to enable him to write, though that has never been confirmed. Little else is known about him, except to say he argues with almost everyone he meets online. Rumoured to have drink and drugs issues, and several websites mention incidents involving the Police.

I will be on your backs about this. When the authors arrive, they are to be treated with the utmost courtesy. Whatever they want, they get. If in doubt, say yes and tell me later. You will not be disciplined if you act on an unusual request. We aim to make their stay – and the stay of the Arkwright Trust – a memorable and comfortable one. I know I can trust you. Thank you.

Cat xx

And that was the first time I came across the Arkwright awards and the four authors.

I was excited already.

I hadn't read a book in fifteen years[8] – to be honest, I cannot remember the book, or whether the gap was in fact, longer than fifteen years; that's just a convenient annuity I use – but still, I felt a charge. Authors. Artists. Creators. A bit different from the sales reps and contractors I am used to meeting, and I was sure it was going to be a most interesting two weeks.

---

[8] I mean, who has the *time?* It takes effort, time and commitment to read a book and, to be frank, with my night porter duties requiring most of my attention, I don't have any of those factors to give. Sorry, authors of the world!

Part Two

Four Authors and an Old Hotel

Pivotal

Apart from those times when I find myself, ahum, between roles, as it were, I have never been absent, and I have never called in sick. I wouldn't know how to ring in sick. Employers generally like me, and one of the reasons is that I don't ring in sick with an hour to go.[9]

My timekeeping is exemplary. Over my entire career, I have been late once, in London, when I was working at The Perez, on the seventh of July two thousand and five.

I think you can understand that. I think you can understand while the traumatised people all went drinking, and the capital drank itself into a calming stupidity after all that death.[10]

I think you can forgive my lateness. But I didn't go to the pub, like the rest of them. I was late for work because there was simply no way I could get to work on time. The tube was down, and the bus system had been suspended. I have never driven a car, so I had to walk six miles and in the end, I was seven minutes late.

---

[9] How can anyone do that? What does it feel like? Are you embarrassed? Do you feel guilty about upsetting your employer's plans and causing problems for your team? I don't understand it. I would have to be at death's door not to come to work. I would have to be paralysed. Can you imagine? A full service hotel without its night porter? It doesn't bear thinking about. The whole place would collapse. I feel nauseous thinking about it. The whole structure, the whole process, the whole ecosystem of the hotel would disintegrate. Everything would fall to pieces, entropy activated. A hotel is like a vampire – it only truly lives in darkness and the Renfield who ensures the continued smooth existence of his master is the night porter, and that is me.

[10] You can bomb the British back to the Stone Age and we'll still come out fighting with anything we can lay our hands on. It is our *Unique Selling Point*, as Cat would say.

The atmosphere in London that day was surreal.

You had to be there to understand.

Time had no meaning. It was as if the clocks had stopped, and all the barometers of the psychological and economic health of the city had been erased. It felt in moments that I was walking through warm treacle.

To this day, I curse myself for those seven minutes. All the way to Kings Cross, I had hopes of making it on time. I failed. It was no consolation to know I was the first one there for the night shift, and none of the management turned in at all.

I *knew*. That was enough.

I tell you this because I was feeling a bit rough the weekend before three of the authors[11] arrived, and I know some less diligent night porters might have rang in sick. Apart from my ethics and morals, I was quite excited and didn't want to miss it. Unfortunately, I wasn't there when three of the authors arrived, and I didn't see any of them till Tuesday night. I wanted to meet and greet Amy, Jo and Frank on that Monday afternoon in November. I could have risen early and withstood the drag and tiredness during the night, but I decided to allow Hayley to check them in herself.

Hayley is twenty and The Saladin's day receptionist. She is an avid watcher of telly programmes. One day, she tells everyone, she is going to be a singer.

She also happens to be a prodigious reader of fiction.[12] I didn't want to rain on her parade, so I didn't.

---

[11]Julian Green had managed to get himself ensconced at The Saladin two weeks early. I didn't know why.

[12]Like everyone else (as I was about to discover), she is writing a novel, 'about, like, a girl singer who becomes a megastar after selling her soul to the devil!' So, really, how could I step in? It would have been churlish. Bless her.

Mary Beth Burnell, the ruthlessly efficient Chair of the Arkwright Awards Committee, is also staying at the hotel. She keeps a room on the second floor, but she doesn't always sleep overnight.

Up till now, she has stayed twice at The Saladin. She keeps several rooms around the area's hotels. Most of the time, she stays at the five star *Crown Palais* in the City.

To get about, she has hired a black Range Rover and, I am told, drives it like a teenager. She is a ball of energy, a real Duracell Rabbit. She simply never stops. She's from New York and has that almost nasal, unsympathetic and severe accent, spawned from diverse generations of immigrants launched by necessity into a world of frenetic competition.

Mary Beth doesn't do pauses. Pauses cost money.

I have never met anyone who speaks so quickly, and I have seldom met anyone so professional. She's organised the whole ceremony virtually single-handedly and puts in hours only someone like, say, a night porter would understand. An Anglophile, she made arrangements to escort the three authors around the hotel on the first evening, the Monday night. I wanted to ask her whether I could come along, but Monday nights are a nightmare, with contractors and reps and businessmen checking in all night, so I didn't do that either.

'You are pivotal to the exercise,' she said to me on Saturday. 'These are combustible people – authors, creators – who can run off at any time. We want them to attend. No table gaps. No excuses on the rostrum.'

'Woody Allen cannot be here tonight, but...' I said, showing I knew what she was getting at.

'You have it, sir. None of that nonsense. I want a major celebration with no gaps. I don't want outside broadcasts. No videotape. The authors know this.'

'How do you know if someone won't deliberately embarrass you on stage or not turn up on the night?'

Smirking, she pulled out her brown leather notebook. 'I've had researchers out there for months. I've made discreet enquiries of anyone likely to be nominated. Anyone whom we thought was a frontrunner, we assessed. Assholes who were likely to embarrass us were – how can we put this – *overlooked* in the final nominations. Cat tells me you're not the type to call the press, so I trust you, but there's one novelist whose work we'd have been proud to showcase, but he's an ass who could start a brawl in an empty room.'

I thought of Julian, whom I had developed a little friendship with.

'Julian?'

'*Green*? I *love* Julian. *Pussycat* Green. My God! He's all Internet and Me.Com. He's all bluster. I so hope he wins the Independent and Contemporary Fiction awards. What a magnificent writer. Oh, My GOD, he's so good. They all say he's just like Salinger.'

'Who does?'

'The papers...the head-honchos on the broadsheets.'

'He says it's just *The Guardian.*'

'Julian is a pessimist. Wait till I see him! I'll kick his pants!'

Julian had caused quite a stir. Already, most of the staff here avoided him like he had just returned from central Africa with the E-Bola virus, but I liked him. So did Mary Beth, apparently, which was lucky for him. 'He's fond of a tipple. Strikes me as a loose cannon.'

'Take it from me, Julian Green won't touch a drop for two days before the ceremony. I've told him. He listens to me. He'll be fine, thanks for your concern. Anyway, on Friday, there is a press conference.'

'He mentioned it last night, yes.'[13]

---

[13]'I'm buzzing about the press conference on Friday afternoon, chap,' Julian says.

'You are?' I say, leafing through a series of memos Cat has written on the subjects of customer service and health and safety. We are at my workstation, and the hotel is relatively

23

quiet. It is very warm where I am, and I wonder whether Cat has turned the heating up. Julian is wearing a Dark Knight tee shirt and Buddy Holly glasses. He has been drinking as usual, but not as much as he had yesterday.

'Buzzing. Have you seen who's coming?'

'No. Who's expected?'

He tells me, recites a long list of local media, national press, and Internet presence. Local TV. 'Not often a writer like me gets a chance like this,' he says.

I nod to confirm I know what he is talking about. I could picture it, though Julian's apparent excitement about it surprised me. It struck me as odd and out of character. It wasn't like him. He seemed too bitter and cynical to be a slave to publicity, the starstruck writer. I would have bet more on the prospect of him not showing up for the conference.

'I know what you're thinking,' he says. 'After all I've said.'

'What am I thinking?' I reply, knowing full well he knows what I am thinking. How I gave it away, I do not know! I must be losing my poker face.

'That I'm the same as the rest of them. A celebrity junkie.'

'Julian – '

'Don't worry, I wouldn't blame you. I'm hypocritical at times, especially when it comes to publicity. Every writer wants their book read, at heart. There's a big distinction. Authors are the professional arm. They're all about the money and the sales. The *reach*. They're all about the rewards and the lifestyle. Writers want their work *read.* We're artists. I couldn't give a Joe Loss about the money, but I want people to read my book. This is an opportunity. This is MY reach, fella. All the press in one hit. My stuff. Me. It's all hypocritical, I know it is, but tell me where I can get this kind of exposure on the Internet? I've told you before. You put your book up on Twitter and before you know it, twenty other authors have put theirs up. It's a bazaar. They're – we – are like lice on a tramp's jockstrap.'

'So you've mentioned.'

'Here is a chance to bust out of that. The broadsheets got hold of my book, but who reads the broadsheets!? Fifty of the best national literary mouthpieces in one room. Of COURSE, I'm going to be excited. On top of the press, you've got the book bloggers connected to Tarzan. The best reviewers in the business, and they aren't averse to self pubs, if they've sold or attracted attention. I've seen the list and I *salivated*, chap. You've got Fiona Faithful from BuyBooks.com. Lenny Cotton from Overtherainbow. Michaela Groves from The Eye. Keanu Lantern from Bigapplelibrary.com is over and attending the conference and ceremony. Private bloggers. Serious judges of literary form. They can spot a good book from a thousand paces. They can sniff one out from the thousands pubbed every month, and they can ensure that book gets out there. Their word is a literary papal bull, a weekly sermon on the mount. A word from these guys, and *readers* will *read your book*. Do you know how many book buyers follow these book bloggers? Thousands of them. Thousands. And their readers buy – they don't just read the reviews and stare blankly into space like lemons. *Veni Vidi Visa. I came. I saw. Out came my credit card.* These are a dream come true, the cream of the crop. It's okay me being Morrissey-like on the top table, but I would be stupid like that. Once a week they feature a book. They put up an extract and they review you. They can make you. They can destroy you. These guys are THE oxygen tanks of publicity.'

'I haven't seen you as excited as this, Julian.'

'I'm on FIRE, chap,' he says, giving me a high five. 'So far, I've been studiously ignored by all of these book blogs, but it's only because they don't know me. I'm on my best behaviour. Can you lend me a pair of your trousers?'

'Seriously?' I ask, alarmed slightly.

'You always look well turned out, you. Not a hair out of place and gold cufflinks to boot. I'll bet you've got some proper clobber in that magic wardrobe of yours?'

Proper Clobber? 'Well – '

'Nah, thanks for offering, but I'm fine – don't want to look like a dog's dinner, wouldn't be good for the *brand* – but I'm staying off the pop for the day, and I'll brush my teeth, and comb the barnet. Seriously, fella – this is a great opportunity for me. I've got to hope they're not just here to listen to Sally Soppybollocks and her pet Action Man. Wouldn't surprise me.'

'Me, neither,' I replied. 'My fingers are crossed for you.'

'I just hope the questions don't go in *two* directions…'

'I told him that if he doesn't behave like a gentleman, he ain't going to NO press conference, no, sir.'

'What did he say to that?'

'Julian agreed,' she says, smiling. 'Brit's putty in my hands. The rest of them will have spoken to the press plenty, incidentally, and for them, it will be a bit of a chore. For Jo – and especially for Julian, even though you wouldn't expect it, it's a big thing. He'll want to make a good impression.'

'I thought he would. He really wants to attend.'

She nodded and looked seriously at me. In her gold spectacles, grey jacket and crisp black trousers, she looked like a headmistress of a girl's school about to talk educational policy on a popular news show.

'You're critical to this. Keep these authors sweet. I've no idea whether they'll win a plugged nickel, but these guys are up there pitching, and the judges mention their names. They need to turn up at the ceremony, so tickle their chins. Whatever they want, they got, right?'

'You can trust me,' I say.

'That's what Cat said.'

'When are you taking them round?'

'Eight on Monday, after dinner. A quick tour. I want to tell them what they can and can't do on our dollars. You know what authors are like!'

'I don't, no.'

'Honey, if it isn't nailed down, it goes in their Samsonite. And as for the free bar? Nope.'

'No free bar?'

She shook her head. 'You'd have no beer left for the locals with this crew. Jo excepted. What a lovely girl she is! If only parents the world over could see how good parenting can produce a lovely girl like Jo. She's exceptional! My own son is sharp, but this girl? WOW! She'd give her last dollar to a passing bum. If it was just Jo, the free bar runs for President, but with the others? Whose idea was that?'

'Yours, maybe?' I laughed.

'Well, maybe. Nobody's perfect,' she says, before disappearing to answer her phone.

The Sardonic, Cynical and Woefully Self-Destructive World of The Writer Julian Green

'I know other authors don't like me,' he says. 'And I couldn't give a bollocks.'

I am always immaculately turned out, shirts pressed and shoes shined. Whatever uniform is supplied, I dry clean. I wear aftershave – proper stuff – and cufflinks. I order shirts online from Jermyn Street, and I never wear them after a year. Even the best shirt starts to wear after that time. Once a week means fifty wears, and a night porter cannot afford to have the tell-tale signs of a frayed cuff, a collar stained with the most imperceptible tidemark, a button missing. The more you wear even the finest shirt, the more entropy reigns, and the more the shirt begins to decay. Each year, I buy ten shirts, which cost me around seventy five pounds each, less discount and add postage. Virgin white and sky blue. Each year, they end up in the charity shop and within a day, they will have gone. The people of Wheatley Fields know a bargain when they see one. I have five pairs of brogues, and they last much longer than a year. An English professional should always invest in English-made shoes. Anything else is a false economy. Uniform is mostly provided, so shoes and shirts are my only expense. I never wear jewellery, save a cygnet ring an ex-girlfriend bought me when I worked in the Gallows Inn up in Newcastle. I wear that on special occasions.

I tell you this not to brag, but to point out that Julian is the total opposite. The absolute polar opposite. He is the scruffiest human being I have seen in The Saladin. You can generally smell him coming before he arrives in the reception.

'Authors are generally egomaniacs who have singularly failed to adapt to the modern world. The vast majority are trapped in a bizarre world of denial, a world governed by an unhinged dictum, which dictates that the ability to write is a skill economically unique enough to make a living. Why should I give a bollocks if someone as crackers as an author likes me or not? Pffft…

Someone is paying for his stay outside the terms of the Awards Committee, but I don't know who. He's been here two weeks already, staying in one of the cheaper rooms. He is out of place at a hotel like The Saladin. Scruffy, drunk, always nipping out the back for a cigarette. Most of the time, he's in the town for a drink.

'I couldn't give a bollocks about other authors. Hacks and Charlatans. Not a *writer* amongst them. Most of the bleeders would sell their mother's soul for a sale. Nah, forget them.'

If it wasn't for his nomination, he wouldn't get within a mile of The Saladin. He's more of a crash-on-sofa-at-a-mates sort of bloke.[14] The Saladin is usually full of cash-rich tourists, Americans, French and Germans, retired civil servants with fat pensions to spend. Not self-published authors like Julian on an extended jolly.

'What can I do? I can't force them to like me, now can I? It's their choice. It's their right. We're a free country the last time I looked. Well, that's debatable, but you know what I mean. And I've never met an author who actually *liked* another author. It's kill or be killed out there, especially amongst the Indies. A pox on them. Yeh, a great big virulent, suppurating pox on them.'

---

[14] Maybe I'm being unkind. I can be, you know.

Who is paying for Julian Green? Out of idle curiosity (and because night porters must always be vigilant), I checked the bookings one night when all was quiet. I discovered that the billing reference data for him had been passworded.[15] All the information had been barred, except, I assume, to Cat.

The next opportunity I got, a couple of evenings later, I collared Cat just before she was about to leave for the evening. I pointed out my discovery and wondered whether this was an anomaly and/or a mistake. She asked me why I was snooping about, and she was quite cold about it. She reminded me of the memo. I was taken aback, and I didn't have an answer for her at that moment. I felt like a naughty child.

Unprepared, I replied that I didn't know.

That information is confidential, she said, turned on her heels and walked off without another word to me.

As far as I knew, for each author, the deal was this. Two weeks at The Saladin, full board plus travel in return for an appearance at the Ceremony. That was what Jo, Frank and Amy were getting. Why was Julian getting an extra two weeks? And why was Cat so defensive? It wasn't like her. Why didn't she trust her night porter with this information? I was slightly aggrieved with it.

---

[15] I have open access to the ICT system at the desk. Night porters often book in late arrivals and nowadays, it is all computer controlled. Many hotels I have worked in have national extranets, but The Saladin Inn is a stand-alone business. Staff and Financial files are locked, of course, and kept in the hotel manager's corralled area. The rest is accessible. I am adept at working with databases, something I learned at college. I am a dab hand, actually. Some nights, I have a good root round. I like databases more than any other of the standard packages. I used to be able to write VBasic and SqL, but I know that I am behind the times and sadly, the knowledge – and worse, the *capability* of gaining the knowledge – is now beyond me, and I shall leave it to the kids.

Why didn't she trust me? Who else knew? My recriminations and bitterness knew no bounds that night.

'I'm absolutely content with my own company. I can go weeks without talking to anyone. Some of the people you have in this hotel – and this town, to be honest – leave *mucho grande* to be desired as human beings. If some of them find themselves any deeper up their own arseholes, they'll need torches.'

Odd.
I quite like Julian. Mary Beth is protective of him. Jo has never encountered him online. Frank has. I'm told Amy knows Julian of old through the Internet, fora, Me.Com etc.[16] Gossip informs me that they were both members of a forum called **The Wizard's Court**. They were massive pals and something happened. No one seems to know what, all behind the scenes shenanigans. He won't have anything to do with her, and she *definitely* avoids him. When she heard Julian was booked in, she tried to move to the Tropics, but Mary Beth told her that it was her way or the highway and Amy backed down.

'I like that Jo, though. We get on, for some reason. She's a top kid. And she can scribble. Not much, mind – lots to learn, but she's not bad. Not bad at all.'

Martin Sixsmith doesn't like him in the bar, possibly because Julian is a left winger, possibly because he is as arrogant as he is and five times as intelligent. Gavin tells us that Julian was like the kids Sixsmith used to beat up at school. He has been known to serve others, even if the author is next in the queue. *There's something about him*, he says. *Something I can't put my finger on. Bloke looks*

---

[16] How can you *know* someone without *meeting* them? It's a phenomenon that escapes me. I am glad I don't network.

dodgy. I'm no fan of the boorish barman, but even if I was, I would reserve my own judgement.[17]

'Nope' he says, 'I couldn't care less whether Amy, Frank or Uncle Tom Cobley like me or not,' and this finally, draws a response from me.

'You don't?' I reply.

'Nope.'

'I can't say that I've noticed anyone dislike you, Julian. I think you're being a bit paranoid,' I say, being slightly economical with the truth.

'Come on...' he says, grinning, almost winking. 'You notice everything. You *see* everything. You're a *night porter*. I'll bet nothing goes off here you don't know about. I'll bet you think it's *your* hotel, don't you?'

I ignore his perceptive last comment. 'I can only comment on what I see –'

'That's what I said,' he interrupts, drunk again.

'– at night.'

'Of course, at night. That's what I meant,' he replies snarkily.

I quite enjoy the company of narcissists. Their lack of interest in the rules of polite conversation means I don't have to try very hard, and I can sit and listen without revealing anything of myself.[18]

He follows up by doing what he always does, which is rant. He is a champion ranter, and I have discovered his favourite target is Amy Cook.

Once he knew she was coming to stay, he sharpened his vowels and laced his consonants with the necessary

---

[17] To be honest, I definitely prefer Julian to Sixsmith: There's something about *him*, if you ask me.

[18] Night porters are generally excellent listeners. It should be in EVERY hotel job description.

poison, the belladonna, the arsenic, the digitalis. I remember when he found out. He was furious. He had calmed down and now contented himself with acid derision he usually shared with me.[19]

Doggerel, As Written By Amy Cook

'That Amy Cook –' he shook his head. '– have you *read* any of her doggerel?'
'I'm not much of a reader, Julian. I've told you this.'
'Wretched stuff. She writes like I can water ski.'
'And can you water ski?'
'I can't swim.'
'Oh,' I reply.
'You don't know the half of it. Passive sentences. Lachrymose dialogue. Plotting by numbers. All the women are beautiful, and all the men are handsome. Nothing like the real world. Look at you and I. Look at the rest of the hotel. Hardly oil paintings…'
I am mildly affronted by his comment, and I think he notices, but Julian just carries on regardless, hoping that I will eventually forget what he said. On this occasion, he is correct – I'm not *that* affronted.
'– adverbs everywhere, like confetti outside a church after a wedding. Metaphors, which clang a big one, like church bells you can hear on the other side of the world;

---

[19] He would have shared much of it online, but he was currently serving bans from at least nineteen different fora and social networks for the crime of repeated abusive postings. There was nowhere he could go to vent about bad authors now – particularly Amy Cook. He told me that the minute anyone abuses Amy Cook or Madeline France, they are banned because all the moderators and panjandra on the sites he frequents, believes the abuser to be a Julian Green respawn. This meant that for the past three weeks, he tells me, Amy Cook could freely visit all these sites in peace and harmony, 'which is something the bloody charlatan does *not* deserve.'

aphorisms, which leave you scratching your head. *Say what!?* Allegories so obscure you want to weep. Plot development like aggravated burglary. Climaxes so inadequately hidden you can spot how her books are going to conclude by the time you reach the acknowledgements. There is no reason to read a book written by Amy Cook writing as Madeline France. None at all. It's doggerel. Even the last one.'

'The one she's been nominated for?'

'That one,' he affirms. 'Overrated. Same rubbish, different day. Don't believe the hype.'

'I've heard –'

'– seriously,' he interrupts, with a hint of steely determination, a belief in his argument. 'It may be feted, but it's just the same doggerel.'

'Okay. Doggerel…' I repeat, not committing myself one way or another.

'Want to hear The Paradox?'

'Go on. I like the sound of that.'

The Publishing Paradox As Explained By Julian Green

'Picture, if you will, the entire stock of the world's fiction paperbacks at one hundred.'

'Just one hundred paperback books?' I nod helpfully.

'A century of books. A ton of books. That's all there is. Past, present, future. One hundred paperbacks.'

'Okay. Will do. I get the concept.'

'In a library.'

'Okay, a library.'

'Or a big box.'

'Right. A big box.'

There is a gap in the conversation, as if Julian is letting the concept circulate in my head. He looks at me with his sharp blue eyes, his unshaven cheeks, the rancid stench of cigarettes and booze irradiating from his black shirt like the heat from a saucepan. He scratches his nose and draws back slightly from the night desk. He leans forward again, as if he cannot make up his mind, and says in a conspiratorial whisper. 'Out of those hundred paperback books, forty seven of them would be romances aimed at a female audience. Forty seven percent. The vast majority simplistic and badly written doggerel of the type presented to the world by Amy Cook writing as Madeline France.'

'As many as that?'

'That's possibly an *underestimate,* depending on how you define romance and whom you read. It's a crying shame. The more doggerel you write, the more you are likely to sell. That's The Paradox. Fundamentally, romance novels like those purveyed by Amy, are the same story repeated time and time again in different novels written by different authors. The same protagonists. The same heroines. The same dark and mysterious lovers. The same dull and worthy heroes, the same dastardly villains. There hasn't been a significant variation in the romance genre since *Wuthering Heights* and here, my friend, is the rub.'

'What rub?' I say.

'– the readers do not WANT a significant variation in the romance genre. In fact, if you write an innovative romance novel, it is ninety percent certain you won't get it published. You will have wasted your time.'

'What about the self-publishing market?'

'That's even worse. Self-publishers tend to ape what publishers do, and they are even MORE conformist than that, so self-published romance fiction is about as conformist as you can get. Therefore, logically, if you produce an innovative romance novel and self-publish it, you are likely to be shunned like a man in a lift who has just eaten a bag of prunes.'

'Gosh –'

'– readers want the same beginning, middle and end, so the mainstream publishers provide it and ergo, the self-publishers provide it. And you know what? *Readers love the familiarity*. They cannot get enough of it. They EAT this stuff. Three, four, five novels a week. Readers want to read stuff that's like their family, familiar, a big comfort zone, the same thing every time, like a Big Mac at the McDonalds. No surprises. Don't EVER get clever in romance: Whatever you do, don't try and be cleverer than the reader. Don't use any words longer than seven letters and don't try anything smart. Never use footnotes or cool chapter headings. Stick to past tense. Stick to what the punters know. Change your style and the average romance punter in ButtPlug, South Dakota will hate you for it, and your carefully created brand will just be so much old newspaper. Romance punters want the rose-tinted nostalgia of the *last novel they read*, and they want it fast – to top it off, they want a novel they can digest in one sitting. Do not, whatever you do, write long books for romance readers. They will hunt you down and give you a jolly good finger wagging. Amy spotted this: *Et voila!* The sterile, unchallenging, all-conquering romance genre. *Et voila aussi!* **Romance Writing 101 as written by Amy Cook writing as Madeline France.'**

I don't quite know what to say, so I say nothing, allowing him to continue. I pick up a peppermint from the dish and take it, roll it around my mouth.

'You've got to hand it to her. You've got to give her a mammoth round of applause. Madeline France books are as popular as a freezing pint of lager on a boiling hot day. The ladies can't get enough of her. Her paperbacks have wiped out forest after forest. Millions of copies. Millions. She's always being interviewed in the magazines. The media love her. You've seen her on the telly, right?'

'Of course, I have,' I lie. I hardly came across her before she arrived at the hotel, but I have no wish to make myself look a fool. 'Can't miss her, can you?'

'Only the other week, she was on *Slappers,* She's something of a heroine to that lot. It's a MILF carpet-munching festival whenever she's on the show.'

'*Slappers?*' I ask, quizzically.

'You don't know *Slappers*? Ladies chat show. On the telly every lunchtime. Women love it. A phenomenon.'

'I'm always asleep. I must have missed it,' I reply, slightly defensively.

My answer satisfies him, apparently, and though he takes a second or two to assimilate the information, he moves on. The grandfather clock in the hallway chimes and whirrs four times.

'It drives me nuts. Honestly. Drives me round the bend.'

'What does?'

'The Paradox, chap.'

'Oh, yes.'

'The worse the author, the more sterile the book, the better it sells. That's The Publishing Paradox. I'm giving the romance hacks a beating, but it applies to all genres.'

'I can see it upsets you.'

'You're not kidding, fella. I sold a hundred and thirteen books last month, and I was reviewed in *The* bloody *Guardian*.'

'The Guardian?'

'Yep. *With this novel, Julian Green finds himself at the vanguard of New British Fiction.*'

'Is that what they wrote?'

'They did. And the review inspired the sale of one hundred and thirteen of my independently published books. Whoopy do,' he said, leaning against the pillar. 'Amy sells one hundred and thirteen of her sterile, not-at-the-vanguard-of-anything novels every half an hour.'

I change the subject to lighten him up. 'I have heard women like to read about vampires.'

'Young birds. They grow into the real stuff at twenty five. Vampire fiction is just an apprenticeship for the romantic sagas loved by their mothers.'

'Oh, okay.'

'Black and red fiction is dead, anyway,' he says, and drifts off for a second.

'These are strong opinions,' I comment.

'You ought to hear my views on thriller authors. Like Frank,' he said. He picks up his phone and types a text to someone. I stand quietly.

'I bloody hate thrillers. What *is* the point of a thriller novel? Why not leave it to the film boys? A scandalous waste of ancient woodland if you ask me,' he mutters.

As he texts, I wonder what the deal is between Amy and him.

His bile towards her work seems more than ego, and no one can get *that* upset about books, surely. He puts his phone away and turns to me as if he is warning me of something. His tone darkens.

'Don't let Amy's jeans and tee shirt approach to high fashion fool you. She's minted, chap. Madeline France, her alter-ego, is the Queen of The Paradox, and she'd need three consecutive lives in order to spend her accumulated royalties. I don't mind that, but please, if she describes herself as a writer, don't forget to piss yourself laughing. She's a hack, like the rest of them.' He trails off and starts to walk to the stairs, taking the scent of whisky and cigarettes with him. I am glad he is going as his bitter rants never seem to end, as occasionally entertaining as they can be, and I have work to do – administrative work, incidents to record.

Mardi Gras. Shrove Tuesday: Is That IT For Tuesday, The Dullest Day?

I book in several guests and take their bags to their rooms. I escort a disabled couple to the bar and make sure Martin looks after them. He gives me a filthy look, one of many I have received from him since I started my job. I speak to a couple of reps I know who have stayed at the hotel before. I feel in control, running the evening business of the hotel from my workstation.

Just when it quiets, and I idly consider a green tea and chocolate, the screen alert flashes on my PC. The screen alert tells me it is Jo, the young author from California.

'I have a problem,' she says, as I pick up the phone. 'I don't understand the shower. Can you help me, please?'

'Of course, Miss. I'll be right up.'

'Oh, would you? Thank you...'

If voices were images, Jo's is ice cream melting on a hot summer's day. I pick up the pager and dash up the staircase. Everyone is smitten by her, apparently. Sixsmith, a skinheaded, fat, right-wing bully who shouldn't be anywhere near the customer service industry, turns into putty whenever she's around. Gavin's the same. Even Kerry, who is as competitive as anyone I have ever met, certainly with other women, warmed to her straight away. A little ray of Californian sunshine. I am soon outside her room, and I knock on the door.

'Come in, door's open.'

I walk in, see her, and reach for the door again: I feel as if I should avert my eyes. She is naked except for a bright green kimono, which barely covers her behind.

'Sorry...I...'

'I can't get these showers to work at all,' she says, ignoring my obvious prudish instinct and heads straight for the bathroom. She is smiling and sprightly. I follow her, her jet black tresses cascading down her back, half-tied in a scrunchie. She reaches up to show me the apparatus that regulates the water temperature. 'I got this to work last night, like, totally random, but I cannot remember how I did it. Showers back home are so much simpler. This is, like, Oh, My God, I just can't...can you show me?' She says, her chestnut eyes beaming, as if I were her dad and she wants a lift somewhere several hours away.

'Glad to.' I switch into professional mode, extricating myself from the unprofessional drooling idiot mode in which I find myself. I reach up into the walk-in shower, step inside, and demonstrate its function while nattering.

'– so, if I pull this –' she says... '– it goes hot?'

'No, this way…' I demonstrate, pulling the lever toward me.

'OMG I've been pushing it toward the wall. No wonder I can't get it hot – and a girl needs her shower!'

'Yes, she does, Miss.'

She leans on the sink and for a second, her kimono opens, and I can see her…but I turn away and grab hold of the temperature gauge for dear life as she talks. I push it, and I pull it, and I scratch my head, and I pretend I know what I am doing.

'I love a hot shower. I feel all tingly and clean afterwards. Don't you?'

'I am partial to being clean, yes. That just showered feeling, Miss.' I reply without looking at her.

I shut the door. She is putting her hair into a swimming cap. It is a process that defies physics. It doesn't seem possible that the opaque, turquoise elasticated cap on her head – which looks like one of those Portuguese Man-O-War jellyfish, only without the legs – can fit all that *hair* inside, but she manages it.

'Is Julian about?' She asks. 'He's a lot of fun.'

Julian? Are we talking about the same person?

'I've just seen him.'

'Wow, he's told me so much about the town, the ceremony. And the press conference as well. He's awesome. He's been so kind'

'Yes, he is, isn't he?' I say dubiously, internally scratching my head in bemusement.

'If you see him, tell him to give me a call.'

'I shall do, Miss.'

'Oh, and before you, go,' she says, her ice cream voice resonating around my head. 'Can you check the TV remote for me? Like, I don't understand how it works.'

'Happy to –'

'And call me Jo, huh. I've not been called Miss since grade school…' she says, laughing, and skipping out of the shower into her bedroom. Spices, fragrances and potpourri colonise the space, and her belongings are already stored away neatly in wardrobes and drawers. The potpourri reminds me that this is a girl's room. There is something about a woman's touch. My flat doesn't have a single extraneous decorative object anywhere in sight. My bathroom is a Bauhaus example of pure Germanic functionalism. Already, the bathroom in Jo's bedroom has a rose in a metallic vase on the toilet cistern head, and this is only her second night.

'I will, M – Jo. If that's alright with you,' I say, picking up the remote.

I demonstrate while Jo sits next to me. She picks up the controls easily. My behaviour is a masterpiece of emotional control because I can see the full stratosphere of her legs from tanned thighs to feet and she has no self-consciousness about it. But then, I am a night porter, and I am trained to control my emotions, and I have been in this situation before. I am ninety percent sure that her largesse and naïveté is non-sexual, but I can never be sure, so I slightly move away from her and lean forward, away from the pillows. An episode of "Dr Who" is on BBC1, with the Scottish actor everyone likes who wears a raincoat with baseball boots.

'I totally love Doctor Who. Leave this on. Do you like the Doctor?'

'Erm, I'm not much of a telly watcher. Always busy.'

'I'll bet you are busy in a great old hotel like this. I'd like to know all about it.'

'Really?' I reply, knowing what's coming next.

'Would you tell me all about its history? I hear it's haunted?

'I'd be happy to, Jo,' I say, standing. 'But I have to get back to the desk, so why don't you come to see me tomorrow night, and I shall tell you what I know.'

'Really? Oh, that would be totally *awesome,*' she replies.

'The hotel is full of ghosts. It's like something out of Scooby Doo.'

'Hey...I thought you didn't watch TV,' she laughs as we walk to the door.

'Everyone knows Scooby Doo, Jo. Will that be all?'

'Just hang on a second while I get in the shower.'

She grins, looks every second of her twenty one years, and skips into the bathroom. 'I'd best be decent, huh!' she says, winking, shutting the bathroom door. I am relieved, despite myself.

Seeing Jo in the shower would be enough to explode my tiny mind, I am sure, but it would be a *spectacular* image to recollect in my dotage.

I hear footsteps, the gentle swoosh of the kimono connecting with the tiles. Then the water, jets of water.

I hear the shower door open, and Jo shouts that it's awesome and thanks, and I return them and leave the hotel bedroom. The pager goes. It sometimes goes like a machine gun in this job.[20]

---

[20] Lots of people couldn't cope with being a night porter because of the anti-social hours, but that's half the attraction for me. I like the contrariness of it. I am so used to it now, I hardly notice. My day is your night. While you sleep, I walk the corridors of some popular hotel. While you work, I'm soaking in dreams (and do I dream. *Do* I dream!). It's all reversed, the yin and the yang. Scarcely notice it, as I said. The first three weeks were hard work but now, my body is attuned to the circadian rhythm of the black night. My health is good, despite what they say about night shifts and poor health. It's not a shift. The answer is in the job title. Night. Porter. I don't work in the day and every day is the same, weekends or weekdays. Weekends are my staple. The type of hotels I have worked in all cater for the tourist trade, like the one I work in now. That means weekends. It doesn't bother me. A Saturday is a Monday is a Wednesday when darkness falls. I like to work sevens. I'm what my father might call a Grabbing Bar Steward, if you get my meaning. I never turn down work and more often than not, I work seven tens. That's ten hours a night, seven nights a week. The hotels I work in – particularly this one – love that kind of simplicity and my bankers love my account.

It's Frank Duke. I am two doors away, and I knock on the door. He opens it.

'That was quick,' he says.

'Can I help you, sir?'

'Got any ice?' Frank and Jo, although from the same country, could not be any different. His voice is deep, almost gruff – a lifetime of beer and whisky and many cigarettes is the usual precedent for a voice that deep. He's not smiling much, and I remember the memo about his predilections, and lack of them.

'I shall bring some up, sir.'

'Hey...' he says, opening the door. He's wearing a white shirt and cream trousers, and he fills the doorway with his presence. I see his laptop in the background, and he's listening to music, though I cannot tell what kind. He's been drinking. 'Anywhere to go round here?'

'To go, sir?'

'Yeh. Out. The pub. A nightclub.'

'Well, yes, sir, but you have to travel into the City...'

'Local. Walking distance. Don't want to travel far.'

I tell him the pubs to go to, but disappoint him on the nightclubs. He nods. It would be difficult to work out Frank's age if you didn't know it in advance. He could be anything from forty to sixty, but he's fit and strong, and

---

In busy hotels like this one, The Saladin, I can choose my own hours after a while and as I already mentioned, I don't get ill. You might consider me sad, and I wouldn't blame you. I don't have much of a life outside my profession. I don't have family, save the aforementioned miniature steps and a brother who lives in Minnesota who I haven't spoken to for eight years. He's a doctor and the first chance he got, he left. I ask you! After all that money the NHS spent on training him! I'd make him pay it back, but he's been gone so long now, I'll bet he's been erased from the official record. Felicity, the woman he married, made it easy for him to go, but where's the loyalty? We never got on, even when we were kids, so I don't miss him.

he has deep brown eyes, which don't leave yours for a second. He's going slightly grey, but he doesn't look concerned about that, the way he carries himself.

'So, what are the locals about?'

'I'm sorry?' I say.

'They lynch black men round here?'

'Of course not, sir.'

'An English dude I am aware of back home tells me there's bigots,' he says, gingerly, treading in shark infested waters.

'In England or Wheatley Fields?' I ask.

'Here. In town?'

'I'm definitely sure that's not the case, sir.'

'What about cops? They see a black man about his business, they shake him down?'

I think of Brophy, but I say nothing. 'Again, of course not, sir. Wheatley Fields is one of the most liberal towns I've worked in. Everyone is fine.'

'Call me Frank. That *sir* is far too Sweet Home Alabama. Only in reverse.'

'Frank,' I confirm.

He leans on the hotel door. 'So, I can go walking to the...Benjamin?'

'Benbow, Frank. The Admiral Benbow.'

'Okay. Safe?'

I think someone has been talking nonsense to him about Wheatley Fields. Either that or he's had a hard life in the South. 'As houses, Frank. It's the busiest pub in the Fields. You might be a bit – er, mature.'

'What does that mean?'

'Lots of young people in there. Mind you, on Tuesday night, they'd be glad of your custom. Come downstairs, and I shall point out the best pubs. You aren't far away. It's nearly ten and some of them shut at eleven.'

The pager goes again, the red light. I know who it is, and I ignore it. Frank notices this.

'Aren't you going to get that?'

'Internal. Dealt with,' I lie.

'Might be important,' he says slowly.

'It's not, sir – Frank, sorry. Frank.'

He stands there and stares straight into my eyes. What he is searching for, I do not know, but he is searching for something. He stands up straight. 'Don't think I'll bother tonight. Going to watch some TV. Do some writing. Thanks for the information,' he says and shuts the door without further ado.

'You're welcome,' I say to the door.

I run down to the reception.

When I get there, I look over the desk to the PC monitor from the customer side. It is number 15. It's Mrs Cook. I pick up the phone

'The mini-bar is er, out of gin,' she informs me nasally and sneezes. 'And I need paracetamol.'

'The mini-bar was filled this lunchtime, Mrs Cook.'

'That may very well be the case,' she replies and trails off, as if distracted by a bird on the windowsill. Mini-bars in each room are filled with eight miniatures. At seven pounds and eighty pence a miniature, the hotel finds that guests tend to leave the mini-bar intact. Most of them, even the prosperous ones, bring their own – duty free, the Community Fayre Supermarket up the road – and we turn a blind eye. I don't blame them. But Amy Cook seems to take bizarre pride in emptying the mini-bar and, as far as I know, she always pays.

'My colleague will fill the mini-bar tomorrow lunchtime. I can bring you a G & T from the bar.'

'That would be most appreciated, yes, it would. Three, yes, three G and T's. Plenty of ice. Bring olives.'

'We have paracetamol in the first aid box. I am not supposed to administer it.'

'Why not! Bloody health and safety regulations. I forgot to buy some. Or I've bloody mislaid them. And I have the most *vicious* headache.'

'Sorry to hear that, Mrs Cook. I can get some, but you would have to sign a release form.'

'I'd sign my own execution docket if it would get rid of this headache,' she replies, an element of irritation.

'I'll be up shortly with your drinks and pills, madam.'

'Be a love and hurry,' she says and puts the phone down.

I do as I'm told. I walk to the bar, nod to an unsmiling Sixsmith, construct the three gin and tonics expertly and place them on the tray with a plate of sliced lemons. I already have the Paracetamol and the release docket in my pocket, and I ascend the stairs to the second floor. As I enter the corridor, my beeper goes, and I know someone is trying to contact me on reception. There is nothing I can do.

I knock on Mrs Cook's door. She beckons me in.

I try to eliminate Julian's opinion of her, and I am successful in doing so. As a night porter, it's important for me to form my own impressions, and I like what I see of her. I experience a twinge when I see her. Not the kind of massive electric shock I experienced when I saw Jo in her kimono, but a definite feedback loop from my head to my lower regions. She's attractive, that's the first instinct, and I didn't expect that.

I expected an iconic Barbara Cartland figure with eyelashes like the legs of hairy spiders and dresses made from curtain material.

That's not Amy at all. Actually, she's wearing jeans and a tee shirt, which says "*Twatter. No-one gives a f**k what you are thinking*". I definitely didn't expect *that.* Short black hair, not tresses or ringlets. Spiked and dyed. She's slim, and young for her age, assuming she's fifty three, which is the only number I know. She's not especially beautiful – she's not flawless at all – but she's not unattractive. Women don't understand that – a man doesn't need unblemished beauty.[21]

---

[21] In fact, flawlessness can send them running for the hills.

I notice her bare feet, and I am momentarily stunned. Strawberry toenail polish and a silver toe ring on the second toe of each foot. Nice feet. Quality. Very well looked after. Cared for – even *supervised* – probably by a regular administration of chiropody courtesy of an expensive professional, rather than a pumice stone in the bath and a rub down with Pound Goblin moisturiser on a towel afterwards. There is a distinct smell of perfume – plus something else, something *earthy* – and the room is a complete mess of trainers, papers, books, printers, and magazines. I notice a copy of her bestseller, *Amelia,* on one of her pillows, with the purple cover; emblazoned with the author's name five times the size of the book title. There are major – and curious – contradictions here.

'You're a lifesaver,' Mrs Cook says without looking at me, a London accent – no, closer to Essex, possibly a touch of Suffolk. Soft and mellifluous. I've worked down there a bit, the Meadsmith Inn, Stowmarket. 'Put them over there,' she gestures to an occasional table by the side of her bed. 'Been gagging for one for an hour, love.'

'You could have called earlier, Mrs Cook. I don't like to think of our guests going thirsty.'

'Bit busy,' she says, pointing to the laptop screen. 'I do wish you'd call me Amy. Less of the Mrs. You make me sound a hundred and fifty.'

'Amy, then.'

She is staring at her laptop, talking on a chat box to someone on Me.Com, the chat facility. I don't really go for social networking, but I can understand it being a necessity for a novelist. I put the drinks on the table and make my way back to the door.

'Do you know, I spend more time marketing my books than I do writing,' she says. 'There's this conference on Friday. I'm always in press conferences, and they always ask the same questions.'

'I would imagine it could be irritating,' I reply.

'And they always want to know who I'm bonking, or what clothes I wear. They never want the work.'

'I wouldn't know, Amy.'

'Bloody press.'

'Yes,' I reply, looking awkward.

'I've been married fifteen years and *still* they've linked me with more men than Katie Price.'

'Do they?'

'Do you not read the papers?'

'I'm afraid I'm a bit busy for the celebrity notices,' I say, which is completely true.

Amy laughs. She turns from the screen, and lit by the powerful laptop, her face is clear and shapely if a little gaunt – my mother would have said she needs a dinner inside her with plenty of Yorkshire Puddings. When she looks at me, I feel that thing again.

What?

Huh?

'I like that. I really like that,' she says. 'Why don't you have a drink? It makes a change to talk to someone in real life for once rather than on these things.'

'I can't, Amy,' I hold up my hands reluctantly. 'Once I start, I'll never stop.'

'Just like me. Bless you. Oh – I forgot. Have you left the tablets?'

I gesture to the tray. 'The release form is there. Please sign it. They check these things.'

'Shall do,' she says, watching me walk to the door. 'Such a shame you won't sip with me.'

I smile.

'Busy, busy, busy. I've just had another call. Must dash. Night porters never stop, Amy,' I reply cheerfully.

'You're a love,' she says, once again, quickly absorbed like a hapless foal in the swamps, in the quicksand that is Me.Com.

I fill in the docket for Amy's drinks and place it in the bar till. The bar is silent, and when the till clicks into place, it does so with a satisfying click.

It's going to be a busy week, with the authors settling in, the press conference, Mary Beth in and out, Cat fussing, making sure everyone is on their best behaviour. I'm going to have to be sharp and organised. In control. Luckily, that's what night porters do, and it is exactly what I'm best at.

Outside in the street, behind the locked hotel door, I hear people walk past the hotel. They are loud, and their piercing exuberances tear through the silence of the night. Focusing on the PC screen, I note the phone call is from Mr Lime in fourteen. I pick up the phone, wondering whether he has also run out of gin.

Storm Clouds Gather Over The Saladin

It had been throwing it down with rain, and Wheatley Fields was awash. An unbroken sheet of black cloud above. Rain so heavy it saturated in seconds. Many conversations in The Saladin early that Wednesday evening recalled the flooding that caused so much havoc a few weeks ago.[22]

Umbrellas for the mobile had proved essential. Me? I came to work in a vintage beige raincoat, which (even if I said so myself), made me look like a detective investigating a particularly gruesome murder. Plus a jet black and silver umbrella, which was made in London in the sixties.[23]

---

[22]Wheatley Fields attracts a weird microclimate akin to a tropical island, and though climatologists have speculated on the reasons why, no one has ever come up with a convincing explanation. The City and, to a lesser extent, Charlestown, never seem to get these deluges.

[23]I love vintage stuff. Though the average consumer has got hold of the notion, thus driving up prices because of increasing demand and relative scarcity, vintage is pure class. Forget this Bangladeshi and Laotian stuff they sell in the chain stores. Just

Thus, because of planning, forethought, caution and prudent use of available resources, I was able to slip smoothly into night porter mode without undue fuss and loss of time. Unlike Sixsmith, who was caught out in it and spent an hour of work's time drying his shirt.

I sit there and am surprised to see Amy and Jo struggle into reception with a mountain of shopping bags. It is a good job I spot them because I am able to sprint across the floor without them calling for me. That would please Cat and the guests. 'Let me take those. You two go and sit down,' I say.

Immediately, they drop the eleven or twelve giant bags on the steps.

'Why thank you, kind sir. We've had a day out in the City. We've been very bad girls and spent a lot of money. Well, Jo has!'

'Hey! Don't be a sneak...' Jo giggles. 'True though. Wow, what wonderful stores!'

'The City is the fourth most popular place in the country to buy quality clothes. People visit from miles around,' I say.

'I think a glass of wine is in order to celebrate our day out, Jo, what do you think?' Amy offers.

'Better make it a beer for me. Wine gets me kinda drunk.' Jo responded, laughing.

'That's the purpose of drink, my love,' her companion says, swiftly removing her raincoat.

I have already brought in the bags and am holding out my arm for the ladies coats, which I will hang up on the coat stand. 'I'll make sure these get dry. I'll order a bottle of wine and a beer for you, ladies. Fire's on and lucky for you, the sofas are available.'

---

don't bother. Go for English-made vintage stuff. Lasts forever, and you can guarantee the stitching is made with adult sweat rather than the tears of crying Asian children.

'You are good. Let's go and put our feet up,' Amy says, guiding Jo into the bar toward the giant sofas in front of the coal fire, which crackled as they approached.

I notice Julian standing by the desk. I hang up the raincoats and signal to him that I would be one moment. He nods. I take the bags into the bar. Sixsmith's face lights up like a lantern when he sees Jo, who is wearing a polo neck, blue jeans and thigh high black leather boots. I walk over and give the order. He assures me that they will be well looked after, and I ignore the undercurrent of what he actually means, the sly dog. I walk over to the ladies, who are examining a bag of expensive Dionysus perfume products. I tell them their drinks are on their way, and they nod in unison.

Julian is wearing a black Motorhead tee shirt, which has seen much better days. One thigh of his jeans is covered in an indefinable pink stain, and he is unshaved. I wish, at times, that I could read him the riot act about his appearance. But I can't. He is holding a gold packet of Benson and Hedges cigarettes and a Zippo lighter.

'Duty free?' I comment.

'You're not kidding. Eight quid a packet here. These are a lot less, trust me.'

'What can I do for you, Julian?'

'Is Jo in there?' He gestures to the bar.

'She is.'

'On her own.'

'No —'

'— that horrible bitch is with her, right.'

'It appears so, Julian.'

'Never mind. Wanted to talk to her about something.'

'Do you want to leave a message?'

'Nah — yes, on second thought, yes. Could you ask her to ring my room? It's about the press conference.'

'Sure, I will. When she comes out.'

'Make it discreet, will you. That hellspawn she's with will queer my pitch and no mistake.'

'I shall give her the message.'

'Cheers. I'm off to the courtyard for a fag.'

'It's throwing it down. Do you want my umbrella?'

'No, chap, I'll be fine, thanks. Is Sixsmith behind the bar tonight? Or is it Kerry?'

'Martin's on,' I say, and notice his immediate disappointment.

'Looks like I'm down The Saddlers later.'

As he goes out into the courtyard, I see Frank come in through the front door. He's not the type of man to need me to help him with his coat, so I let him beat the rain out of his coat onto the mat. Frank wears a Homberg hat, a black one. He's with someone, a girl. A local girl I half recognise. I have seen her around in the square. Frank comes over, and she accompanies him. He's been drinking, but he's not drunk.

'Any messages?'

I check in the pigeon holes. 'Sorry, Frank.'

'Nothing from the NY Times?'

'Nothing at all, sorry.'

'Goddamn. I called them for a reporter on Friday.'

'The conference?'

'That's right. The press conference. I noticed a distinct lack of Stateside coverage.'

'I'll keep an eye on the messages, Frank.'

He acknowledges me. 'That's straight up. Send a bottle of wine up, would you?'

'Any variety?'

Frank defers to his young friend. 'What colour wine?'

The girl, who is no older than twenty and wears a tracksuit, shrugs her shoulders. 'White. Red brings me out in a rash.'

'House wine, madam?' I say, wanting to condescend to her so bad it makes me tingle with anticipation.

'That's fair enough.'

'And for you, Frank?'

'Bourbon. A bottle. I'm out. Any Woodford?'

'Doubt it. I'll ask Martin. Jack Daniels do?'

'Sure you not got Woodford?' Frank says accusingly. I have not seen him smile yet, and I am not sure whether it's me he has an issue with.

'As I say –'

'Check. This is Lucy. Showing her my novel.'

'Hello, Lucy.'

'Hiya,' she says, smiling, half ignoring me.

'C'mon. You can help me write a story,' Frank says and gestures her upstairs. She dutifully follows.

He stops.

'Got peanuts?'

'Salted, Dry, or Honey roasted.'

'All three. And olives. Like olives, Lucy?'

'No, but I like nuts,' she says, half giggling.

The King of New York

It occurs to me at that very moment who Frank looks like. When I was a student, I watched a DVD called *King Of New York*.[24]

I hadn't thought about the film until this very moment for many, many years. He reminds me of the gangster in it, only much broader.

I cannot remember his name, but he's the spit moral. That same heavy lidded look. That same sense of me first, you nowhere. The disdain. The obtrusive, deliberate cool of it.

He puts his meaty paw on Lucy's back and ushers her upstairs.

---

[24]There is a magnificent scene where the gangster walks into a fried chicken shop and orders the entire menu for him and his gang. I smile at the memory and the chutzpah. I love *King Of New York*. I'm going to have to buy it now.

Midnight Run

I go to see Sixsmith and ask for the bottle of Jack Daniels. He is perched on a barstool scanning the Wheatley Fields Free Press classified ads. I think he runs an online auction business on the side.

'We're out,' he says, without looking up.

These are not the words I want to hear, particularly delivered by a man who is clearly not making much effort to hide his disdain, delivered in a rural Midlands accent, with a burr, the emphasis on the vowels. There is no hierarchy on paper, but I know where I stand. 'Can you nip up the Community Fayre and get some?'

'No. Busy.'

I look around the bar. There are two punters enjoying a pint. A fire well on the way to ash and ember. The TV showing a football match.

I press on. 'Cat says –'

'– bollocks to Cat,' Sixsmith says, emphasising everything and delivering it slowly. 'I'm busy, you go.'

'Listen, Martin. Frank wants a bottle of bourbon. He gets a bottle of bourbon. If you don't go fetch a bottle of bourbon from the Community Fayre, or the One Stop, I'm calling Cat.'

He looks up from his paper with menace. 'You do that, mate. You do that. See what happens.'

'Don't be so ridiculous, Martin.'

'I'm not going out in that rain,' he says, aware he is pushing it as far as it will go and softening a little. He isn't stupid: He's behaving like it – nasty and stupid, malevolent even – but he isn't.

'Okay. Send Kerry.'

'Yeh. Send Kerry. Where is she?'

'Don't know, Martin.'

'You find her and send her,' he says, returning to the paper and chewing on a peanut.

Annoyed, I see Kerry and rather than ask her to go to the supermarket, I ask her to hold the reception for fifteen minutes. She says she is due to go home, but says yes. I put on my raincoat. It is lashing down, so I take my umbrella. I race up the High Street to the off licence, order a bottle of Jack Daniels. They will bill me – this is not the first time this has happened, and we have a proper arrangement. I pick up three bags of peanuts, giant bags. This means I can ask Gavin for olives and not Sixsmith. I've had enough of him for one night. The Polish girl behind the counter takes all the details, and I am soon racing back along the street, nearly slipping outside the chocolate shop, half twisting my ankle. I am reasonably fit, so the race back is over in a jiffy, and although I am sopping wet, the job is done, and my sense of professionalism is satisfied. I run to the kitchen and ask for a jar of olives. Gavin is cooking steaks, and my mouth waters. He gives me six on a glass petrie dish from an already opened jar, which is fair enough and soon, I am ready to take up the goods. Kerry is talking to a guest, and I don't want to interrupt, so I take up the bottle, the nuts, and the olives myself. I am soon outside his door and knocking.

Lucy answers the door. 'Hi.'

The TV is on, and I can see Frank's chocolate and pale strawberry coloured bare feet hanging off the edge of the bed behind Lucy, who, now I see her in a different light, has also been drinking most of the afternoon. She sways just a little, a blade of grass in a light breeze.

'Frank's order, madam.'

'Is all this for us?'

'Yes. All this for you.'

'Awesome.' She nods. 'Yeh, awesome.' Takes the tray from me and kicks the door shut gently without saying goodbye.

My pager goes, and it is Kerry. I signal I'm coming back. I check my watch. It is past eight, and I have another twelve hours to go. I feel as if I have been working since eight in the morning instead of two hours.

When I get downstairs, Jo is waiting with her shopping bags. Amy is on her mobile phone underneath the portrait of Charles I by the door. 'Would you help me up with these?' Jo asks sweetly.

'My pleasure. Shall we take the lift?'

'Totally,' she says, relieved.

Jo waves at Amy, who blows her a kiss. I pick up the bags to Kerry's consternation. I know Kerry has to leave, but this is business. She is noticeably frustrated. I carry the bags to the lift, and Jo walks behind me, slightly pickled and giggling. She burps and swiftly apologises for it. 'My God, I so didn't expect that to happen. What must you think of me?'

'I didn't hear anything, Jo.'

'You're such a gentleman. I love England. Everyone has been so nice. I love it, my God, you are all so cool.'

'Thank you, Jo. My country appreciates that.'

We get into the lift, and I press a button.

'Apart from the weather, that is. So amazing the rain, Wow. Never seen anything like it,' she says,

'By the way, Julian asked me to ask you to give him a call in his room when you get the chance.'

'Julian? What about?'

'He said he wants to talk to you about Friday.'

'Oh, cool. I am *so* nervous. Me at a press conference. I've never done that before.'

'Me neither,' I say, and Jo laughs, as she is meant to.

I manage to get the bags into her room. She tries to tip me. This is the first time any of the guests tries this.

'No tipping here, Jo. My compliments.' Many hotels permit tips – The Saladin doesn't, compensating the staff with an assumed tip in the hourly rate.

'Oh, My God – no TIPPING? How cool is that! I kinda can't believe how awesome this is. We tip everywhere in the States.'

'Not in The Saladin. Will that be all?' I ask.

'Sure thing. Okay. And thanks.' She says, her phone going off, a vaguely familiar ringtone alerting her to a call. I smile and shut the door behind me.

I walk past Frank's room and hear music I don't recognise. By the time I get back to the desk, Kerry is irritated and storms off without saying goodbye to me. I'm not offended: Any rage I have, though internalised and controlled (and hotter than molten steel), is aimed not at her, but at Sixsmith for humiliating me. He knows I won't tell Cat. He knows I have a minimum contact policy with management – I made the mistake of telling him. Give a bully the right amount of information, and he will make it count. His mask slipped tonight.

Why? Why tonight? His resentment toward me has been bubbling under the surface, it always has been, but why did it blow tonight?

It just doesn't work with Sixsmith and me. Maybe it's some chemistry thing. Maybe it's an unstable reaction that's never going to work. We just don't mix. I came here in March around Easter time. I don't think we ever enjoyed a honeymoon period. He was off with me from the Induction stage onwards – the limp handshake and the cold stare.

Awkward, those awkward moments.

We've never had a bloke chat – football,[25] music,[26] women, politics – and yet, I've seen him hold court in the

---

[25] Chelsea. Despite being born and bred in Wheatley Fields, despite three local League teams, and without any apparent family connection, Sixsmith is a fanatic Chelsea supporter, spending long hours in front of the telly, and a fair amount of his monthly wages on a Sky subscription, supporting his favourite team. He also plays golf on Sundays. I don't know his handicap because I just don't care.

[26] Madness, The Specials, The Beat, The Jam, and all that eighties mod thing. Talking about these groups can send Sixsmith delirious with joy.

bar until three in the morning about Chelsea and Rory McIlroy, and how David Cameron isn't tough enough on benefit claimants, and what he would like to do to Megan Merryweather, the eighteen year old *Loaded* model everyone natters about at the moment.[27] He's never done that with me. Initially, I felt a bit left out.

In the early days, I tried to sit and talk to him when it was quiet in the hotel, but while he was garrulous and bluff with everyone else, he would turn into a Trappist monk with me. And it got worse as time has progressed. Sometimes you have to accept the way things are. Not that I want to discuss Chelsea, or Seve Ballesteros, or Ian Duncan-Smith's inability to control the welfare budget, or the precise dimensions of Briony Baxendale's voluptuous boobage. It's just…well…I like people to like me, and I feel awkward if they don't.

It's normal, isn't it? To want people to like you?

I think it is, anyway.

Amy, whom I notice, has just the two bags, picks up her raincoat and comes over to talk to me. I am beginning to suspect – and I mean this in the most politically correct way possible, and also the most professional – that she enjoys a drink. Her eyes flicker when she talks, and there is a slight slur.

'Is Frank available,' she asks. 'Don't tell anyone I asked, mind. I fancy a chat – and you're always busy.'

'Yes, Amy. And I'm afraid Frank's indisposed.'

'Really?' Amy exclaims. 'Why?'

---

[27]He's a big sociable Nazi, the type you get in hotels the world over, chatting to businessmen and contractors about the Four Topics of the Masculine Apocalypse. **Sport, old music, women** and **right wing politics** – most recently immigration. Carry on drinking long enough with a male bar manager in a full service hotel from Plymouth to Aberdeen, and said manager will eventually hold court on each of these themes.

'I've no idea,' I lie. 'He left instructions that he is not to be disturbed.'

Amy glances at me.

'Nothing to do with that young girl he's with?'

I feel as if I look silly and don't respond. I feel something else also, the inverse, the paradoxical opposite of the creepiness I felt last night. It felt like anti-matter might feel if it were real, rather than an abstraction.

She smiles and lets me off. 'I was at the Ladies when he came in. You are very confidential, and I trust you. So, I guess it's me, myself and the mini-bar. Did that Julian say anything about me. I saw him lurking about.'

'Of course not, Amy.'

'You wouldn't tell me if he did, would you?'

I don't reply.

'It's okay. I admire that. I know he hates me and one day, I might tell you why, when I am less drunk and more disposed. Tally ho and off we go!' Amy says, walking toward the lift.

'Good night, Amy.' I reply.

Julian's Opinion of Frank Duke (and Thriller Writers in General)

He's in front of me now, half cut, but not that far gone. Julian is sitting on a bar stool he's dragged from the bar. He is slightly slurring his words, but as drunks go, and I have met hundreds, he's a good one, who can hold his drink. He's the type of drunk who cannot be killed by conventional weapons.

Despite a few things, including her obvious interest in Frank and the fact Julian and I have become quite friendly, I don't want him to criticise Amy any more, and I am prepared to stop him doing so. A night porter, above all things, should be impartial and balanced, especially when it comes to guests, and while Julian ranting about Amy was perfectly okay when I didn't know her, when she was an abstract concept in the distance, I know her now, and (the twinge) that knowledge has changed things. It doesn't change how I feel about Julian – but it certainly means he cannot launch into her with impunity. It wouldn't be fair.

So instead, he sits on his bar stool and talks about Frank.

'What do you think of Frank?' he asks. I notice his black tee shirt with an album cover on it – Japan, *Gentlemen Take Polaroids* – and ripped jeans and (oddly, for the weather), pink flip flops. He's sipping a malt whisky – a large glass I served him earlier.

'He's a nice man. You're not a fan, I've noticed.'

'No issues with *him* at all. It's just he can't write. That's my problem with the concept of Frank Duke.'

I play Devil's Advocate. 'How come he's been nominated?'

'Publicity. He sells a million copies minimum. It's good publicity to have a pop novelist like him on the show. While you are at it, add Cook to that caper, too.'

'You don't think Jo can write?'

'Don't get me wrong, if you're a kid, she's Shakespeare, but you don't mature into a writer until your mid-thirties. What does Jo know? What can she tell us about the world we live in? Yeh, she can construct a sentence, and those that know, tell me her dialogue is spot-on, but she shouldn't be lauded like this. She'll get complacent. She'll never write anything *substantial* – that's assuming there is anything substantial left to write. Did you know Amy is the favourite for the big prize?'

'Amy?'

'Bookies have her 6/4 favourite. She's that popular.'

'Her last book is supposed to be very literary.'

'Yeh, right. And I'm Chairman Mao's pet monkey.'

I get on my guard. 'That's what I heard.'

'Still the same old Amy Cook she was last year,' but, for whatever reason, he doesn't launch into her in the way I expect him to. Instead, he switches subject.

'I like Jo. Did I tell you I'm taking her to the races.'
'Wheatley Fields Racecourse?'
'That's right. That's what I wanted to tell her about. I've got a taxi at twelve. Do you like the horses?'
'I do, yes.'
'Why don't you come?' He asks, genuinely.
'Can't. I'm having a suit fitted in the City.'
'Don't tell me you've got a tailor?'
'I have, indeed,' I said, and Julian starts to laugh.
'I knew there was something cool about you, Mr Porter. That *is* cool. A tailor…I don't even have a *suit.*'
'Work, Julian. Got to look the part.'

We chat about the horses, work and suits in a sort of jumbled order. He also talks about Jo. Had Amy not got in first with the shopping trip, he would have taken her to The Three Steeples Church today.

We talk about Jo for a bit, how nice she is, how refreshing, and I go to the bar and refill his whisky. When I return, he is subdued: This is the problem with conversing with a drunk – the massive mood swings.

'Frank. He hates me.'

I pick up a boiled sweet from the complimentary dish. 'I can't say that I blame him, Julian.'

'Me, too.'

'He served in Vietnam –'

'Did he? I read his bio. One of the last tours ever assigned before the fall of Saigon. I wonder how much action he saw. I'm sceptical. He was a guitarist in a top band. There is something wrong about that guy.'

'What do you mean?'

'He's done *far* too much with his life. Nobody packs rock guitar, Vietnam, and writing novels into one life, do they. Nah, it's all a bit –'

'Fake?' I interject.

'– scripted. Yeh, scripted. Frank the Action Man. It's not about *him* though. I'm sure he tells a good joke, is kind to animals and all that. He just can't *write*'

'That's your objection?'

'They fill up the shelves with crap and no one gets to see the good stuff. He's a cheerleader for that. I hate these people who think they can write when they can't. The *public loves them.* Can't they *see?* It's the Paradox.'

'What price are you in the betting?' I ask, genuinely curious and eager to stop him ranting before he starts.

'For the big one? The Gold Award?'

'Yes.'

'I'm in the Bar price.'

'You mean an outsider?'

'Online, Betmarket have me at 580 for pennies. No market. No public. No publicity value.'

'I read that piece you told me about.'

'Jeavons in *The Guardian*?'

'That's it. The vanguard thing.'

'He's a nice bloke. Barking up the wrong tree sadly. You know how he got to read the book?'

'Bought online?'

'Even if he does buy Indie – and he doesn't – the odds on him finding my book at random are millions to one. Let's face it, everyone is writing a book nowadays thanks to Tarzan. There are ways you can narrow the odds, but, sadly, there are millions and millions of books out there now and about half a million authors. He would never have found it.'

'So how?'

'Someone bought a paperback from Tarzan and sent it to him. Someone he knew and trusted, obviously, because he read it.'

'Who. Do you know?'

'Nope. Never found out. He must have bribed Phillip Jeavons to read the book, whoever it was. I was just some Indie.'

'He loves the book.'

'Unlike the author called Dyanne Rebus, of Arkansas, who described it as the most depressing experience of her entire life.'

'Reading this made me want to kill myself', she wrote on Tarzan. *'I hope I never come across this man's work again in my lifetime.'*

'It could have been someone you have annoyed.'

He shakes his head and sips his malt. 'Nope. I'd never heard of this woman. Jeavons was the opposite, though. He thinks it's great and afterwards, I got nominated for an Arkwright. Two, actually. Independent and Contemporary. And if I win one, I'm in with a shot at the Gold. All that press and publicity. Exciting, innit.'

'Must be.'

'Let's be honest, everyone's writing a book these days.'

'Are they?

'You're not kidding. Millions of authors. It's not so much the book, or the writing, it's the getting it in front of the reader's minces.'

'What?'

'Minces. Mince pies. Eyes. The reader's beady eyes.'

'Yes. Mince pies. Hence your excitement about the press conference.'

'F'in bonus. Sadly, Amy Cook and Frank Duke have got more chance than I have of winning something because they are household names, but a nomination is a bonus, and a conference to discuss the nomination is a Brucie-double-bonus.'

'Okay, understood.'

'Glad you're keeping up.'

'So, what are Frank's odds?'

'For Best Thriller? Quite well fancied. Five-to-one.'

'And Jo?'

'Quite fancied for the YA prize. Can't remember precisely. Seven-to-two, I think. The judges love her. There is a Halo Effect about Jo.'

'A Halo Effect?'

'Yeh, from psychology. It's about the equation between looks and behaviour. It seems we associate beauty with goodness, handsomeness with gallantry. Good looking people get lesser sentences in court, better marks in class, the benefit of the doubt whenever it is needed. Also works in publishing.'

'I remember the Halo Effect.'

'Ah!' he says, looking at me as if he was staring down a sniper's scope. 'But do you know Duncan's Dictum?'

I shake my head. 'Got me there.'

'Glen Duncan. Brilliant writer. He famously prognosticated that a publisher looks at the author photo before the manuscript and uses that to make their publication decision. That puts Jo bang in the lead for her prize. I've seen the rest of the field for YA Author of the Year, and she's the peach in a basket of conkers. I've had a decent bet on her this week. You should. But, as I said earlier, she's not ready for the two main prizes, and if she carries on writing about vampires, or gargoyles, or succubi, whatever kid's nonsense it is that she writes about, she is never going to achieve anything *substantial,*' he said, waving his arm about and finishing his malt. 'Any chance of another?'

'Last one, Julian? It's late.'

'Okay. Make it a large, in that case.'

The bar light was still open, and I opened the bottle of malt he'd been working his way through. I was glad he didn't rear up on me for gently suggesting an informal last orders.

I had to be careful with him, his capacity for drink, and his tendency to annihilate himself.[28]

---

[28] A week ago, they had to bring him in from The Saddlers. Big Keith (the landlord) drove him round and dropped him off outside. He collapsed, and the landlord had to park on double yellows to make sure he actually made it into the hotel. I spotted the situation and helped. He's not heavy and it was easy enough. What was harder to take was his vomiting into an antique brass bucket, which dates back to the mid eighteenth

century. It's a copy of one George III might have used. Keith – a hard man – wanted to tell me to tell him that it was all over at his pub, and ten years ago, he would have been barred, but in today's day and age, you can't bar a drunk who gets completely munted on beer costing three pounds and fifty pence a pint. Most young people hammer themselves on supermarket vodka and tins of Thor's Hammer before they go out, but Julian is a pub man through and through: He needs to hold court. Drinkers and bystanders are his mirror. That kind of brain damage must have transferred thirty quid minimum into Keith's till – plus the tiny tots he was fond of (the vodkas, the malts, the Jack Daniels), all at a minimum three quid a pop. Keith helped me upstairs with him. He reeked of beer, fags, congealed vomit and, weirdly, air-freshener. We threw him on his bed face down, the correct position for someone in that state, and he never murmured a word. He got up in the morning as if nothing had happened and off he went into the City. Alcoholics can handle that kind of physical abuse. Me? A sniff of the barmaid's apron, and I'm asleep in the corner. A ginger wine at Christmas and a tot of whisky for the Queen's Speech. The rest of the time, I'm on juice. I had to clean up his mess and spent most of the night shining the brass with a special chamois leather. I made it my business to tell Julian he owed me. Two nights before that, he was thrown out of the Benbow for punching a bouncer. The bouncer came out much the best and that was the end of that. Barred and bruised. A night before that, a girl slapped him in the Haywain for making an improper suggestion. At the weekend, he didn't bother coming back to his room, partying with all the students at the college, some fifteen years younger than him. He's out of control, and I know he is. I hear him wailing in his room sometimes when I walk past. I hear him chuntering as he walks upstairs. He's unsettled. Something bothers him. If it wasn't for the Awards, he would have been barred from the hotel by now. He's smashed glasses (accidentally, he says, clumsily, he says) in his bathroom. He's fallen into the mini-bar and nearly put an elbow through the shower door (accidentally, he says, clumsily, he says). I wish I could coach him. I can't interfere though – I'm the night porter, not a counsellor. I'll clean his mess up and sort his bill when it's time for him to go back to Hell.

I hand Julian the half full glass of malt.

'Hey, I was thinking of something the other night."

'Yes?' I reply, sitting down behind my desk. I was suddenly thirsty and admonished myself for not pouring a fruit juice when I was at the bar.

'There's a film about you. Have you seen it?'

'The Night Porter? With Dirk Bogarde?'

'That's it,' he said. 'By Cavani. Seen it?'

'I have.'

'I thought you weren't a film man?'

'Not really. I *have* seen that. You look surprised?'

'I am.'

Julian laughed. 'All the Charlotte Rampling stuff?'

I laughed with him. 'Not quite, Julian.'

'Why? The film is a training DVD for night porters. I'd be very surprised if any night porter worth his salt hadn't seen it. Compulsory viewing.

'You mean the hotel, the style, the *immaculatum.*'

'That's it.'

'Hence, the tailor.'

'Hence, the tailor, indeed.'

The pager vibrated and sung. It was Mrs Appleby.

Julian grinned at me.

'You're a good man, Mr Porter. You're a damned good man.'

'And I take it you're off to bed?'

'Via the lift, chap. See you in the morning.'

I still don't know who's paying for the hotel.

Cat's had words with me. Guests have complained – everything from his smell, to his mad staring eyes in the bar, his ranting in the bedroom, his ghostly pallor, his clumsy stumbles in the corridor into unwelcoming doors – but Cat says his benefactor just says send me the bill. I sometimes wonder whether it's Mary Beth Burnell, but she's no millionaire and she's too – I don't know, it's all wrong. Someone is paying the tab and someone will be left to pick up the pieces.

Let's be honest…

'Let's be honest. Everyone's writing a book nowadays.'[29][30][31][32]

---

[29] All the following novels were submitted to the Arkwright Trust for inclusion and selection in the Independent category – and ninety percent of them were self-published on Tarzan. Mary Beth gave me a copy of the list. There are more, but I did not include the disqualified – over seventy others, which did not meet the criteria. As an initial filter, "a slush pile panjandrum", as she described herself, chuckling, Mary Beth read at least the first chapter of each nominee. Pass that stage and she would read on, and pass them to another eight judges. The octet would pass their five selections to a final five judges. All the occupations come from the initial entry form. This is how the writers of these novels – which are each at least 50,000 words long, 50k words being the minimum criteria for selection – describe themselves. Notice how not one of them described themselves as an author? I have not seen the entry form – and maybe that self-description was not permitted – but I found that surprising. Especially the unemployed. It must be so easy to describe yourself as an author in that case.

[30] Shine Regan, (Student), *My Vampire Lover,* Michael Michaelson, (Solicitor), *Case Dismissed,* Leif Way, (Repairman), *I, Frankenstein,* Brian Cantrell, (Draughstman), *Drawing Them In! My Life As A Technical Artist,* Nathan Leader, (Student), *Murder Times Five,* Louise Lance, (Lawyer), *Courtroom Number Nine,* William C Best, (Retired), *Lunar Landing on Lecos 945,* Scott A Dixon (Retired), *Martian Memories,* Mitchell B Jung, (Retired), *Something Astral This Way Comes,* Petra Nightbird, (Student), *Your Kisses Are Sweet,* Kendrick G Happy, (Retired), *Stranger in a Stranger's Land,* Laura Clipp, (Housewife), *On My Knees For Him,* Makko Isumjo, (Student), *Syzygy in Blue,* Craig Knutt, (Student), *Cheltenham Axe Murders,* Pauline Finch, (Housewife), *Letters of Love,* Paula Peters, (Student), *Castle of Dragons,* Abraham P Wilden, (Farmer), *Running with Stonewall Jackson,* Graham March, (Librarian), *Harper Into Africa,* Francis Francis, (Housewife), *The Glass Castle,* Elizabeth Bean, (Civil Servant), *Giants In The Mountains,* Brian Trout (Fishmonger),

Trays of Ice: A Life With Fish, Amanda Flint, (Student), *In Love With A Killer Werewolf,* Noosha Venus, (Student), *Chained,* Jack "Peanuthead" Wilson, (Taxi Driver), *Cabbie!* Joy Meadows, (Housewife), *A Winter's Love,* Mildred Leech, (Post Office Counter Assistant), *Loving Letters; A Working Life At The Post Office,* Mo Kristiansen, (Student), *Parties of the Glamorous Dead,* Martina Nirvana, (Retail Manager), *The Ludo Box,* Cal Dench, (Unemployed), *Zombie Adventures,* Alan Pike, (Chef), *Clive's Restaurant,* Alan X. Jarvis, (Retired), *Sauron Fourteen,* Bob Harvey, (Car Mechanic), *Adventures in the London Motor Trade,* Pam Kent, (Housewife), *Sex and the Over Fifties,* Mary Ann Lewandoski,. (Retired), *Fallen Leaves,* Valerie Sherbert, (Librarian), *Passage to Tibet,* Kiki Crisp, (Certified Accountant), *Enslaved,* L.Mugg-Phillips, (Architect), *Space Station Number Eight,* Fallon Foulds, (Student), *Revenge of the Aknaten Trolls,* Brian Hand, (Unemployed), *Force Ten Attack on Guadalcanal,* Kelly Dunne, (Student), *My Big Black Boss,* Lana Reid, (Student), *Noone Saw You In The Trees,* Morgan Naismith, (Retired), *Astronauts and Aliens,* DJ Creed, (DJ), *HipHop Gunmen.* Bob Fortune, (Bookmaker), *The Gamble,* Meaden Lynch, (Farmer), *Fields of Dreams – My Life In The Farm Belt,* Lulu Balls, (Freelance), *Sexy Girl and a Big Bad Boy,* Barbara Lynch, (Retired), *A Cruise In The Caribbean,* Ruth Johnson, (Retail Worker), *Bachelor Billionaire,* Ruth Falco, (Housewife), *Barbara's Billionaire,* Kelley Lunt, (Student), *Billionaire Paradise,* Rachel Porter, (Student), *Enslave Me and Make Me Beg,* Rachel Du Pont, (Accountant), *Love in Louisville,* Renee Smith, (Housewife), *Kiss of the Vampire,* Gil Jennings, (Unemployed), *I, Vampire Slayer,* Barbara Fitton, (Grandmother), *Moll's Court,* Crystal Tipps, (Housewife), *Dominated in the Master's Bedroom,* Maxwell Heath, (Unemployed), *Washington Warning,* F.Lyons, (Fitter), *A Colony on Mars 398,* Brett West, (Male Model), *Carla's Angels,* Matthew C Wilhelm, (Stockbroker), *The Kansas City Project,* Janie Januszek, (Loss Adjuster), *Forty Shades of Crimson,* Antonia Mars-Delphi, (Party Organiser), *Antonia's Sexy Parties,* Ann Winterton, (Housewife), *An Eternal Romance,* Alana Beast, (Unemployed), *Sex Mad Brighton Barmaids,* Amy Tent, (Pharmacist), *Blue Ophelia,* Gary

Whitehouse, (Lawnmower Salesman), *Supergrass! My Life in Lawnmowers,* Bing Quickstep, (Estate Agent), *I, Zombie,* Mark Fulsome, (Sales Rep), *Johnny Bravo,* Zoe Planchette, (Student), *The Grey Gargoyle,* Zoe Feast, (Solicitor), *Detective Truman Investigates: In The Boneyard,* Fatima Ali, (Optician), *Blood On The River,* Paul Feely, (Unemployed), *Chimp Dixon,* Manny Kaltz, (Ex-Footballer), *In Defence,* Porter Phoenix, (Waitress), *Dinner for One,* Lenny Watkins, (Unemployed), *Welcome to Gun City,* Peaches Allen, (Department Store Sales), *BDSM Stands for Sex,* Una Forbes-Nelson, (Housewife), *The Prince and the Princess,* Janine Balls, (Flower Shop Owner), *Daffodils and Dahlias: High Jinks on the Flowery High Street,* Jim Forest, (Salesman), *Gay Nights,* Candle Wright, (Student), *Mirror Lies The Vampire,* Jack Phythian, (Unemployed), *Zombie Flesh Hunters,* Peter Zinc, (Fitter), *Death Zombies On The March,* Neil Wood, (Student), *Zombie Killer,* Suzanne Screwdriver, (Student), *I Married A Zombie Flesh Eater,* Malcolm Barnett, (Butcher), *I've Got A Big Chopper! My Life In The Retail Meat Trade,* Catriona Kennedy, (Cosmetics Distributor), *Dragons and Dance,* Ally McBeal, (Student), *Crucified and Stripped,* Phoebe McBride, (Housewife), *Swept Off My Feet by Dr Neat,* Bruno Nkomo, (Student), *Daktari Nights,* Zoe Love, (Student), *Kissed By A Gargoyle,* Malcolm Muggleton, (Newsagent), *Sleepless in Swansea – Early Morning Life as a Newsagent,* Caitlyn Phillips, (Student), *Weep Weep: Single All My Life,* Rachel Rho, (Office Manager), *Tales of a Part Time Stripper,* Rachel Reid, (Teacher), *At His Mercy,* Rachel Ruff, (Student), *Gargoyle vs Vampire,* Leonard Kent Rachel III, (Retired), *Star System Alpha Centauri,* Binden Lasch, (Electrician), *Sparks Fly in Cincinatti,* Cal Munt, (Unemployed), *Vampire Flesh Eaters,* Rachel Whitemoor-Unkala, (Housewife), *My Giant Black Lover,* Julie Pilgrim, (Student), *Crystal Castles In The Sky,* Alison Ponder, (Delivery Driver), *Pole Dancer,* Josephine St Clair, (Freelance), *WHORE! My Life As A Low Rent Prostitute in Pittsburgh,* Wilma Creep, (Librarian), *Hungry Games,* Lawrence Erikson, (Geologist), *Tyler of the Trade Winds,* Mark Wade, (Unemployed), *Gun Battle,* Enid Del Motto, (Retired), *Golden Locks,* Quuna M'Bele, (Student), *Zulu Massacre,* Marion Borna, (Veterinary Nurse), *I Married A*

Gunslinger, Peter Cotton, (Civil Servant), *The Gunslinger,* Colin Maverick, (Medical Sales Representative), *Blood Red Gunslinger,* Barry F Salt, (Retired), *Gunslinger's Dawn,* Nigel Maverick, (Plasterer), *Kill All Aliens,* Bonnie Wilson, (Housewife), *Fields of Golden Dreams,* Kyren Keith, (Student), *Dark Cravings,* Queenie Morpeth, (Trainee Teacher), *I, Gargoyle,* Lily Lanchester, (Student), *Gorgeous and Gagged,* Marlene Michaels, (Solicitor), *The Haunted Courtroom,* Penny Peters, (Office Manager), *Saturday Night Is For Ironing My Knickers!* Harry Li, (Chartered Accountant), *Immobile Parallax,* Pauline O'Callaghan, (Unemployed), *Slave To My Black Master,* Fred J Stronach, (Civil Servant), *Star System Moonax,* Tess Kay, (Warehouse Distributor), *I Deserve My Punishment,* Barbara Mead, (Retired), *Roses For Me, Just Love for Him,* Nigel Woodhouse, (Painter and Decorator), *Splash! Painting My Way Through Life,* Lena Solvitzky, (Student), *Dragonfire Tales,* Banfield Mozart-Jones, (Unemployed), *Effervescentium,* Lorna McCloud, (Shopworker), *Quest for Fire – A Dragon's Tale,* Pete Hall, (Car Mechanic), *Drinking And Other Man-Bollocks,* Caravelle De Priest, (Artist), *Raphael and Me,* Brian P Messerschmitt, (Retired), *Space Shuttle To Star System S-129,* Younis Ahmed, (Student), *Interpol Incident,* Max Cherry, (Advertising Executive), *Judy's Luck,* Ali Day, (Artist), *Dragon's Scales of Gold,* Xal Fenchurch, (Student), *Quest For The King,* Rose Winter-Fitchney, (Housewife), *Seven Days With My Billionaire,* Mungton Parsnip, (Unemployed), *Mungton Parsnip – A History,* Lulu Gray, (Cosmetics Retail Assistant), *The Man With The Iron Manacles,* Vera Fox-Mappelton, (Interior Designer), *Stripes and Pastels. Decorating For Celebrities And The Rich,* Snowdrop White, (Student), *Me, Luke and Lucifer the Dog,* Carrie Box, (Student), *The Daughter of Satan,* Erick E Wolfe, (Retired), *Alien Landing,* Kennedy Krush, (Consultant), *Lipstick Lesbian,* Margaret Bosworth, (Housewife), *Kisses On The Golden Veranda,* Amy Eagle, (Student), *Young Lovers Cry,* Vaughan Volpa, (Telesales), *I Hate You For Hanging Up On Me,* Eunice Miller, (Housewife), *A Doctor's Heart,* Callum Biscuit, (Unemployed), *Zombietrap,* Mick Livingstone, (Site Manager), *Making It Work - My Life In Projects,* Maureen Laverty, (Catering Manager), *Harder and*

Harder, Cane Wilson, (Student), *Microsex,* Stephen P. Gallagher, (Retired) *I, Cyborg,* Eric Peach, (Government), *Detective Carroll Investigates,* Jane King-Welbeck, (Homemaker), *Carrie's In Love,* Bernice Cavendish, (Civil Servant), *Bluff King Hal's Last Hunt,* Florence King, (Bar Staff), *Loving The Gargoyle,* Georgina Rhys-Nkana, (Secretary), *Amelia's Teardrops,* Bryn Brindle, (Van Driver), *Confessions of a Delivery Driver,* Mark Margarson, (Unemployed), *The Walking Nightmare,* Hazel Harvest, (Student), *I Love Sex,* Keelan Wince, (Financial Analyst), *The Washington Zombie Murders,* Marie Wood, (Estate Agent), *Rhapsody in Rose Pink,* Fenny Chambers, (Housewife), *Black Cock,* John Ramp, (Police Officer), *O'Bannon,* Xantos Kelly, (Student), *No-one Loves Me,* Jenny Milton, (Housewife), *Escape To The South Hams,* Hayley Lu, (Student), *Bad Boy Boogie,* Carla Lime, (Housewife), *Bad Boy In My Bed,* Rue Vale, (Cosmetics Sales), *Bad Boys,* Phillippa Pye-Meadows, (Quantity Surveyor), *Baddest Boy in Town,* Iona Flint, (Commis Chef), *I, Lesbian,* Adam Allen, (Taxi Driver), *Late Nights and Alienation in St Albans,* Adam Alchemy, (Student), *The Wizard,* Adam Kesteven, (Forestry Worker), *Save The Goldfinch,* Ken Lumbsden, (Retired), *Managing My Affairs. Things I Have Seen In Factory Management.* Mara Kauntz, (Student), *I, Vampire* –

[31] – and finally, possibly the best of all, and very close to being nominated, I hear, was a great YA novel by the wonderfully named American called Scarlett Byron, (Student) – and if that's her real name, I would marry her tomorrow, sight unseen – about a reluctant vampire. The novel is called *Comfy Gravestones*.

[32] I'll let you count them. And when you think self-pubs are notoriously reluctant to submit anything to anyone, for fear of criticism and censure, what kind of percentage is this? Ten per cent? Twenty? This is only British and American authors. Over ten percent of the Icelandic population have written a book.
The population of Iceland is 302,000, give or take the odd Viking. Thirty thousand people minimum.

The Magic Bookcase

On Thursday evening, Cat, with a grin on her face as wide as the Thames, stops me before I can sit down at my night porting station and log on. I am in a good mood. I had spent the afternoon cleaning my flat to a rare shine while watching horse racing. I had chanced a bet on my online account on the twilight card at Kempton – a horse called Kuanayo – and it had won quite easily at seven-to-one. I backed the horse enough to pay for a couple of new shirts and subsequently, I bought and paid for two from a London-based online retailer. Both are beautiful shirts – one snow white, the other fuchsia. They will arrive next week, and I am excited by the purchase. I walked the short distance to work with a smile on my face.

'Come look at this. It's awesome,' Cat says. 'It was delivered and fitted today.'

She's wearing a cream suit for some reason, a light blue blouse, and a pair of black high-heel patents I've not seen before. I wonder if she is going out after work. It is 7pm. I follow her. I see Frank Duke up ahead, and he's looking at something, a book, which he holds in his hand. We stop in front of a bookcase.

Frank, I notice, is studying one of the books. He doesn't say anything to us as he leans against the wall. When he sees us peruse the case, he moves away and sits on one of the occasional chairs in the corridor. Cat looks at me, raises her eyebrows and turns to the case.

'Look at this. Mary Beth asked me whether the hotel wanted one. What do you think I said! It's so cool.'

The case is striking and attractive to the eye. I stand back as far as I can go and assess the item in front of me with a critical eye. Six feet square, encased with two glass doors. Carved gargoyle heads grace the top two corners. It is a mahogany colour. I walk forward and look closer at the wood. Run my fingertips across it. It is sublime, but it isn't mahogany. At least, I hope it isn't. I will have to check with Mary Beth. I will not be amused if it's mahogany despite its beauty. Mahogany and other hardwoods are always more beautiful as trees. Still, I examine it closer. Running fingertips along its patina leaves no after-impression. The varnish shines intensely (as do the glass doors, which, I suspect, are reinforced and super-glazed). Concentric whorls and interlocking whirlpools cascade from top to bottom just below the level of glance.

There are five shelves, big enough to fit a substantial novel (but not a coffee table book), each lined with silver and gold braiding and all full of modern tomes, nothing leather-bound, no folio editions, nothing faux-trad. These are colourful, almost artistic, paperback books. The bookshelf is newly crafted. It is not antique, so the fact it houses paperbacks doesn't jar – and it is important to note that these aren't charity shop paperbacks. These are pristine, immaculate, some with matte covers and some with gloss. Some large and weighty, others small and petite, small enough to fit in a clasp bag. Another quirky aspect of it is that I hardly recognise the names. I am drawn to the ones I do know and, yes, all those of our guests are here.[33] [34] Madeline France, *Amelia.* Frank

---

[33] Later that night, when it was quiet, I counted the books. Taken as a whole, a coagulated, multi-coloured mass, a patchwork of words and colours, I noticed that each of them was embossed with a tiny symbol – A^t – in gold on a white background shaped like a teardrop. I guessed that that must have denoted an Arkwright edition and I realised these were all specially commissioned.

[34] Mackenzie Knight, *Cypress Hill.* Emma Edwards, *Sanguinary, Imbrued, Ensanguined,* Katie Oliver, *Prada and Prejudice.* Debi Smith, *Chocolate and Romance,* Brenda Perlin, *Burnt Promises, Shattered Reality, Brooklyn and Bo,* Frank Duke, *Shakedown in Chicago, Apocalyptic, New York Shakedown, Bombsite, Invasion USA, Bankjob, Nuclear Attack,*

Wendy Steele, *Destiny of Angels,* Billie Jones, *Snake Typhoon,* Susan Buchanan, *The Dating Game,* Viggo Jones, *The Far Side of Consciousness,* Lelani Black, *Bosses With Benefits, Gone Greek. Doctor, Doctor,* Marcia Brake, *Maxilon Five,* Mary Ann Bernal, *The Briton and the Dane, Concordia, Timeline,* Phil Naessens, *The Reluctant Sportswriter,* Dawn Smith, *Crimson Fury,* SK Whiteside, *Inheritance,* Karenne Griffin, *Beyond The Island, The Valleys.* Rae Gee, *Mars On The Rise, The Glory of Joshua Jones,* Cleetus Christmas, *Parallelogram,* Renee Sweet, *Billionaire in Love,* Ngaire Elder, *The Adventures of Cecilia Spark, The Mystic Mountains of Terra, Dragon's Star,* Terry Tyler, *Nine Lives, Dream On, Nobody's Fool,* Ken Hoss, *Storm Warning,* Matt Posner, *The School of the Ages,* Sarah Tipper, *Eviscerated Panda, Back in Bamboo, Death Metal Maniac,* Cheryl Ramirez, *Texas,* Nigel Fink, *Blood Wedding,* Danielle Belwater, *Of Fire and Rain.* Elise Van Cise, *Don't Touch,* Otto Mann, *I Left The House One Day and Returned As A Rabbit,* Alan Potts, *The National Hunt,* Sue Lobo, *Poetry, The African Wilderness, Lollipops of Dust,* Eric Rada, *New York Symphony,* Mark Barry, *Carla, The Pandemonium Sisters, Hollywood Shakedown, S & V,* N. Bryan Hamilton, *My Life as a Peanut,* Kim Scott, *Regarding Ruth,* Brian Palmer, *The Curious Case of Kenny Gillett,* Christy Foster, *Bluffing The Devil,* Suzanne Van Rooyen, *Obscura Burning, The Other Me,* Wayne De Priest, *Angeltown,* Bill Jones Jr, *The Stream, Hard as Roxx,* Sinead MacDughlas, *Learn To Love Me,* Yvonne Knutt, *Antonia, Anastasia,* Vickie McKeehan, *Pelican Pointe, The Bones Will Tell,* K-Trina Meador, *The Knights of Dixie Wild, Journey to Freedom,* Paul Ducard, *The Other Side of Satan,* Madeline France, *Amelia, The Wind in the Trees, Rachel's Love, Rose Red, Rhapsody in Fuchsia, Love in Vegas,* Josephine Jackson, *Gettysburg,* Gladys Quintal, *The Man Of Your Dreams, Succubus,* Stefan Xerxes, *Fast Food and Hard Times,* Louise Gornall, *In Stone,* Jessica McHugh, *Pins, Song of Eidolons,* Shane KP O'Neill, *For Whom The Bell Tolls, The Dracula Chronicles,* Jo Marron-Saint, *Heart and Soul, Sonia the Succubus, Sonia and the Vampire Wolf, Sonia Goes to Hell, Bloodshot,* Kyra Dune, *Elfblood,* Donald Key, *Stained Glass Heart,* Kenneth J Grant, *Ulysses; The Magnificent Journey,* Forlan Jentz, *XO,* Julie

Duke, *New York Shakedown.* Jo Marron-Saint, *Sonia The Succubus* – and I was pleased to note the chromatic blue spine of *Notes,* which Julian had shown me earlier.

'Arkwright-nominated books from the past six years. Hotel guests can take them up to their rooms,' Cat says.

'Seems a shame to actually read them,' I commented. 'The case is a work of art on its own. What about theft?'

'We're lucky. We can easily replace them. They keep multiple copies stored in the old Euripides Clinic. They are building a library of books down there, a British Library of modern fiction. I've been invited next week, and I cannot wait. They've donated these to us, and we can have as many as we like, and if one of the guests gets light fingered...so? We can replace the copy. What do you think, Frank?' Cat asks the reading author, excited. 'Isn't it wonderful?'

'Yes, it is. It's a striking addition to the hotel. I'm proud to have my books as part of the collection,' he replies, his bassoon voice filling the corridor. Today, he

---

Cassar, *Ruby Blue,* Jasmine Bath, *No-one's Daughter,* Carla Meyer, *Destined,* Ruth Watson Morris, *Fantacia,* Mande Matthews, *Shadowlight,* Linna Drehmel, *H.E.A.R.T,* Paul Palance, *Jewel Thieves,* Caroline Faulkes-Newton, *Love in a Cadillac, Roses are Red,* Bathsheba Dailey, *Tales of Romeo,* Keith Nicholls, *Virginia Waters,* Ken Lights, *Everglades,* Max Thomson-Jones, *Warren Hill,* Monique Rockcliffe, *The Sword Bearers,* Rosie Lola, *Renegade Lover,* ST Bende, *Entranced,* Kyle Hannah, *Time Assassins.* Lenny Dollar, *Casey's Story.* Michelle Miller, *Lovetide,* Britney Eugene-Smith, *The Sparkling Crypt,* Brian Dobbins, *Corryville,* Michelle Gent, *Ancients and Gods,* Adam Tithe, *Europiated,* Toi Thomas, *Eternal Curse,* Maggie Secara, *Molly September,* Val-Rae Christensen, *Of Moths and Butterflies,* Kaitlyn Dean, *The Witches Sleep,* Kelly Grealis, *The Descendant,* Colin Canister, *Elegant Waves of Eternal Being,* Jenny Worstall, *Make A Joyful Noise,* Mackenzie Brown, *The Book of Souls,* Jeanette Hornby, *Candy's Man,* Zeus Bracchus, *Extreme,* Nathan Squiers, *Prince of Darkness,* Alesha Escobar, *The Gray Tower.*

is dressed like an English gentleman, with a pinstripe charcoal grey suit and magnificent brogues, the leather shined to a mirror polish. From where we stand, you can see the soles of the brogues, and they have not seen concrete – though I doubt he bought that suit off the peg. He stands, towering over us, both physically and metaphorically. He puts back his book neatly. 'I'm going to win Best Thriller this year. I know it. I can feel it. I hear you were talking odds the other night with the English writer,' he says to me – and I immediately wonder how he knows.

'Just a small chat in passing.'

'I inquired at Ladbrokes.' He pronounces it Brokes, as in Pokes, rather than Brooks. 'They have my book at eleven-to-two. Man, I scooped up that price, and I called some guys back home, guys who play the hoops and the NFL, to open accounts. We hit those suckers, and they'll pay. *Shakedown in Chicago* has sold three million copies. There is a historic correlation between the winner of that prize and sales,' he says. 'Ladbrokes have me at thirty-three-to-one for the big prize. I guess they have that kinda cool. Some of these ladies and gentlemen here –' he says, pointing at the book case, '– are far more deserving in terms of literary prowess, including my very good friend, Mrs Cook, but I doubt anyone has written a more exciting book this year,' he says, with a striking lack of modesty. 'And that's what we are here for, isn't it?'

Cat is spellbound. I have not heard him speak at this length since he's been here, and his voice gets deeper the more sentences his discourse contains. It slows down.

'Er, is it?' She says, confused. 'Why are we here?'

'To excite,' he says, looking intently at her.

'Yes.'

'To entertain.'

'Okay. I see,' she replies.

'And to energize. The asshole English self-publisher has been vocal about Mrs Cook and I. And friends of mine online. About how we can't write. About how he can. He's been unkind. I have read his comments on the Internet, and he and I today discussed those comments.'

I say nothing. Cat looks at me for reasons I don't understand, but stay silent.

'His work is good. It is magnificent, in parts. I will be prepared to admit that he is a far better author than me, but as for his work –' He pulls out *Notes* gently, as if he has a reverence for books, an understanding of both their strength and their fragility, and taps it with the fingertip of his right hand. He has big hands, an artisan's hands, I notice. '– it is *not* entertaining. It is *not* exciting. It does *not* energise the reader. It will win nothing. Nada. He can criticise, and emote, and theorise about my work all he likes.'

He puts back *Notes* in its place on the shelf. 'I am impervious to him. Does the mountainside cry at the beat of the gull's wings on its edifice? Now. I must eat.' And without saying goodbye, he walks past and into the reception, leaving Cat and I staring at the case.

The bookcase is a beautiful piece, but I'm not sure about the position – it is too close to the kitchen for my taste, but I can see why Cat has had it placed there, halfway up the wall. The entrance hall is packed with clocks, portraits and artefacts. I wonder whether enough people will see this. I would have put it elsewhere.

When Julian saw it, he was the least interested of the quartet, and hardly spent any time at all looking at it. Of all the authors to see that bookcase, he was the only one who left his own book alone. It was as if *Notes* wasn't there. Make of that what you will.

'Love books,' he said. 'All kinds. Real bibliophile, me.' I have to say that I wasn't convinced. To be fair, he was in a hurry.

'It's a nice case,' I said.

'The real work of art is the book. Much rather the case remained a tree. Some classics in here; some big, grey, dumb, feathery, clucking turkeys as well, mind.

How the heck did some of those novels get in there! The Arkwright panel *do* like those penny dreadfuls that *sell*.'

'I hear Frank had a chat with you today?' I venture.

'Oh, yeh. He grabbed me after breakfast. I let him yawp on at me about stuff, but I threw a deaf un. Just sort of nodded to keep him going. In one ear, out the other. Thriller authors, as I have said, don't know what they are talking about when it comes to the noble activities of the scriptorium. Haven't a Scooby. An ironing board talks more sense than Frank. Not just him. I'd rather lose a foot in an industrial accident than have a conversation about writing with a thriller author. Off for a pint, guv.'

With that, he popped off to the pub. I didn't think to ask him which one. I assume The Saddlers.

Jo, when she saw the bookcase, was over the moon. 'OMG, that is SO beautiful. And LOOK –' she jumps up excitedly. '– there's SONIA! OMG!'

'Good, isn't it,' I say.

'WOW. That is awesome! Imagine – that's ME on there with all these fantastic books, all these wonderful authors. My visit here just gets better and better...' She jumps up and kisses me on the cheek. 'Thank you for being so wonderful,' she says.

'Erm, it's all part of the service,' I reply, nonplussed.

'This hotel – my stay, this country, it's just wonderful. And to see my books in this awesome case is the icing on the cake.' She says goodbye and heads off for something to eat.

Later, well after dinner, I spot Amy looking at the case. I walk over. In her jeans and plain grey tee shirt, she looks anything but an author and more a hiker resting after the fifteen mile walk through the hills. 'Like it?'

'It's strangely beautiful.'

'Your book is in there.'

'Several, look,' she says. 'There's one out of place.'

'So there is.' I organise her books together in a jiffy. It's often difficult to know what Amy is thinking, but I always remember Cat's briefing. On a bad day, she could have seen the misplacing of her books as a walk-out offence, but since she'd been here, she'd been polite and friendly to all the staff. Especially to me.

'Thank you. It jarred a little.'

'I can imagine it did.'

She removes *Notes* and peruses it for a while. Reads the blurb intently, as if she was in a library and was deciding whether to borrow the book. 'Julian is unbelievably rude to me. It makes it difficult for me to like this book. I do, though. I can't help it. Authors are notoriously fragile, yet a writer's ego is a monstrous thing. Vile and bloated. Criticise a writer and they will eventually destroy you.'

'Do you get criticised a lot?' I ask, and instantly regret it, as it is an inane fanboy-type question.

She offers me the slightest of smiles, as if to say she has recognised the inanity, but has forgiven me.

'I get kicked on the Internet. Romance authors do, you know. We take a battering for what we write.'

'I can imagine.'

'We're seen as shallow, and irrelevant, and feminine, and inconsequential. Our prose is ridiculed for its simplicity. Our ideas are criticised for plagiarism – but how many stories can you write about falling in love, huh? How can that be plagiarism? Everything from our covers, to our plots, to our dialogue, is savaged by the critics. So yes, we get it more than most.'

'I bet it hurts to be criticised like that,' I ask, mindful of Julian's review of *Amelia* I saw yesterday afternoon.[35]

---

[35]'Don't believe the hype, ladies and gentlemen. It's still the same old Madeline France. If you think this is literature because Madeline France has taken English lessons for the first

'You're talking about what Julian said about me? Not really. You want to see what my readers are saying about Julian. They are hopping mad, and have leaped to my defence,' she laughs. 'I didn't have to say a word. I felt sorry for him, actually. They really got stuck in.'

'I'll have to check that out.'

'Three hundred and sixty rebuttals on Tarzan.

'What's a rebuttal in that context?'

'Readers can tick a button to say whether the review is helpful or not. Apparently, his comments weren't considered all that helpful.'

'Three hundred and sixty. That's a lot.'

'My fans and friends came out in force. I felt chuffed. Proud. Romance authors are a tight bunch, mostly good friends, a team, almost a tribe – and that includes the readers. Fanatics. Bloody hooligans, some of them. I've

---

time in her life, you have no idea what you are talking about. This is the stuff of cheating, literature one-oh-one.

Worse, with all the hype, it's a wolf dressed as a sheep. France is still as shallow as ever. It's the same drippy stuff. Boy meets girl. Girl meets boy. They fall in love. There. Are. Problems. They Split Up. They Reunite. They Live Happily Ever After. There is nothing new here. This is romance novel number one million.

The usual Madeline France problems can be seen once more: The dialogue is stilted. Her climax is farcical and clichéd, a repeat of a million similar climaxes. If the word plagiarism hadn't been invented, I would have coined the phrase Francing. I thank *yew*. There are inconsistencies in plot you can drive a cruise liner through. It's migraine inducing, with eyeball-bursting prose. Custard pouring slowly onto a slice of tart has more dramatic tension.

Seriously, people, there is nothing to see here, move along. If you're going to buy this abject, overhyped bitch drivel, prepare for a billion brain cells to die screaming. God above, I wish someone would have the balls to hunt down and kill Madeline France's typing secretary, so I never have to read the labours of her idiotic mistress again.

got readers who've been with me for twenty years. I've got readers who still write to me longhand and snail mail, like they used to in the old days. Every author I am acquainted with has rebutted that review today. They've given Julian hammer all over the Internet. So how can it hurt to have so many readers, followers and friends?'

'I can see that,' I say.

We look at the case for a while. She leans against the wall with one of her novels in her hand.

'You know, it's a real pity,' she says.

'What is?'

'Julian's abuse of me. It's counter-productive. It makes people dislike him. Potential allies.'

'Is he envious of you?' I fish, hoping she may tell me something juicy about the two of them, but she plays it with a straight bat.

'Julian is such a brilliant writer. He simply writes in an unpopular genre. It frustrates him. Even the best contemporary fiction authors don't make much of a living. I can see The Paradox inherent there, but I'm not going to grieve. I'm here to entertain my readers, not to educate them.'

'I'm beginning to understand The Paradox.'

'The Publishing Paradox Theory is patronising. Writing should be about entertainment, and story, and plot. Especially romance. Romance writing might be simple, and the stories homely and easy to follow, but they *comfort.* They are *welcome* in the lives of my readers, like a visit from an old friend. Readers don't want to read about the flawed and jaundiced inner life of the artist, their tortured souls, or the gruesome state of the world. The horrors within. The darkness. They don't want to consider the human as a parasite intent on destroying the earth. Who would want to read all that? Readers *live* with it. They want to *escape* from all that for just a few short hours on the sofa with a box of chocolates and a cup of cocoa. Sometimes, I think that I don't care about this award, you know.'

'You don't?' Amy surprises me.

'Love, I get an award every time one of my readers writes to me and say they *adored* my book. Every time I get a review on Tarzan, I am proud. I get a *buzz*. That's the type of award I relish. The respect of my readers.'

I nod, but say nothing. She turns to me, puts her arm on my shoulder. She is much too close, and I can smell her. Unperfumed, she emits earth and sweat, as if she'd just – well, as if she'd just had sex, not to put too fine a point on it. That was the smell I picked up on Tuesday.

Earthy.

A deep, inner, unwashed sex smell.

She needs a shower, but if she were my girlfriend, I wouldn't let her shower again, ever. That *smell*. Sublime. *Sublime. Sublime. Oh, dear. I am the night porter. I should not be having thoughts like that about a guest.*

Amy whispers conspiratorially. 'I want the prize, love. Don't get me wrong.'

'Thought so. Otherwise, you wouldn't be here.'

Amy glances at me, an ethereal, impish glance.

'Perceptive, aren't we,' she says and walks away, leaving me with peculiar thoughts.[36][37]

---

[36] Who was she sleeping with to emit a fragrance like that? Must be Frank. And how can anyone who had received a review as caustic, as acidic as that, be so magnanimous and balanced. What about "the monstrous writerly ego?" Amy was a contradiction wrapped in an enigma. I started to think that she and Julian, as weird as it may be, had once had a relationship, and she had dumped him. It was my best guess. He behaved like a scorned lover – a *badly* scorned lover.

[37] Later that night, I began to realise that my feelings for Amy were moving beyond those a night porter has for one of his guests. I began to wish that she would call me to refill the mini-bar, as she often did. I thought about that at home the next morning: *Wonder whether she will call me up to fill her mini-bar,* I thought, lying on my quilt. It took me an age to get to

Some Nights Are Perfect.

They don't happen often, but when they do, a night porter should savour them. I had one later that night, after speaking to Amy at the bookcase.

You remember them for a good while afterwards, and you anticipate them happening again in the future.

You may try to manipulate the variables, which lead to those nights – though it is not easy, and the opportunities to do so are almost always limited by the circumstances of your employment and the randomness of the life of the hotel in which you serve. In most cases, it is more prudent to wait for the perfect night to happen to you. That way, you are not disappointed, and the faultless night is never subject to the law of diminishing returns.

On those nights, you are unhurried.

You are settled. Unflustered in the comforting space inside your work station. The telephones are dead; the screensaver on your computer screen rotates infinitely. Guests in the rooms remain still, like the gargoyles of ancient churches, sleeping the night away in a Heaven (or Hell) of their own making, and of which you are no part whatsoever. Requests for mini-bar refills and junk snacks remain marvellously non-existent. Sleepless drunks, unable to separate themselves from the bar's endless supply of expense account hooch, do not harass you. They do not solicit your opinions on the attractiveness of certain women, nor ask you to predict the outcomes of

---

sleep. I began also – horror upon horrors for my professional status – that she may have had a tiny, *tiny* interest in my good self. Obviously, Frank was a BIG problem in that sense – and after seeing her tonight, by the bookcase, my feelings about Frank had also taken a turn for the unprofessional. Only in the opposite direction.

sports matches. They do not harangue you on the subject of politics, nor ask you to play three card brag.

You are in your natural state.

You are alone.

In solitude, you can meditate. Mull over. You can contemplate at your leisure. Even better – and you do not know how this happens – as if you have been given the gift of precognition, the ability to see the future, on those unspoiled nights, you know that this state of night porter Nirvana is going to last, and that it will last until the morning comes, when it is time to go home.

Around you, in the spatial nexus of which your workstation forms the core, the hotel has the atmosphere of a house where a lover has departed after a week of ecstasy. The absence of real emotion, vacuumed and erased, creates a strained beauty, like a single violin string eternally bowed. Emptiness is the king (and mournfulness the queen) of all he surveys.

On nights of perfection, you are able to embrace its melancholy and, for a brief moment, never let it go.

The silence in a hotel on a flawless night like this is unforgettable. A silence so strong it overwhelms the whirring of the hotel's central heating system, the crackling of the dying embers of the coal fire. No cars pass by on the streets outside. Your past remains in abeyance, your guilt suppressed, your haunted memories trapped underneath a subconscious stratum a million feet thick and made of soundproof concrete. You are tabula rasa and your universe can be reduced to an immutable, unbreakable, unfalsifiable formula.

There is You.
There is the Hotel.
Then there is the Night.

You are Completed.

Prelude

Everyone talked about the press conference all week, and there wasn't a single dimension where you could avoid mention of it.

I got told things.

The authors. Cat, Kerry, Gavin. They kept me posted on happenings in the hours of daylight before I emerged from my velvet-lined coffin to take my post.

I heard that the press called constantly for rooms. We had none, and they were always disappointed. Most of them planned to travel from their bases in London or take rooms in The City. Even that was a tight call. Getting a room at short notice in The Fields was almost impossible. Hayley and I fielded many, many calls – some abusive, some manipulative, some flattering, some begging – but in the end, what can a staff member do?

There are rooms.

Or there are none.

It is as simple as that.

Martin Sixsmith discussed the press conference with all his cronies in the bar as if he knew the journalists personally. He talked about the authors, and only Jo came out of his discourse with credit. He knew that if he told tales out of school though, Cat would crucify him, so he kept his poisonous comments very much to his Inner Circle of mechanics, barmen, gamblers, farm boys, unemployed, bouncers and gym-dwellers, most of whom came in dribs and drabs at lunch. The rest of the time, he played it with a straight bat.

Hayley told all her friends that the hotel was full of celebrities and every now and again, some of her friends came down from the agricultural college to have a drink and see whom they could recognise.

Journalists. Authors. Artists. TV celebrities. Kids loved them. Kids wanted to be them, without precisely understanding why.

The allure of fame. The X-Factor.

As far as the authors went, they were never harassed, but they were in demand. Naturally, Frank Duke was popular, and every now and again, he would be asked for his autograph in the bar, or in the street, and to his credit, he always said yes. Amy Cook, but not as much as Frank. Jo, took some attention from knowledgeable kids from The Three Steeples School, and she spoke to them with equanimity and real enthusiasm. *Heart and Soul* had reached plenty of sixth formers. She signed plenty of books and never turned down a request. After all, if it became excessive, she would just go back to her room.

The only person who never got talked to/about, approached for an autograph, chatted to, or deliberately sought out for advice and experiences, was Julian.

Despite having a great book, he was a total unknown, and I knew it was depressing him. I suspected also that eventually, a man with an ego the size of his, would eventually burst like an overripe melon. On the Friday morning, before I went home, I prayed that Julian got his moment in the sunshine at the press conference. I liked the man, but it was obvious that he'd made a lot of enemies, inside and outside the hotel.

I wasn't counting my chickens.

Press Conference Blues

I did not see any of the authors for a few hours when I got into work on Friday evening. It was throwing it down outside once more. In the west of the country, flood warnings were in force. Thirty thousand homes were without electricity. There had been deaths.

Gales battered shipping as the low pressure over Great Britain showed no sign of lifting. In Wheatley Fields, we never saw extremes like this because of the topography of the area, but it was bad, the rain, and the wind. Sudden drops in the temperature led to hailstones, which dented bodywork on passing cars and rattled windows. You needed layers; you needed an umbrella and a raincoat just to walk the streets.

Cat spoke to me briefly about hotel business and left via taxi. Sixsmith was his usual surly self. The reporters at the press conference had scarcely bought a pint, and they definitely didn't eat the bar snacks he and the kitchen staff had prepared. His comments on the press were largely unprintable.

Mary Beth would have told him, as she told me, that the media didn't splash the cash anymore. At one time, an Independent Freelance would charge up to three grand for a half page article in a broadsheet. Now, because of the Internet, they'd be lucky to get twenty percent of that. That left little room for expense account ale drinking of yore, the long Fleet Street lunches, the late nights, the broken marriages. None of that would have placated Sixsmith. He wasn't much of a thinker. He was more of a...well, more of a *Sixsmith*.

Gavin was in a better mood as a full hotel and the rain meant guests didn't go out as a rule (though Amy and Frank had braved the weather) and ate in the Jerusalem. I jibbed and jabbed, ducked and dived, and did my stuff until eleven, when I finally made contact with an author, and I knew whom it was going to be.

Julian calls me on the reception telephone.

By now, it is 11pm. A few Friday night drinkers remain, and the groom's segment of a wedding party ensuring the groom enjoys one last night of freedom.

Outside, drinkers and revellers brave the November rain as they amble their way to the Benbow for the late night disco. I notice a group of young girls and marvel at their fortitude. I estimate it to be around two to three degrees. Despite the rain, and despite the presence of flimsy umbrellas, they are wearing belly tops, high heels and acres of pale, rain spattered skin. If they are eighteen, it can't be by much. A savage fight broke out earlier outside the King's Crown and the aftermath ripples – the Police shuttle to and fro from their station near the memorial. A guest told me earlier that it was football-related, a remark about an incident during last week's local football "Derby" between Wheatley Fields City and Follow Field United. A disputed penalty, he understood. Accusations of a dive leading to the winning goal. Several arrests were made, and two young men will be spending the weekend in hospital having stitches in head wounds. The King's Crown is now shut, pending investigations – something which will cause havoc to the landlord's accounts on a busy pre-Christmas Friday.

Julian.

I pick up the phone.

'Hello, Julian. What can I do for you?'

'You would think they would ask me one question, wouldn't you.'

'At the press conference?'

'They didn't ask me one question. Not one.'

'Not one?'

'No. It was like I was invisible. I was ritually humiliated.'

'What happened?' I am genuinely interested. He sounds terrible, his voice a rasping, nicotine-coated bassoon. He's been drinking. I realise that I haven't seen any of the authors since I arrived at work. This is the first mention of this afternoon's press conference I have encountered.

'I'm gutted with Mary Beth. What a sow. I thought she was a buddy.'

'Julian. Start at the beginning.'

There is a silence. 'You busy?'

'I can't leave the desk. The bar's busy, and I may need to help out.'

'I'll come down. I need to talk. Do you mind?'

'Of course not,' I reply.

'Anyone on the armchairs?'

'No. All in the bar.'

'That gobby wedding party. Birmingham. That's a city spawned in Hell if ever there was one. Rude people. On the pop all afternoon. Mary Beth had to tell them to STFU because Her Majesty's Press couldn't hear themselves think.'

I remove the receiver from my ear and listen. It is peaceful in the bar. The occasional burst of laughter. The odd joke. 'It's fine now. I think the worst of the drinking has come and gone.'

'Be there in a mo,' he says and puts the phone down.

As he does so, Amy and Frank come in the door. She has her arm in his, but that could be interpreted in many, many different ways. My mind interprets what it sees in the way you would expect it to. 'Hello, you two.'

'We've been to Pietro's for dinner, haven't we, Frank,' Amy says. She's wearing a peach coloured suit and an expensive fur coat. Her hair is dyed blonde. Frank is wearing a suit, blue, a thin, inlaid stripe topped with his flat racing cap and trench coat. They are both smiling and happy – evidently, a successful night out.

'Sure have.' Frank adds not quite as laconically as I have come to expect.

'Nice dinner,' Amy says. 'Have you eaten there?'

I shake my head and plead the negative.

'You should. Do you like Italian food?'

I aver that this is the case.

'They cook a brilliant steak, don't they, Frank?'

'They sure do,' he says. 'And supply some of the damndest wine I have ever tasted.'

'Barolo, Frank. Ought to have fetched a bottle home. Do you like Barolo?' She asks and I confirm that I do.

A bitchy, tortured part of me that came from the acidic, jealous part of my soul wants to spoil the rosy glow emanating from the couple like a nuclear blast by mentioning that Amy's husband, The Major, the good and honourable Major Benson, had called earlier. I leave it and ask how the conference went.

'Oh, brilliant,' Amy says 'I got lots of attention, didn't I, Frank?'

'You sure did,' he says.

'And so did you. My, they like you over here, Frank, don't they!'

'So they do,' Frank says. 'Apparently, I am popular in the UK.'

'More plugs than an electrical supplies warehouse, huh, Frank! Your sales will go through the roof. That girl from the Post likes you, doesn't she, Frank? She undressed you with her eyes.'

Amy laughs and tugs on the arm of Frank's coat. He's smiling, but I have no idea what he thinks of her adoration, which, if looked at in a certain way, could be seen as parody. I suspect she's patronising him, but then, I would do, wouldn't I.

'I didn't notice that, Mrs Cook,' he says in that deep profundo American accent. 'Now, let us leave this gentleman to his *ting* and go do ours. What say we go upstairs and have a natter with Big Jack.'

'Big Jack, huh.' Amy replies. 'Hmmmm, can't wait to meet big Jack. I'm a *terrible* fan of big Jack,' she looks at me again, this time down the sights of a wagging finger, pointed at me in ironic fashion: 'I hope there's enough ice in the fridge. Otherwise, I'll be sending for *you*.'

I assure Amy that there is an iceberg's worth of ice in there. She is drunk, and this is the first time I have ever noticed. Frank doesn't look sober either. They must have enjoyed a better conference than Julian, who comes down the stairs just as the two of them ascend.

The three authors cross, unluckily.

Julian doesn't acknowledge them, and they return the favour. Strangers to the scene, which had just transpired would not have known that the three of them shared a panel at a hotel press conference not six hours before.

'Where have them two been, I wonder, dressed in their fine furs and diamond studded britches?' he says. He is wearing a new Silver Surfer tee shirt,[38] jeans and a pair of vintage Forest Hills trainers. There is a smell about him covered up by hastily applied deodorant, and I am sure he's lost weight since he has been at the hotel.

'He's banging her, you know.'

'Is he?' I say, burning up inside. I don't want to hear this. I would rather Julian not tell me, but it turns out he is just talking off the top of his head.

'Dunno. I was just provoking you into agreeing with me, thereby soliciting information from you. I thought you might know,' he says, and my relief is tangible. 'As we have discussed, you know *everything*, Mr Porter.'

'They're just friends. Companions.'

'Think so? Amy lounged about in Kenya while her husband was out with his elephant gun chasing the Mau Mau through the jungle. It wouldn't be the first time that Amy Cook had gone over to the dark side,' he says bitterly, sneering.

Julian follows up with something scurrilous and acidic – spectacularly over the top – and I feel as if I have to slow him down a bit.

After I do so, he looks directly at me, and for a split-second, I think we are going to come to blows. I would hate that to happen, but my loyalties have changed since Julian and I began our endless night conversations.

It's a subtle change, I must admit, but I can't have him say what he did about Amy. I just can't.

In the immediate aftermath, I watch him tense.

Then Julian shrugs his shoulders, a *comme ci, comme ca* gesture, indicating that he may have been wrong to say what he had just said about the romance author,

---

[38] I know it is new because the decal on the front is pristine and unmarked by the usual Julian issue beer and food stains.

which, had anyone but me heard it, may have gotten him scolded, punched or, in some circumstances, arrested.

He sits down on the big purple armchair. I notice he's carrying an energy drink in a silver tin.

I sit down opposite him.

'So, what occurred earlier? Take me through it.'

'I was really looking forward to it, as you know. Buzzing, I was,' he says. 'My first conference. You saw the list of delegates. Everyone was going to be there. All the broadsheets – *the Times, The Gruniad, The Independent, the Telegraph*. All the tabloids bar *The Star*, whose readers like books with pictures. Billy Kent of the *Daily Mail. East Midlands Today. Radio City.* All the radio stations, Jason Loftus from *Trent Sound. Kemet.* The book reviewers I mentioned. All the supplements, all the specialist journals. You saw the list…'

'I wondered whether the room would be big enough.'

'It was cosy, put it that way. As it happened, quite a few people didn't turn up, which Mary Beth seems to have anticipated, but there was a good thirty press there. I was well on top, I really was. The four of us took our places on the big table at the front. They erected lights and a series of boards behind us with the Arkwright logo. You know, like the ones you see when football managers are interviewed after the big match.'

'I know those.'

'And do you know what?'

'What?'

'I didn't get ONE question.'

'What, not one?'

'Not one question.'

'Amy? Frank?'

'Jo, too. She got loads, which is something. Me? Not one. It was like I was the *help*. It was like I was the guy who set the tables and the lights up. Halfway through, I offered to make the tea.'

'What about after?'

'After what?'

'The formal conference? Was there a meet-and-greet? A mix? A party?'

'Nope. Mary Beth ushered us out, and the gang went off to another function to meet some more authors. I understand Amy arranged an interview or two, and so did Frank, but I was already off to The Saddlers by that point. I thought I had been set up. I didn't need to be there. I was making up the numbers like some dickhead.'

'None of the bloggers ask you anything?'

'They never turned up. They sent minions. Bloggers. Self-important –'

'– I'm surprised they didn't come, even to meet –' I nip his coming choice epithet about bloggers in the bud.

'– Amy? They'll meet her at the ceremony. It's Friday in the North. Southerners: They can't be arsed. Munchkins rather than Names.'

'That must make you feel a bit better?'

'Nah. It's the wordage after that's important, not the Names, and you just know I won't be mentioned in anything more than the most basic of terms. I'll be laughed at. *Who He*!? What's da *help* doing in the photo? *Where da writers at*?'

'I'm really sorry to hear this, Julian.'

'Worry not. Got a few beers down my neck and Jo was sympathetic,' he winked.

'That's good.'

'Still not good for my book, though. I'm going to have a pint. I'd offer you one,'

'Long night ahead of me, Julian. Thanks anyway.'

The Ritual At The Gates Of The Temple

In her room later, after calling for more gin, Big Jack evidently not to her taste, Amy tells me the same story, but with subtle differences. Frank had gone back to his room – tired out, apparently.

'Julian has not made himself any friends, you know.'

'Hasn't he?'

'He thinks what happened down there is all about his book or the fact he's self-published. It's not. It's about *him*. I think the reason they ignored him boiled down to two major issues, one personal and one industry.'

'Okay.'

'Julian leaves a trail of destruction wherever he goes. In his quest for some illusory literary perfection, he destroys everything that moves, and he has offended hundreds online, and they remember. They talk. They *network*. Half the people in that room this afternoon detest him and his insults. He's vicious, you know.'

'I've encountered that, Amy. But he can be nice.'

'He seems to like you.'

'Yes –'

'– but, well, so do we all.'

'Okay –' I say, a touch embarrassed.

'Well –'she says, grinning, an impish look in her eye. '– Frank's not *that* keen on you. You're a bit *English* for his tastes, sweetness.'

'Thanks for telling me,' I respond, crestfallen. Even though I knew Frank and I were not hitting it off all that much, the confirmation hurts. My head starts to ache a little. I don't like it when people feel like that. It jars.

'I'm just kidding you. Frank likes you plenty, just in a different way. A more subtle fashion.'

'Okay,' I say, totally unconvinced.

'Anyhow, back to Julian. They ignored him deliberately because of who he is, not because of his book. He is cutting and destructive, despite all those superhero tee shirts, his Mockney rhymers, his geeky glasses. He's a case. I wish he would stop because I am sure it's all just insecurity.'

'Insecurity?'

'About self-pubbing. He's not been through it.'

'Through what?'

'It.'

'What is 'It', Amy? Enlighten me.'

'The Ritual At The Gates Of The Temple.'

'What's that?'

'We've all been there, all us mainstream published authors. All us authors you see in bookshops. All us slaves of the Big Eight. We withstood the Ritual, and now we belong. Julian doesn't belong, like the rest of them, all the Sparkies.'

'Sparkies?'

'Authors who self-publish. We call them Sparkies.'

'Okay.'

'The major problem with self-publishing – apart from the ferocious competition, the lack of sales, the lack of money, the ridicule, the imbalance between effort and reward, the people who think they *should* be writers, but who, in fact, shouldn't be within a mile of a word processor, the relentless marketing tactics necessary to make a sale, the hundred and twenty hour weeks, the lack of media exposure and the unavoidable fact that most self-published work is considered to be inadequate by the mainstream, and because of that, we don't take the sector all that seriously – is the insecurity,' she says.

'The insecurity?'

'Yes. Julian is pathologically insecure, and because of that, his tendency is to attack, like a wounded animal. Strike first and ask questions later. He doesn't know whether he's a good author or not.'

'*The Guardian* said –'

'– The Ritual,' she interrupted. 'He's not been through it, and it kills him. He has a fear of rejection. He's scared. The Ritual cures you of that. You see, I *know*. I'm an author. I have no insecurities because my work has been examined and judged. Not just by readers, but by professionals. It has survived the slush pile. It has been laughed at, rejected, beaten, shunned – and this is by *friends*. It has survived editors. Some of whom are more vicious than Julian will *ever* be. That isn't because of inherent insecurity, that's because they are bad; plain, ordinary, bad people. My early novels were savaged by a bully, you know, and it is only because of the intervention of the fellow who actually ran the publisher itself in this country that I'm here now. The editor assigned to me all those years ago *hates* me more than Julian. I survived him. I survived. Julian doesn't know his merit or the merit of his work, and until he undertakes the Ritual, he will never know.'

'The Ritual of Publication?'

'No,' she says. 'The Ritual of *Selection*. Remember the Benedictine monks?'

'I can't say that I do, Amy.'

'In the 6th and 7th Century, becoming a monk was a most desirable option in a world just recovering from the Justinian Plague. Three meals a day, shelter and a purpose. But you had to be really devout. You had to desire it more than anything else in the world, and the Benedictine Order was *the* pinnacle. If you wanted to be Benedictine, you suffered for it. You had to *want* it. Those fellas made you *suffer* for your art. You visited the monastery to apply. You would rap on the gates. They would ignore you for hours and hours. You would stand outside the Gates in all weather. To attention, no slouching. They would come to you and, at first, they would beat you with sticks. They would knock you down, and you would get up. They would knock you down again. Those that got up and stayed up, they would chastise and mock. They would abuse and insult. All the monks inside would come out and laugh at you. They would laugh and laugh. They would beat you, chase you away, all the way down the road you came on. You would be psychologically tortured. Day and night you would wait. You would be repeatedly assured by the same Monk, an Abbot of standing and rank that you would NEVER be invited through the Gates of *his* monastery, and by standing at the gate, you were wasting your time. That would happen repeatedly. You. Will. Never. Belong. Time would pass. Snow, and hail, and storms, and rain. They would not feed you. You would not be given water. This Ritual would be repeated for days and days until you left the Gates. If you withstood all that, all that violence, all that abuse, the Gates would open, and they would accept you as a Novitiate. That is their Ritual.'

'Nothing worth having is given for free, yes?'

She stands close to me now. 'You see, Julian is as good a writer as there is. His book is sublime. His use of language is first class. He pees all over me as a writer, but he's never faced the Ritual, and he will always have that hole inside him, that sense of emptiness, that sense of being on the outside of something. It's nothing to do with the quality of story or writing – it's whether you are tough enough to face the Ritual.'

'Were you rejected?'

Amy rolled another cigarette and sipped her gin. 'My first novel was rejected by thirty six different publishers.'

'Whoosh. Like JK Rowling.'

'Classic example. JK. I've met her, you know. Terrific woman. She hawked Harry Potter everywhere. Every publisher in the world before someone bit. Years and years, she hawked that. The Ritual, you see. Yet, the numbers of publishers knocking her back wasn't the worst of it. She very nearly gave up, you know.'

'Did she?'

'Can we go for a fag in the toilet?'

'I'm not supposed –'

She put her hand on my arm. '– please, love. It's either that or the yard, and no more stories.'

I smiled. 'Okay.'

'And you won't tell?'

'Of course not.'

I can smell her as she passes me on the way to the pot. She is barefoot, and I cannot take my eyes off her feet. She sits on the toilet seat and lights a roll-up with a Zippo.

The bathroom ether becomes smoke and petrol.[39]

She sits awkwardly, with her legs either side of the toilet seat and leans forward, gesticulating occasionally with her cigarette as she spoke.

'Towards the end, one publisher kept JK's manuscript for eight months. Her agent continually assured her that they loved it, and were going to publish it, after all that effort, the fish had finally, *finally* bitten. This is a Big Eight pubber, a proper jobbie, none of that small press stuff: They're one step up from self-pubbing. This was the deal. She tells all her chums that Harry is going to be published. She starts spending – and she hardly had any cash, bear in mind. She celebrates, parties. One morning, she gets a parcel in the post.'

'Oh, no. Don't want to hear this,' I say.

'It's her manuscript with a rejection letter. They're not bothering after all.'

'Is this true?'

'It is. Bang on. It nearly broke her. *The Ritual* nearly broke her. I've heard her interviewed, and she said that she would have given up, the lowest point, the point where the world is at its darkest. It just goes to show how brutal publishers are.'

'She nearly walked away from the Gates of the Monastery?'

'I think she did. I think they got her. Mentally, she couldn't stand it anymore. All the rejection. All the rest of it. The next morning, someone else who had previously read Harry, and who heard about the unfortunate business of the rejection, calls her agent up, and accepts the manuscript on the spot. And the rest is history,' Amy says, putting her fag down the toilet. 'I had similar experiences. King had similar. Grisham. Gregory.

---

[39]There are no smoke detectors in the rooms of The Saladin – only in the corridors and areas where chemicals are stored, plus all the other places you might expect, i.e. the kitchen.

Steele. All of them, all the authors the self-pubbing wannabes venerate. All of them suffered The Ritual. The Sparkies? Deep inside, they will never know what they're made of. Who they are as people. Who they are as authors. It's tough to say this to people like Julian, but until they go through The Ritual, they will never be taken seriously. Even the ones who've made money or even the ones who can actually write a sentence. Like Julian.'

I stand there for a bit, not saying anything. She walks over to her writing table and taps something out on her laptop. My pager vibrates, and I say I have to go.

'Amy?'

'Yes?'

'Thank you for that. I learned loads.'

'A pleasure. Can you bring me up some olives? You forgot,' she says.

'Right away,' I say, grinning because even though she is staring at the screen, I can see that she is smiling.

I am surprised that I am taken with Amy, more so than Jo, who is younger than me and very beautiful. Astonishingly beautiful and *nice*. An almost impossible-to-find combination.

Did I prefer the older woman? Had I discovered something about myself? Was there some maternal cathexis buried deep inside me? My relationships had been, so far, unremarkable. And it had been around six years since my last serious girlfriend, the odd fumble and fling apart. Six years. I had never wanted an older woman, but I find myself thinking about Amy more and more, the more we talk. I should not do this, but no one will know, and I will never tell, nor will I act on it. I am a night porter and a professional. I will never fraternise sexually with a guest. I am unable to do so.[40] It doesn't

---

[40] In the great Roger Moore's debut Bond film *Live and Let Die,* the character played by Jane Seymour is able to accurately prophesise the future, but only if she remains a virgin. I

stop me *feeling* like this. I am human. I am whole. I am a man. And I am attracted to Amy. I suspect also – despite Frank – that she is also attracted (in a fashion) to me.

Even if she *loved* me, it can never be. I met her at work. I met her while porting. Amy Cook will always be a hotel guest, and it can never *be* because of that. That's the tragedy of it. Even if she never visited The Saladin again, even if she never told anyone where we met as long as she lived, we could never be – because I would know. I would remember.

There is the obvious: Her husband might have something to say about the matter. However, he hasn't played much of a part in the story so far. She never talks about him, at least to me. He never calls her. He is a ghost. In many ways, I am liberated by the futility of my attraction (crush?) because I can fantasise about her. About us. Looks-wise, Jo is far superior. On the face of it, there is no comparison. Jo's beauty has that American wholesomeness, that Californian perfection. Young, fresh, a lovely figure shaped by papaya and mango. A creamy tanned skin and chestnut brown eyes. There is that burnished voice, almost lacquered, like the meniscus on Japanese ceramics moulded for a month, glazed repeatedly for a decade and left in the sun for an eon. I could listen to that voice for hours – Jo could read the Baja telephone directory to me, and my concentration would hold – but Amy shades it, despite the smell of fags, her imperfect, angular face, her aging eyes.

There is…there is – something.

---

struggled to comprehend the mechanics of that as a child. What did it mean? It was only when I became a night porter that I understood: If I slept with a guest, I would be unable to carry on my career. My days of porting would be over. My vocation. The horror of what I have done would overwhelm me.

I don't know what or why. It's an aura, a presence about her. It's something you need to experience rather than see. Julian's hatred of her shows no sight of abating, but at least his recent bans and his friendship with Jo keeps him distracted and away from his online (and offline) campaign of terror.

What does Frank think of her?

He never says anything to me of significance. They could be friends. They could be lovers. They could be friends with benefits, lovers of temporary convenience.

I would like to find out.

I would also like to know – you know, the *answer,* but I daren't ask.

About her and Julian. A direct question.

But it's not in me. Not *in* me.

The Lost Weekend

Jo is waiting for me when I arrive at work. Jeans and trainers, her hair in a ponytail. It's around 5.45pm, and I realise that I am getting earlier and earlier to work. She looks anxious.

'Have you seen Julian?'

'I've not, Jo. I've been at home.'

It occurs to me that if these authors were regular guests, I would be better off staying in the staff quarters, which are largely unused. Other places I have worked, the staff quarters have a waiting list, but not here. I have stayed there one night when I arrived from Chichester. I had no choice and was swiftly out. I know night porters who live in, but I have never fancied that. I need the separation, the clear blue water between my profession and my private life, such as it is. It's just lately. It all seems to have gone a bit, well, pear. I'm *always* at work.

'He was supposed to take me to the City, y'know. Like, to the football match.'

'Was he?' He hadn't mentioned it to me last night.

'He said it was a big game, and I would enjoy it. I hope he's okay.'

'I'm sure he is, Jo. I saw him last night, and he was fine.'

'He was upset, y'know. About the press conference. They were lousy to him. Lousy.'

I remembered what Amy said about the true reasons why. 'So I heard.'

'I hope he's not out there getting drunk.'

Because that's what Julian does. That's how he handles things. Benders. That's what he does. That's exactly *where he is now.* 'I do, too,' I reply.

'If he arrives, can you ask him to come see me?' Jo said, starting to edge toward the stairs.

'First thing I'll say, Jo.'

'That would be terrific. Thank you so much.'

With that, she skipped upstairs. I have never taken Julian's mobile phone number (I'm not sure I have ever taken a guest's number, though I have been offered it many times, for many different reasons), so I cannot contact him.

He wouldn't miss an afternoon with Jo. That interaction had been the highlight of his time here. The two of them had become decent friends. Jo had not stopped going on about her afternoon at the races, and the two of them had nattered and joked in the early evening on the armchairs over the past two days.[41]

---

[41]'Make no mistake. The monster brand that is Amy Cook AKA Madeline France is a serious contender for Best Writer,' Julian says. 'It pains me to say so, because, as you both know, I really do not like her or her work, and I do not wish her well in the slightest, but it's true. She could win this.'

I'm the first to respond. 'Think so?'

'I'm serious. The jungle drums are beating so loud I'm having to wear ear plugs.' Secretly, I'm pleased.

'That's great,' Jo says. 'But how do you know?'

'She's favourite in the bookmakers for a start.'
'She is?'
'Six-to-four. It's no value, but the bookies aren't stupid.'
'What does that mean?' Jo asks, bemused, but fascinated.

The Englishman explains the concept of odds and chances to her, then sums up. 'It means she will probably win, and gamblers with plenty of money will make even more money.'

'It's awesome. Read it two nights ago. Well…half of it,' Jo says, giggling guiltily, contradicting, almost excusing herself like so many readers do when discussing literary fiction. 'I was, like, so tired…'

'Amy has three things in her favour. One, she's famous. Two, she's popular in the UK. Three, she's tried to write a book, which moves fiction forward. I don't think she succeeded, and everyone knows I'm not a fan of her work at all. It's massively flawed, like a bad diamond, but she's at least *tried* to write a serious book, I shall give her that.'

This was Jo's impact on him. It stuck out like a sore thumb. There is no way in the world he would have said this a week ago. 'According to the critics, the novel works. That made me take notice when I was coming to a conclusion.'

'For your bets?' I comment.

'And for an Internet thing I wrote the other week. A tipping piece.'

'Classy,' I grin.

'None classier than me, chap,' Julian winks ostentatiously as he replies and then, gets straight back on the horse. 'The critics didn't give JK a lot of love when she wrote *Casual Vacancy*. They usually slap down pop scribblers like Amy when they try to break out of their comfort zones, but they didn't this time. They *adore* the novel. You should read what Lucille Pinner said in *The Times*. Giles Hanratty in *The Guardian*. These are two of the most caustic critics on the planet, and they're talking about Amy's book in terms favourable enough for the Booker, not just the Arkwright. Hanratty called it groundbreaking. He once hated a book so much, he called the writer a four letter word beginning with C in print. You have to be something special to survive his Thursday column, and she did. Take all this into account and voila, the 6/4 quotes on the Arkwright market. It's a short book

– a major boost. It's sold well, been in the papers. Lots in her favour. I can see why she's favourite and if I were her, I'd be confident.'

'That's a powerful combination,' I say, picking up on his earlier analysis. 'A best seller with literary qualities.'

'Literary? Let's not get too excited,' Julian says. 'But she only has three other writers to beat?'

'I thought any of the forty writers could win,' Jo adds.

'Theoretically, Jo. In practice, it's a four horse race according to the bookmakers, and they don't give money away. Here's the field. Len Castle, Alia Jiwali, Susan Limehaus and Amy,' Julian states with some authority. 'The rest are huge odds with the bookies. Name your price.'

Jo has no idea what he's talking about, and Julian explains to her once more about betting. Only these four writers are quoted below twenty-to-one.

'If I walked into a bookies with ten grand and asked to back me, you or Frank, they'd take my money with no fuss. For the authors I've just mentioned, they'd have you thrown out the shop.'

'Your book is wonderful,' Jo says to Julian.

'How far did you get, Jo?' He replies, slightly embarrassed.

'Well, er –' She grins.

'Come on, you. How far?'

'Like, about ten pages!' Jo laughs and Julian laughs along with her. 'Man, you write some fancy words. I spent most of the time looking them up on the e-dictionary!'

'My wonderful unread classic! My Underworld. My Ulysses. My Infinite Jest. Jo, no one knows me, no one read the book, save one big literary critic by some fluke and a generous reader. Arkwright judges like to see sales. It's part of the deal. They don't mind a popular book. My book ain't popular.'

'I'm really gonna finish it, Julian.'

'Save your eyesight, Jo. Hey, look at this.'

He reaches into his pocket and pulls out his battered black leather wallet. Three cards fall out onto the table. Several ten pound notes in various manky states follow.

He pulls out a slip of paper. 'This is a betting slip. Have a dekko at this,' he says, and passes the slip to Jo, who unfolds it with a distaste she tries to hide as it is smeared in brown sauce.

Then she smiles. 'OMG, it's me. You bet ME to win Best YA. One hundred pounds! OMG!' She says, excited. Leaning over, she kisses Julian on the cheek and bounces up and down in her seat. 'How much will you win?'

'A couple of hundred. Look –'

He points to the slip. 'There are four runners in each race and according to the bookies, you're two-to-one, second favourite of four.'

'Who is ahead of me in the race?' Jo asks, clearly – and surprisingly – not having studied the field.

'Renee Padwick.'

'OMG, OMG, OMG, I'll NEVER beat Renee. She's totally *awesome*. She writes great books. I've read all her work. She's, like, a totally cool writer. I'm totally in LOVE with Renee!" She exclaims, without a trace of disappointment.

Jo seems genuinely pleased, and I know she will cheer if Renee wins on the night. 'She's so good. I hope she wins.'

'You'll win,' Julian says confidently. 'You've got all the momentum. Everyone loves your last Sonia book. 'It's top stuff. It's short, fun, the critics like it, and the kids buy it in shelfloads. I'll top this bet up before the ceremony. You're a shoo-in...'

'Julian –' Jo asks, bemused again.

'I mean, you will triumph, gal.'

'That would be so fantastic. Are you betting Amy for Best Writer?'

He shakes his head. 'She'll win, but – well, you know,' he says. 'Dwinkies?' He asks, shaking his pint glass.

Jo picks up her handbag and stands up. 'No way, I'm bushed, Julian. OMG, I've had such a manic day...'

Julian looks disappointed. 'Just when the night begins to unfurl. Well, in that case, rather than sit here and get seriously munted, as is my wont, and as is my custom of an evening, I shall walk you home and then retire early to my rest, madam,' he says, offering his arm.

'Thank you, kind sir,' she says. And the two walk upstairs.

Hence the energy pop and the late night malt whiskies after Jo had gone to bed. She had mellowed him, but the press conference had hit hard, that much was obvious. He would *never* have stood Jo up.

Frank and Amy go out again to the Italian restaurant. They leave about eight. I don't bother asking them if they have seen Julian for obvious reasons. They are casually dressed in jeans and trainers – even Frank has dressed down for a British Saturday night. I am pleasant to both of them as they leave, but inside, my guts are churning. I was surprised the other night when Frank went to bed, but the odds are against a late night call-up.

The bar is chokka: Kerry is helping Sixsmith serve the drinks. The hotel is completely full, and I am kept busy with requests – in fact, it is a busy night – and people are nice, and people are pleasant, and I listen to their issues, and I have short and sweet conversations with people I would ordinarily talk to in more depth, but I only want to talk to the authors.

It is completely unprofessional (but let's face the truth, my professionalism has waned somewhat in the past week), but that's the way it is at the moment. Cat's fault – she told me to treat them like the Qatari royal family, and that's what I have done (that is MY excuse!).

Until 1am, the night becomes a series of defragmented snippets, unconnected episodes, and I realise that I will miss the authors, and when they go next Sunday, hopefully chockfull of awards and trophies, the job here isn't going to be anything like as fun as it had been. In fact, if it was going to be anything like this jagged, disconnected Saturday night, I wouldn't be happy. Was this how it was before I met them? I can't remember, and it had only been five days.

The fragments are a reflection of a shattered mirror. I don't see Jo at all. I want to go up and see her, but what would be the point: there is no news. I notice the hotel phone from her room is constantly engaged, and I guessed she was phoning home; that, or she had knocked over the receiver. Sixsmith gives me a filthy look when I tell him I cannot help out behind the bar. He calls me something vile. Unforgivably, he calls my *profession* something vile. Gavin brings me a steak sandwich and tells me about a horse he had backed, which won him £200 at Sandown Park. A resident tells me that Notts County had lost at home again. The rain outside is sporadic, and the wind knocks a window box from his awning. I go outside in the wet to pick it up.

Fragments. Frank and Amy return home and chat with me, but all I can see is that they are holding hands like a couple in love, and my emotions are sore and swollen, but I know they don't notice.

And at 1.30, Julian staggers through the door and launches himself onto one of the armchairs.

Three things happen.

One, I race over to get his car coat, which is soaking wet and in danger of soaking the armchairs.

Two, I refuse to get him a drink.

Three, I realise that the fragmentation was over, and I feel complete.

Julian was home.

In sixteen years of being a night porter, I had never felt like this. Not remotely like this.

'Where have you been?' I ask, like some nagging fishwife.

'Is Amy in?' He slurs.

'Why?'

'Coz I'm gonna ey the bitch...'

'Julian, stop being stupid.'

'I'm just kidding...' he says, grinning ostentatiously, drunkenly, removing a can of Special from his jeans pocket. How it fitted in there, I do not know. I could not have him down here in this state, I knew that.

'I'll take you upstairs.'

He stands up aware, seemingly, of the situation. There is mud on his jeans, and he smells vile. He has fallen on grass. There is no way they would let him stay here without the Ceremony.

'No need. I'm fine,' he says, swaying as he walks to the lift, muttering under his breath. 'Shouldn't have done what she done,' he says.

'Julian, do you want coffee?'

He shakes his head, sipping at his can. 'She shouldn't have done it,' Julian says, and the lift arrives.

At least, he is safe. I can comfort myself knowing that.

And on Sunday

He did exactly the same thing again, only this time he got himself arrested outside the chippy for attempting to punch a local in an argument in the kebab queue.

He came off worst. Spent the night in Wheatley Fields nick before being released on the Monday morning, without charge.

Really, Julian couldn't deal with it. None of it. The brilliance of his writing. The lack of success. The success of others less brilliant than him. The press. The ignorance. The bitterness inside him.

And there was something else.

Something deep inside.

Something that caused him to drink and cause havoc wherever he went. Something that caused him to hurt the ones that liked him, respected him – in this context, Jo, in particular.

Like a suicide note in weekly parts.

And on the Monday, it all got on top, as they say, down South.

On Top, As They Say, Down South

On Monday night, I get into work, and I am frazzled. My neighbour was playing his music loudly all morning – strident enough to make it through the walls of my noise cancellers and after the fuss with Julian this weekend, I could have done with the rest. He is a student at the local agricultural college, a Londoner. His body is covered in tattoos, and he enjoys listening to hardcore dance music. Euphoric trance, they tell me. Played at concert amplitude. It's not a problem for me at night, obviously, but in the day? I have asked him on several occasions to stop, but he just says okay geezer in that harsh accent of his and carries on.[42]

I am not good without sleep.

You may find that odd for someone who stays up all night, but behind the scenes, I hit the pillow.

I don't wake until I have to go back to work.[43] [44]

---

[42]The first stage for anti-social neighbours, which he is, is a quiet chat in the courtyard. If that doesn't work, try again. It's the Police. You CAN call 999, and they will pop round to have a word, but they may take their time. It is not a priority. They will tell you to contact Environmental Health. This service varies from Council to Council. Some have noise units who will come out, issue a warrant backed up by the courts. If the neighbour continues being anti-social, then they will ask for a warrant to remove their equipment. It doesn't usually reach that far. The procedure lasts forever. I have considered contacting the agricultural college about him, but that is a last resort. I will use it if I have to, if I have many more days' sleep like this one.

[43]I sometimes feel my entire life is spent at work.

[44]It reminds me of Shakespeare, my life as a night porter. It has Shakespearean qualities in many aspects, but the All The World's A Stage quote sums it up for me. You know the one.

Today had been a nightmare, and I dreamed, so when Cat is waiting for me at the desk, I'm wired and not myself. I feel in turmoil. Head tight. Eyes like slits. Guts churning.

What's wrong? I do not NEED this!

'Evening, Cat.'

'Evening. Your pal, Julian...'she says, archly, gesturing with her head over to some non-specific point in space. I follow the direction of the gesture, and realise he must be upstairs.

'I just talk to him, Cat...' I say, instinctively, sick of him. I knew it was him. I knew it.

'Mate, you know what I mean. He's off his nut.'

'Drunk?'

'Completely munted. Launched into Amy earlier in the bar while she was munching a packet of Twiglets.'

'Is she okay?'

'Verbals. I didn't see it or hear it, but Martin called me in. It was a row. Amy gave as good as she got.'

'I'll go and see Martin.'

'I don't want Julian on the beer tonight. They're all down for dinner.'

'I know. They've been looking forward to it,' I say, remembering what Jo and Amy said last night.

'Gavin is cooking something special. I don't know what, but it smells nice. Arkwright's is paying. They are in the Jerusalem at nine. Julian has been de-invited, if you can do such a thing. Make sure he stays out of the way. I've got Gavin to plate-up his dinner. You can take it up to his room. Alright?'

'Does Mary Beth know?'

'She read him the Riot Act. Not a happy bunny,' Cat says ominously. 'I don't want fuss here. You know that.'

Managers.
Idiots.
All of them.
Idiots.
Idiots.

Cat.

Idiot.

I don't know whether it's me or whether everyone feels like this, but whenever a manager says something *general*, like that final addendum (*you know that, you know that, you know that*), I think they are pointing the finger at me.

I wasn't even in the building.

How could I be responsible for Julian getting trolleyed … how … how … my head feels tight, and I am close to saying something, but I haven't got this far as a night porter in top full service hotels by displacing my paranoia everywhere like a big kid arguing with teacher, so I just nod, and mouth a professional's platitude with no trace of irony. It hurts to do this, but I put that down to lack of sleep. 'I do. Sorry, Cat. Won't happen again. I'll keep an eye on him.'

'It's not your fault. Just keep him off the ale tonight and out of the Jerusalem. Mary Beth will sort him out.'

'Do you know what the argument was about?'

'Martin said it was the usual author's stuff.'

'I'll ask him, as I said.'

'You do that. Now be very careful.'

She pulls out her Organiser and moves onto other business in the hotel, none of which is as interesting as the fight between Amy and Julian. I wait patiently for its end. When it does, I nip up to the bar. See Martin.

'Hi, Martin.'

He is sitting on a bar stool. There are two drinkers in the bar. Oldies. Locals on the Bishop's Mitre.

I will give him this, the bar is immaculately clean and tidy. A roaring fire blazes, and I hear the coals crackle as I sit down. The bar manager mumbles a hello in return but doesn't look up from his crossword (simple).

'What happened earlier?' I ask.

'That Julian is a c___. He really is. I'd bar him tonight. I'd kick him out,' he says while continuing to ignore my gaze. He really doesn't like me, and I feel awkward, but I need to know.

'What were they arguing about?'

'He was out of it. I wasn't listening. All these authors are arseholes anyway. Heard more commonsense in the Benbow on a Saturday night. A set of monkeys. Except that Jo ... she's –'

'– you must have heard what he said?' I interrupt him, perhaps too edgily. He rears up on me.

'What's up? You in training for the Filth?'

'Martin –'

'– feel like you're interrogating me.' He folds his paper neatly. He is drinking a tall glass of water, with a slice of lime floating on the top like a mini water lily. Takes a sip and dismounts his bar stool.

'Just asking, Martin.'

'Look. I know he's your buddy, but he was bang out of order and wants kicking out of the hotel. I tell you now; I'm not serving him again. He can go f__k himself.'

'You have to…'

Martin leans toward me. I smell garlic and mustard on his breath. His lips are large, and his cheeks are stubbly. He is built like a rugby player, and his eyes flash darkness. 'Mate, I can serve who the f___ I want. I can also NOT serve who I want.' He points at himself, though I know he would rather punch me. 'I. Am. The. Bar. Manager.'

'– the memo –'

'F__ the memo. Cat don't know what she's on about. Green's lowering the tone. 'All them crappy writers are lowering the tone. Bitch laid into him an'all. Foul-mouthed cow.'

'She gave him some back?' I am impressed, but the positivity is soon stamped upon by the barman who is slowly revealing his true colours as time goes on.

'What the f___ has all this got to do with you, anyway? You're the *night porter*. Just get on with your job. Why are you always talking with these freaks? You don't talk to Mr and Mrs Appleby, do you? You don't talk to Jeff the plumber, or Bill the Paint Rep from the Handicentre? You can't be arsed with them. Honest folk. Ordinary folk. Bloody writers! Bloody f__ ups. What is it? Is it because they're celebrities?'

'No. I –'

'If you don't mind, I'm busy. Go and tidy a f___g room, or something useful, something you're actually *paid* to do, mate.'

I want to hit him.
I want to bash his face in.
I want to bite into his fat cheeks.
I want to launch into his corpulent, bald, rugby playing, cueball, rural, yokel, stinking Wheatley Fields face.

Fat.
Fat.
Fat.
Fat.
Fat.
I want to pick up the glass he left behind, smash it on the oak bar, and jab the jagged edge into his fat
corpulent
ugly
fat
bullying
and make it
bleed
a river
a river of blood
flow
river
flow
river
an explosion of blood
(hit him)

    (NUT him)
    plasma
    watch the bully cry
    bully
    bully

but I don't, I am a professional, and I watch him disappear toward the kitchen before I dismount my bar stool and amble back to my work station.

Cat sees me before she leaves. I am working on something on the computer. She's wearing her raincoat, which means she is on the 100 to the City for a meal or a night out, rather than driving home.
    I like her high-heel shoes – black patent, new, expensive.
    'Martin tell you what went on?' She asks.
    'He did, yes.'
    She looks pleased.
    'Good. Mate, keep an eye on him tonight. See you tomorrow.'
    'Bye.'

After that start, the first two hours of my shift are horrendous, and I am snappy and unpleasant to Gavin and Kerry, but as the night develops, I start to feel better, start to get into it. I apologise to both of them, and they admit to being surprised at my chippiness. Sleep deprivation, I say, overlooking Martin's input into the basic formula of my snippy aggression for political reasons. They accept my apology, and Gavin offers to save some of the dinner he is cooking with some enthusiasm. I ask what it is. He says it is a surprise, though I can smell beef, and there is a hint of cinnamon around the kitchen area. Martin sticks to the bar like spreading glue. I have no plans to go in there.

Frank, Jo and Amy come down to dinner together. They look to be in a great form, and the girls are laughing and joking. Amy breaks away from the trio and comes over to see me.

'Are you around later?'
'Of course, I am, Amy. I'm at *work*.' I say, cheekily.
'Only, my –'
'– mini-bar?'
'Empty, love. Wait for me to get back.'
'I will.'

She is dressed for dinner, drunk and daring. I thought for one moment she was going to give me a kiss, which would be just silly. I like her dress and shoes, but she can't touch Jo tonight, who looks utterly magnificent in a lime green trouser suit, the likes of which I have not seen for many years. Her hair is down, and the jet black simultaneously reflects and absorbs the lights from the ceiling. She walks with majesty across the floor, holding Frank's arm. He is casually dressed in trousers and a pale lemon sweater. He is wearing his blue wide-brimmed racing cap. I really like that cap. In fact, I covet it, but I have not seen one like it.

Just to make sure, I go upstairs to see Julian. I knock on his door, but there is no answer. He is obviously fast asleep, so I leave it. I have seen the writer drunk on five or six occasions now. He is a colossal drinker, but he will have to stop, at least round the hotel. He's getting on people's nerves, as he has done all weekend, if the truth be told. The press conference: As unfair as the media were to him, he's dealt with it badly, and I, as I stand outside his door vow to discuss it with him.

It's all in the coping and Julian cannot cope with

(rejection?)
(other writers?)
(people?)
(reality?)
(*anything?*)

The options cascade, and I realise helping Julian to cope may not be as easy as I make it sound, so I disappear back to my desk, and smell Gavin's delicious dinner in the Jerusalem.

The night passes. About ten, Mrs Appleby calls me to her room. She has discovered a damp patch behind her bed, and she is berating me. The damp could get on her chest, she says, and she is desirous of an immediate move to another room. I am wondering how she noticed whether it is *really* an incidence of damp or something else, and whether Mrs Appleby, whose husband sits quietly and slightly sheepish near the dressing table, is a serial complainer, and is looking for a discount on her bill, when my pager goes off. I assure Mrs Appleby that I shall return, and she is not amused. Even if it is damp, the odds on such a small patch of it getting on her chest are fairly long, so she is safe. I say that I will be back up tomorrow with a hair dryer as that is the only solution I can think of.

Adamant that she wishes to move, I tell her that I will refer her complaint to Cat. Promptly, I leave the room to the sound of her obvious frustration.

Gavin is outside the room biting his fingernail.

'Best come quick,' he says in his usual clipped, staccato delivery. He looks very worried, more than usual.

'What's happened, Gav?'

'The writer – the drunk –'

'Julian?' I interrupt. 'What about him?'

'He's back. Been out. On the pop.'

'That's impossible! He was in his room. I would have seen him'

'Hammered,' Gavin says, ignoring me. 'On the pop in the BumbleBee. Thrown out for arguing. My friend texted me.'

'Where is he – no, he's not –'

'Yeh. In the bar.'

'With the others?' I say, feeling my belly turn to ice.

'Authors,' he nods, confirming my fears. Immediately, I race downstairs and into the bar. Julian, wearing a Judas Priest *Stained Class* tee shirt, is staggering. He is gaunt, face red as a beetroot, but I know all that (that Julian is death warmed up, a zombie, a health hazard), the new stuff I need to be aware of as a night porter, the *professional information* I need to act upon, is that he is pointing at Amy and ranting...

'– fucked your way to that contract; you did; hundreds of writers slave, and slave, and write, and write, and no one ever notices, and they rot, and they fester, and they stand ignored in the gutter, good writers, BRILLIANT writers, writers who deserve a shot at the money, and there's you, a HACK, a romance HACK, not a bloody writer at ALL, and you cheated and fu –'

'– I didn't, Julian,' she interrupts, angrily. 'And what you are saying is libellous and outrageous,' Amy replies, but Julian isn't listening.

'– plagiarising, and shagging, and brownnosing, and using every contact you've got to beat the slush pile like some crappy stand-up comedian, Julian Cleary, Dawn German, Alex Hayle, all that lot of talentless pricks, useless, privileged, ghost-written fakers, and copyists, and you, and you –'

Jo is nearly in tears. 'Julian, please, please –'

But he ignores her. Sixsmith, the bully, handy with his fists and with no idea what is being said, is hovering, and he would like nothing more than the opportunity to punch Julian, so I stand in between him and the ranting novelist. I put my hand on his shoulder...

'Julian –'

Roughly, he throws me off. '– circumvent every rule we have to play by in the game, every Cluedo principle, every Monopoly instruction, every Chess move us poor writers have to live by, but you, you, talentless sow –' He is furious, and there is no irony in his voice. His fists clench. He is not going to stop.

Amy stands. '– say one more thing to me, and I will consult solicitors, Julian. This time I won't stop until they have the lot. I mean it...'

'Here we go, look, not only talentless, but a *bully*! Consult solicitors? I wish you'd have consulted a writing school before you inflicted your crap on the world, you amateur goon. I know for a FACT you copied *Amelia*, or f'in paid someone to write –'

Frank stands up next to Amy. He slightly pushes her back and approaches Julian.

'Shut your mouth, asshole,' he says.

'Ooh, Amy, the Black Knight has arrived to defend your corrupted soul.'

'I said shut your mouth,' he replies.

'Please, Julian, come with me, this is so freaking bad...' Jo interjects, but Julian turns to Frank, ignoring the only person in the hotel besides me who likes him.

'What you going to do, Frank? Send your rapping James Bond copy after me. You're another plagiarist. I bet Ian Fleming is turning in his grave. Bloody thriller writers – tossers, every one of you. Cheats and tossers.'

He advances once more. 'Shut your *mouth*.'

Julian laughs defiantly. 'Look! He's going to beat little me to an English pulp. Pretty much like what you lot did in the war, eh, Frank?'

'F__k the war. You've made this between us,' he says, moving closer. Sixsmith barges me out of the way and stands between Frank and Julian, a natural barrier.

Julian looks over the bar manager's shoulder. 'You would say that, Frank, seeing as our little country has only just stopped repaying yours for the alleged 'assistance' you gave us in the Second World War, Frank. That's why we didn't join you over in 'Nam, Frank. We couldn't *afford* to because you BLED US DRY throughout WWII.'

'I'm warning you,' Frank says.

'And you joined in the festivities late, Frank. Your cousins, Old Blighty, had been bombed to a pulp by the

Germans, bleeding, battered and half dead, and you could have helped us out from the beginning, but you bricked it, Frank. Cold as ice, you waited until we were half dead so you could take over all our markets for your FRIED CHICKEN AND COMICS, Frank. That's Yankees, Frank. Cunning bullies and calculating shitters.'

Enraged, Frank lurches forward, but Sixsmith stops him. Everyone is everywhere at once, shouting and arguing, pushing and shoving, a big melee, and I find myself in front of Julian who is still ranting.

'I'm half your size, Frank. You'd beat me to a pulp, but when you think about it, that's what you Yanks do, isn't it? You're a nation of bullies. That's why you write cock-extension thrillers about secret agents because a nation of farmers wearing slippers kicked Uncle Sam's fried chicken lardy arse, just like the Afghans are kicking it now, a historically undefeated nation of ragheads living in caves on husks of rice and haunches of dog kicking your nuclear-powered, Superfortress Yankee Doodle Dandy arses, Frank. Is that why you write this thriller stuff, Frank? Boost your country's self-esteem because everywhere you go, you get your arse kicked by brave little people who don't want to fight in the first place?'

'One more word and I'll kick –' Frank says, furious.

'– you put it about you were in 'Nam, Frank. Bollocks. You were in the pay corps, weren't you, Frank? While all your countrymen were getting hammered by little people in slippers, you were back in Buttf__k, Arizona sending out cheques. At least your pals had a pop in the tunnels – not like you, sitting there, safe as a bug in a rug, behind your desk, listening to Englebert Humperdinck, with your hand down your overalls having a crafty wa –'

With a roar, Frank throws Sixsmith out of the way and jumps onto Julian, the momentum of his lunge throwing him to the floor. Frank punches him twice in the face, a pair of meaty, sturdy blows, the impact of which could be heard in the corridor. Sixsmith, Gavin and I pull him off before he can hit him again.

The tableau is gruesome, more Benbow than Saladin. Behind him, Jo and Amy are screaming. Tables have tipped and glasses smash in the melee. Guests from the Jerusalem come in to see what the fuss is about. Frank is heavy, boxer heavy, but he allows himself to be lifted off. His body is softer than I thought, and the struggle is not a difficult one. It is as if he is a willing participant in the lift. He is angry, and his teeth are bared like an animal, but he doesn't struggle. His language is profane, and he shouts at Julian, threats and interlocutions, insults and slang, but he doesn't go in for the kill.

Julian's nose is bloodied, and his glasses are smashed. 'You see. You just can't resist it, can you, Frank?' Julian gets up on one elbow. Jo bobs down to see if he's okay. He is rubbing his leg, and I realise that Sixsmith had stamped on it in the melee. 'You've even got the Yokel here at it, Frank –' He nods at Sixsmith. 'Don't think I didn't see what you did, yokel boy. Have you been listening? Have you? Aw, you have. I'm surprised they teach you English in this rural shithole, never mind History. Now get back behind the bar, you shocking knob, and pour me a refreshing pint of lager. Chop chop, there's a good chap,' he says, still on the floor.

Sixsmith is enraged. 'If he's not kicked out of the hotel tomorrow, I quit,' he says to me.

'It's not about you, Martin. Calm down,' I say.

The look he gives me is indescribable. Perhaps I should have backed him up, but I don't like him after the fuss earlier on, I just don't, and I'm not much for *esprit de corps* and that. I turn to Julian. 'I'm taking you to bed,' I say, and instantly regret it.

'Oooh, I'm on a chutney promise, lovey,' Julian says before one final shot at Amy. 'See what you caused, bitch. Everywhere you go, you inflict pain and misery. It's part of you. Cynicism, misery and manipulation.

You're the Daughter of Satan, chubby cheeks. The beauty of love and romance? You are a fraud Amy. A fraud. Poxed – everywhere you go, someone suffers.'

He points at her angrily, climatically, a drunk's climax, something that had been clearly bubbling inside him for hours, days, maybe years. 'You know what you did, Amy. You KNOW.'

She shakes her head, seemingly shocked.

'You're a drunk, and you know nothing,' Amy replies, and it is hard to tell from her guarded, stony glance whether he had hit a bullseye.

Julian wipes the blood off his nose and face with the back of his forearm. 'I do, Mrs Cook. Oh, I do. I SO know – and so do you,' he whispers audibly, a sound more akin to a hiss.

Julian glares at Frank, and tries to look threatening, not altogether convincingly. 'I've got mates, you know. BIG bastards. I'd watch your back if I were you,' he says and allows Jo and I to walk him out of the bar.

Unlike many drunks, he doesn't try and run back to continue the confrontation. He rubs his leg and wipes his nose on the tee shirt. Mutters drunkenly to himself. Staggers from one side to another. The smell of drink, cigarettes, and body odour coming from him is considerable. Jo is in tears, but Julian doesn't seem to notice. The three of us queue for the disabled lift and listen to it whirr, and crank, and clank, as it arrives.

The damage he has done is considerable. Two tables broken, one plate and one leg. Four glasses lie smashed. A bottle of wine has stained the carpet blood red. Frank is livid. So is Sixsmith (and not just with Julian). Amy is in tears.

Several other drinkers in the bar are stunned, half appalled and half thrilled by the unexpected Monday night entertainment.

It is not yet eleven...

...
...
...
...
...
...
...
...
...
...
...
...
...
...

that night, about five am, on my rounds, answering a call, I found Julian Green on his hotel bedroom floor, dead, face down, underneath the windowsill.

Someone had hit him.
Someone from the hotel.

I knew that I, as night porter, had failed in my duty to protect the Ceremony and The Saladin. I turned away from the scene and went back downstairs, and began to make the necessary calls....

Part 3

The Aftermath Of The Arguably Justified Attack On Julian Green

The Second Tuesday

I am a night porter, but this morning, I am staying at my post, even though it is the daylight hours. It was I who found him after all, and I called Cat, Mary Beth, and the Police. In that order. I am central to the drama, and that generates enough adrenaline to keep me going until at least midday.

And Cat had best not ask me to take the night off. I wouldn't miss this for the world. I'm already on seven nights a week, and I am seeing this whole thing out to a conclusion.[45]

The Saladin hadn't seen a night like that one since Charles I sneaked in through the stables disguised as a priest. Public squabbling, fighting in the bar, drunken celebrities and attempted murder.

Or a murder.

We don't know.

Julian was scarcely breathing, and his eyeballs had disappeared. I thought he was dead. He looked it. I'm no Detective, even though I have the raincoat, but I think it's a safe bet that someone hit him on the back of the head with a heavy object and left him to die. The writer drank industrial quantities of alcohol throughout the evening. Probably drugs. He had been hit from behind as he went to refill his drink. There was no possibility of a fall.

Once he had taken my statement, Brophy, the avuncular Irish Police Sergeant who ruled the town of Wheatley Fields with an iron fist, arrested Frank Duke.

I've met Brophy before. It was long odds-on that he was going to pull Frank, not *just* because of the punches in the bar after the dinner. The Irishman never even

---

[45] I'm not walking out halfway through the film. Sorry, putting the book down half way through the story.

bothered with the girls. Or the other guests – though he said he would return.

Brophy is an unpleasantly violent traditionalist, an old school copper who spends much of his time drinking with his huntin', shootin' and fishin' cronies in the Haywain up the road.[46]

Frank left the hotel in handcuffs while Brophy took a call from the Assistant Constable on his mobile phone. The hotel's morning team watched, curious, as Frank walked proud and tall to the car outside. He smiled at me, the thinnest of smiles, but generally, as you would expect, his face was tense. Scared even. I couldn't begin to interpret what that glance meant, and I didn't try. This is not the first time I have come across attempted murder in my career as a night porter, but it is the first time I have encountered it amongst celebrities, however C-List.

And I was sad. I liked Julian. He was unpleasant and vicious last night, and I probably wouldn't have spoken to him for a couple of days. Looking back, had I been stronger physically, I should have manhandled him out of there before Frank hit him. I know he wouldn't have shopped me to Cat, and he may have thanked me for it. His abuse of Amy and Frank was a thermonuclear bomb made of violent sentiment, and its impact lingered. His exploding bomb radiated the kind of words that can never be unsaid.[47]

There is no way Amy would ever be as magnanimous about him again, as she had been when we talked in front of the bookcase. In all likelihood, Frank would never even *attempt* to speak to him. Worse, he had probably

---

[46]After giving you this information, I'll leave you to work out why the tall, handsome and black Frank Duke might be a hot favourite for the collar.

[47]The Chinese say that there isn't a racehorse fast enough to catch words racing from an angry mouth.

damaged his emergent friendship with Jo, who cried tears for an hour afterwards, and had her dream holiday in Great Britain unutterably spoiled, all the dreams, and the memories, and the good will shattered.[48]

There is something wrong with him, something deep in his core, somewhere suppurating with bile. I have never met anyone who uses words as weapons like he does and rather than hate him, I find myself feeling for him. He seems to me to spend his entire life in pain. The drink. The prescription drugs.[49]

Where it all leaves the Awards Ceremony, I don't know. And as for Cat...

'Well. Goody gumdrops. Goody, goody gumdrops,' she says as I tell her the news at my work station.

'Yes, indeed,' I reply.

There is a short gap. She speaks.

'We, my night porter friend, have buggered it up. We've turned it over good and proper.' Her face, normally open and expansive, is pinched and bitter, her eyes, slits; like a snake hunting supper.

'It looks a lot like it,' I reply once more.

Another gap. 'Well, that's it for the bonus.'

'And the ceremony.'

---

[48] But she was remarkably forgiving. I was surprised. Maybe there is a religious element, an American Christian thing. Or maybe she really *does* like him, however hard that may be to believe. The other idea I had was that she didn't like Frank and Amy much either. I could have been half right there, but I discounted it as embellishment pretty shortly after I had the idea.

[49] Hey. I'm talking about him as if he's alive. He might very well be dead, and it's bad luck, and ill manners to speak anything but good of the dead. Julian, if you are dead and watching me now, behind my night porterly desk, you were a brilliant writer.

'Not just that. That's it for the winter. That's your lot.' She throws her clipboard upon the reception. 'It's all over. You may as well get your online application in for McDonalds. The Dick Whittingtons will be crawling all over us like lice on a tramp's jockstrap. And I'm the tramp's cock.'

Even though I was furious with her – a man is critically ill in hospital after all, a man I like – I shut my mouth and let her rant.

Divorcing my personal feelings from my professional veneer, I realised she was right. After all this publicity – arguments, drunkenness, drugs, fighting and an attempted murder just before the major awards ceremony they finance – Arkwright's would rather house their shortlistees in a homeless hostel than The Saladin again.

'There's something about authors,' she continued. 'Dolly Bluestockings.'

'What?' I queried.

'Dolly Bluestockings. Whiter than white. Miss Jean Dolly Bluestockings Brodie. They've got to be whiter than white. They let their books tell the stories and stay in the background. Name an author who destroys hotel rooms? Name a drug addicted author who gets six months for possession?' she asks. 'You can't, can you!? All clean as whistles. And that's why Arkwright chose us. We're the cleanest whistle in Wheatley Fields. And we're now as dirty as a mechanics –'

'– overalls?' I interjected.

'Those, too. Rest of the guests okay?'

'Fine. Obviously, Sergeant Brophy arrested Frank and is interrogating him up the road at the station. He wants to see you in an hour, Cat.'

'I know all this. How are the guests?' Cat responds, with a note of irritation.

'Fine,' I say, fighting fire with fire. 'The real question is, where are the press?'

'What?' Cat says. 'Oh, balls, the pr –'

'There won't be any press, Cat.' A voice to the left of me interjects.

Mary Beth Burnell stands there fresh as paint. Houndstooth jacket, black trousers. Carrying a vintage tan leather satchel, which must have cost a grand at least.

'Mrs Burnell. Thank you for coming,' Cat says. 'I am SO sorry about all this…'

She waves Cat away cordially. 'It isn't your fault. We're not blaming the hotel. We've had a meeting at the Theatre this morning. Can we talk?'

'Yes, of course.'

Mary Beth turns to look at me. Immaculate in her thousand dollar golden spectacles, she looked like the PA to someone very powerful, indeed. Which, as the Chair of the Awards Committee for the Arkwright Trust, was not far from the truth. She had an efficiency and authority about her, and she didn't seem fazed by the news. I was surprised to see her refer to me.

'You saw it all last night?'

I aver that I did so.

'You attempted to intervene?'

'I did, yes. Frank was pretty angry...' I say, almost apologetically.

'And you have no idea who went into Julian's room?'

'None. None at all.'

She turns to Cat. 'I have something to tell you. Cat, can he come into the meeting with us?'

Cat looks at me, and I can tell for a split second that she is not happy. However, she is on a salvage mission, which might just save the hotel from the clutches of the Dick Whittington chain, so she nods. 'Let's meet in the bar. The fire's roaring, and it's a lot warmer than my office. I'll order coffee.'

Mary Beth sips at her hot drink. Her accent is cutting and abrasive, and she speaks swiftly. 'The Arkwright Trust is one of the most powerful elements in Wheatley Fields culture,' is her opening salvo. 'I live and work in

New York and I have seen power up close, but I've seldom come across a more powerful influence than Arkwright is here. They own land and property stretching south down to the City and up north to Sheffield. It influences Councils and employers. It invests and supports business. For instance, you may be surprised to know that the Trust have purchased forty per cent of the equity in this hotel, and they did it three days ago, through one of their many shells. They are secretive and court no publicity in their financial dealings, so you can tell as many people as possible, and it could get into the papers, but Arkwright will know it comes from you, as I would never tell anyone, because I am a professional and this situation requires professionals.'

'So why tell us?' Cat asked.

'Because I have just saved your job. You so owe me.'

'Really?' She replies, shocked.

'Yes. There's a heck of a lot of anger down there, but I handled it.'

'Oh, okay.' Cat says, knowing full well she had nothing to do with any of it. Presumably, Mary Beth had saved mine, too. The sense of gratitude is enough, Mary Beth assumes, to prevent us contacting the papers, and she is right for both of us.

'Essentially, as regards last night's shocking events, Arkwright have become directly involved.'

'In what sense?' Cat asks, fascinated.

'A very high level sense. For instance, the City's Assistant Chief Constable is having breakfast with Lucas Arkwright –' she looks at her Rolex watch. '– about now at *Hearts,* in the City. The conversation will be about crisis management, I am sure.'

'And it is a crisis,' I say.

'The type of crisis management that involves the press,' she continues.

'The press?' Cat parrots.

'TV, newspapers, radio mainly. A press blackout on the incident has been agreed for three days, until after the ceremony. Arkwright's could theoretically keep the blackout going forever, but someone will put the gen on Me.Com or the other networks and the bloggers will...well, you know.'

I think about what this entails. It's big. Huge. Corrupt.

'The Editors of the local press have agreed to a blackout on condition of an exclusive on Monday, which I will manage. I'd like you two to be the face of The Saladin, by the way, when they come.'

'We'd be glad to, 'Cat says. I sit there, like a rabbit in headlights, saying nothing. I detest any publicity. I certainly don't want my name in the paper – I'm strictly backroom. I love my invisibility, and I will be talking to Cat about that.

'Julian is like a son to me,' the American continues. 'We've been corresponding for a year or so, and I love him dearly, warts and all. I have never read such talent, but I know his weaknesses, and I am aware of his bitterness. I have arranged for a twenty four hour guard and private nursing staff to take over from the socialised staff down there at your hospital.'

'What do you mean by socialised? You mean The Prince Charles?' Cat queries.

'That's the hospital. National Health System. Socialised medicine. The one for everyone.'

'It's Service, madam,' I say.

'Pardon?'

'National Health Service.'

'That, too. I don't trust it. There's a saying in New York – pay peanuts, get monkeys, so Arkwright has taken over his care. Any nurse who saw him admitted this morning will be sacked if they tip off the media. All Me.Com feeds will be scrutinised. It's been organised. Luckily, Julian isn't well known and so far, so good. Nothing is out there. We may have gotten away with it.'

'What about Sgt Brophy?' I add. 'The Sarge is a notorious presence in Wheatley Fields life. He drinks here on occasion. He likes a natter. I've heard him say he's got contacts in press and TV.'

'Is that the Policeman who arrested Frank Duke?'

'That's him.'

Mary Beth takes a note with her pen and leans back on her sofa crossing her legs as she does so. 'Sgt. Brophy has just been arrested by City Detectives on suspicion of planting evidence. Frank has been released and will be coming back to the hotel any minute now.'

'You've had the Sarge arrested?' Cat asks incredulously.

'Not me. Arkwright.'

'Arkwright, then.'

'With the co-operation of The Assistant Chief Constable, yes. Thank God you contacted me at six. It gave me time to work.'

'But Sgt. Brophy? He's innocent.' Cat says with genuine concern.

'I assure you he's far from innocent, Cat – the man is quite the rascal – but he shall be released on Sunday after the ceremony with a compensatory sum in his wallet courtesy of Luke Arkwright. Plus an impenetrable, legally binding gagging clause. I'm glad you contacted me first, before you called the Police. There was fuss two years ago with a suspected murderer and sex offender. The Sgt. was much too *assured* in his judgements about the fellow. The local Police learned lessons from that, and one of those lessons was that Sgt. Brophy is a liability who needs careful monitoring.'

'There's bound to be a leak,' I say. 'Has to be. The hotel guests who saw the fight. The authors themselves.'

'The Arkwright Trust will deny everything, and refer the queries to a Public Relations firm they engage from time to time. Brilliant firm. They will tie it in knots. Rumours and gossip. And don't forget, the authors will be up for a significant prize. One of the authors here is a front runner for the big one,' Mary Beth says calmly, taking a sip of coffee and luxuriating in front of the fire.

'Amy?' I suggest.

'Indeed, Amy. I'm going to have a word with them all today to emphasise the importance of tact and discretion. They will listen. One other thing we're doing...'

'Which is,' Cat says, bitten and absorbed by curiosity.

'The generic Independent Award is being abandoned. The three other shortlisted authors are being told now.'

'They must be furious,' I say.

'Apoplectic. If they complain – well – there is always next year. They've been compensated. And even if he recovers, Julian won't win Contemporary this year.'

'How do you know?' I ask.

Mary Beth looks at me as if I am an idiot. 'We have withdrawn him, pleading an irregularity in nomination.'

'If Julian recovers, he'll be livid.'

'If I may be so bold, the man has behaved like an asshole. He is going to have to learn that some things are bigger than his ego. Call it a punishment.'

'That's harsh,' I comment. 'The Press Conference unbalanced him. And he could die.'

'It's the politics of the ceremony,' she replies, with phlegmatic finality. 'It is touch and go whether he will recover from the blow he received. I am praying every night he does because I love him like a son, but no one is bigger than the ceremony, and I won't have no-shows. There is no way Julian will be able to attend.'

I nod and don't respond further. It seems harsh to me, but I'm the night porter, so I understand politics. Rules are rules. I guess it will be a bigger result for Julian if he recovers. I also believe that the three of us are in shock and are thinking with our heads and not our hearts.

We sit quietly for a while. Cat interrupts the silence with a quiet implication. 'The hotel –'

'– what about it?' Mary Beth interrupts.

'Will...will –' Cat was tongue-tied. This meant a lot to her. '– we be chosen next year for the Prime?'

'Of course,' Mary Beth says, standing and putting away her personal organiser. 'After all, your new bosses sponsor the ceremony, don't they? Now, I have authors to see. Can I have their room numbers, please? I won't take up any more of your time.'

'Those numbers will be yours,' I say, standing.

'I'll bet you are shattered.'

'I am, yes,'

'Go home and get some sleep. The Police will be back, but not till later. I shall liaise.'

If Cat was upset by her interjection in the organisational chart of The Saladin Hotel, she didn't show it.

'Yes, go home and we'll see you tonight.'

'I'll come in early. About six.'

'That's a good idea. I shall feed back to you what happened with the others. You are going to be critical for the next few days. They like you and trust you. They have already told me in conversation. It is now Tuesday. On Saturday, we have the ceremony. You need to look after the authors in the evening. The heavy drinking is over – even for Mrs Cook –'

'– that is going to be tough to impose,' I say.

'I am aware of Amy's recent drinking problem, but she can control it. She will need to. I know the press will get wind of what happened. Cat, I need to be informed of any new guests for the next two nights.'

'Hotel's full and will be till Sunday,' Cat said. 'But the bars and restaurants are public access.'

'Then you –' she says, nodding in my direction, 'will be critical. Keep an eye on anyone asking questions. Keep the authors safe and warm. Try to encourage them to stay in their rooms. Forget the racetrack, forget shopping, forget wandering about in your magnificent winter countryside. It's all over until Sunday. I'm serious – I shall impose a curfew on pain of disqualification if I have to. Both of you need to reinforce the importance of this. If the news of the attack on Julian *does* get out, we can control the earthquake from inside the hotel. We cannot protect them from the inquisitors outside.'

'What if –'

'– Julian dies? Way ahead of you. Sad as it may seem, the passing of a minor self-published novelist like Julian won't cause a single ripple on its own – and I adore him, as I said, warts and all, like my own son – but hand the press the notion that a bestselling author like Jo, Frank or Amy might have been responsible for attempted murder and that's a completely different matter. The ceremony becomes a farce. Arkwright Trust spend about six million Sterling on awards night. Probably more. If this news gets out, that's the end of it. They are secretive people. Good people, but secretive. Joshua Arkwright loved literature and sponsored many, many authors in his heyday a century and a half ago, when the British Empire was at its very peak. Now, his ancestors honour his memory with this award. It would be a shame for that to end, wouldn't it?'

Realpolitik or not, her tone grated a little. I felt I had to say something. 'Someone tried to kill Julian,' I said. 'We can't erase that, Mary Beth.'

She steeled herself. 'I know that. I know that well.' A tear appeared in the corner of her eye, and she dabbed it with a handkerchief. I felt bad for saying something.

'I'm sorry, ma'am.'

'Don't be. I believe in God, and justice, and we WILL find who did this. But God willing, it can wait until Sunday.'

'Mate, haven't you got a home to go to?' Cat interjected, stern and slightly annoyed at my comment.

'I have. I shall see you both at six.

I tell Cat that I am taking the advice, and I go home, out into the wind and the rain of the winter's morning. Already, I know I will not be able to sleep.

Six came, and I was at the reception desk on the dot. Cat had sent home Hayley who staffed the reception throughout the day. I have hardly ever seen her except at staff meetings. Night porters are self-contained people and happy with that. Other team members tend to be, relative to the night porter, like ships that pass in the night. In the past, I have responded to many job advertisements, which ask for a "team playing" night porter. I make a point of asking who writes the adverts – only after I have landed the job, of course. There is no such beast as a team playing night porter, and if anyone tries to convince you they exist, they are playing head games with you.

Mary Beth and Cat update the situation, which can be summarised thus.
1) Julian is stable, but still unconscious.
2) Mary Beth has laid the law down with the authors. There will be no further issues.
3) Forensic Scientists carried out a battery of examinations in Frank's and Julian's rooms. These were discreet tests carried out by staff in plain clothes rather than the snow suits of TV lore. Amy and Jo have not been tested. No other hotel guests are under suspicion.
4) Bearing in mind point 3, Mary Beth relates that all the guests in the hotel will be questioned by Police over the course of the next few days. All the staff present – including me, Gavin, Kerry and Martin Sixsmith, will be interviewed over the next week.
5) A potential leak on a nurse's Me.Com page at lunchtime was quashed, and the nurse suspended. When contacted by press, hotel administrators denied the story. Mary Beth denied the story to a journalist following it up. Cat, when the Chronicle contacted The Saladin, also lied out of her back teeth. No further press leakage had occurred today.
6) Mary Beth reiterated to me that I am to keep an eye on the situation. I tell her that as a professional night porter, I will do my utmost to remain vigilant.

Mary Beth was dressed to the nines as she was off to dinner with the City Chamber of Commerce. Cat looked tired out. She'd been with Mary Beth all day bar two hours, and I can imagine that being demanding. Not only did she have to look after the Police, she had to cater to Mary Beth, and also keep an eye on the day-to-day running of a fully booked, full service hotel. Several guests paid for full board. And Gavin went sick, leaving her to locate (successfully) an agency chef. I suspect Cat is looking forward to normality returning to The Saladin. A peaceful life without being harassed by staff questions – and the stern New York scrutiny of the new part-owner's representative. I definitely wouldn't like that: She's a total professional and misses nothing.

I wonder whether this whole experience has changed Cat's view on climbing the ladder. She is unsmiling and weary. Shadows, semi-circular divots the colour of cigarette ash coat her sockets, and she smells strongly of perfume, as if she has splashed it on with a sponge to hide the smell of stressed-out armpit odour. Red ears and a creased blouse add to the I Am Not Enjoying Work Today look.

Seeing her makes me realise once more that I'm glad I am the night porter and not the manager.

The Return of Frank Duke

An hour later, after Mary Beth and Cat had left for pastures new, Frank comes to see me. I see him hovering around the bookcase, pretending to read something. I can't see what it is. He is wearing a black and white Adidas tracksuit and tennis trainers, completely unbranded. When I look at him close up, he is tired and drawn, and his eyes are red rimmed.

'I didn't do it.'

'I know, Frank. But you have to admit –'

He ignores me completely, and I regret having an opinion. I resolve not to have such a thing again.

'That cop is racist,' he says.

I say nothing, but aver subtly with a nod.

'I do my disagreements in public. I would never hit anyone from behind. Cowardly. It ain't me, man.'

'I understand, Frank.'

'I was *ragin.* You heard what he said. He insulted Amy. I couldn't have that. It was *wrong* what he said.'

'And you.'

'What?'

'He insulted you. And your country.'

He shrugged his shoulders. 'What an asswipe! Nah, that ain't a problem. It was Amy...he upset her. I can see why they have beef.'

'Beef?' I query.

'Yeh, issues, as you guys say over here. *Issues.* I got *issues.* He got *issues.* She got *issues.* Everyone's got *issues.* All I ever hear from Amy is *issues.*'

'Isn't that an American thing?'

'What?'

'Calling everything an issue?'

He looks at me.

I look at him.

He speaks.

'I found out why he hates her. Amy told me. It's a beast. *Jehoshaphat,* her news knocked my head off.'

'Can you share?' I ask

'Never. I can never share. It's bad, man. It's bad. I almost feel sorry for the guy. Almost, but not quite.'

'When did she tell you?'

'Last night. I was with Amy. Drinking and talking. In her room.'

'Ah,' I say.

'There ain't nothing going on,' he says, immediately, clearly reading my mind.

'Didn't say there was, Frank.'

'Just comfort. We talked, y'know. Just talked, listened to some sounds on my laptop. Cops can check my computer. I was with Amy.'

'Hitting Julian in his room would be obvious,' I say.

'Jesus, they'd be crawling over my ass, and they would never stop until I was on death row.'

'No death penalty over here. And he's not dead.'

'No death penalty?' He looks surprised.

'Life imprisonment. If it was you who whacked Julian, you'd be in the City Prison and out in eight.'

'Life is eight years?' He mirrors me, bemused.

'Approximately, I understand.'

'I got acquaintances who seriously need to be here.'

Frank still looks nervous. I cannot see Frank as the guilty man. I see the mugshot in the paper, I see the Police photo in my head, and it isn't Frank I see in the frame. 'I know it isn't you, Frank,' I confirm.

'Thanks,' he says. 'That's a reassurance.'

'Mind you, watch Brophy.'

'Asshole is a racist. I'm going to need a big lawyer.'

'Have you sorted one out?'

'I've e-mailed my lawyer in Chicago. He's on the case. They have an office in London, and when they interview me again on Monday, he'll be here. Amy's done the same thing. I don't know about Jo. She won't leave her room, poor kid. Jo likes Julian for some crazy reason. Chicks, huh.'

'Indeed, Frank.' I made a mental note to go and see her after this. Take some food up.

'Frank?' I ask.

'Whassup?'

'Were you really in Vietnam?'

'Last year in 75. I was on one of the last copters out of Saigon. There's a photo you can see on the Internet. I'm on it. On the copter. I was in the Embassy protecting some guy, and we got out together. I wrote about it in one of my books. It's not fiction. That's, like, fact.'

'And did you really meet Hunter Thompson?'

'I did. *Asshole*,' he replies and moves on. 'Dude was out of his gourd, so maybe I shouldn't judge him that harshly, you know what I'm saying. Never saw nothing to change my opinion. Next question.'

'Julian never believed those things,' I say.

'I guessed.'

'Julian told me you made it up to improve your marketing profile.'

Frank, for the first time, laughs. And laughs. He holds his belly. Booming around the reception area. Tears fall.

'Marketing profile. Jesus Christ, these Tarzan boys. They have no motherf____in clue. No clue at all. I got me a publisher who does all that stuff. As if I need to improve my profile! I gone sold eight million books in eight years, and I have to pretend I was in 'Nam and knew Thompson to sell those things? Yeh, right. Sure I am! Pay corps? Jesus H Christ, that guy is an asshole.

The grandfather clock whirrs and chimes seven o'clock. I noticed my pager go off, but I ignore it as it is just Gavin in the kitchen, and I am with a guest. Frank leans on the desk. 'That Englishman is full of hate. Full up to the BRIM with it. Can't help feeling sorry for the guy now, but last night – Jesus, he pushed my buttons so *bad*. He got zero respect. I'm going to have dinner and go see Amy. She's shaken up.'

He holds out his giant paw. 'Hey, thanks for listening.'

I shake his hand. I so want to say something cool like *de nada* to him, but I remain professional.

'You're welcome. Anytime.'

With that, he walks off in the direction of the Jerusalem restaurant.

Did Frank hit Julian over the head with a hammer?

I don't know. No. It's too obvious. The laptop thing explains nothing. He could have turned on the music, left his hotel room, knocked on Julian's door, and hit him with his back turned. It would have taken no more than two minutes. Amy as an alibi? She could have been in on it. She could have watched. After all, she has the biggest motive. Julian said evil things to her and is never going to stop for reasons only they – and Frank! – knows. The Police should be interested in her. And that information. She could have departed her room, and wiped out Julian in two minutes flat, and no one would be any the wiser. Where's the hammer? Where's the weapon? Arkwright must have *major* influence to ride roughshod through established forensic procedure. Whoever hit Julian has a whole week to rid themselves of the weapon, a whole week to come up with an alibi. Why? It's as if they know whodunit and already have the evidence in hand.

Later, I go up to see Jo with a tray of soup, and toast, and a bottle of glucose pop. I knock on the door. 'Jo? It's me, the night porter. I've brought some food.'

Surprisingly, she opens the door straight away. She's had a shower and the room smells of oils and unguents. Again, surprisingly, she appears cheerful, but I suspect that's a mask. She is wearing her shiny emerald green kimono with an ornate white dragon on the back and, again, I suspect, nothing else. I find her astonishingly beautiful and to my knowledge, I am the only man who gets to see her like this in the Hotel. Julian, had he done so, would have said something to me. Her hair is tied in an orange scrunchie, which, on closer inspection, as I follow her to the sideboard, is a pair of her silk peach panties. I do my best not to think about it.

'How are you, Jo?'

'Fine. Thank you so much for the food. I have been meaning to come down, but, like, I've been watching TV. Dude, you guys have *bad* TV.'

'Not good, is it,' I comment.

Jo slides into bed, still in her kimono. 'How's Julian?'

'Stable, Jo. Still unconscious, though.'

Now I know her cheerfulness is just an act. She raises her knees underneath her quilt and folds her arms around the caps, like a giant hugging a mountain. She buries her face in the quilt and cries. I hesitate to put my arm around her, so I take the soup over to the table next to her bed, remove her iPhone and leave it there.

'I've got a really good feeling about Julian, Jo. I think he'll be okay,' to the sound of her sniffles.

'He was so nice to me. He treated me, like, amazing. He was a real gentleman. That day at the races. It was just so awesome. I mean, amazing. All the horses. All the people. He made me feel so welcome. I used to live near Santa Anita as a child, and my dad used to go, but he would never take me, and I always wanted to go and see the horses. He didn't want me around gamblers, but I would never have noticed. I just wanted to see the horses and the mountains. Wheatley Fields track is so cool. Y'know, I won three races…a couple of dollars a race…and a couple of them were favourite, but I won. Julian advised me to back the horse I liked as they walked round in the paddock. I so love horses. One of the horses nodded at me through the railings. Julian said I had to back that one, and I did. Y'know, he put fifty quid on that horse and it won…it won.'

'He told me about that,' I said. He didn't mention to me that a horse's reflexive nod was the basis of the selection, though, and I grinned a little.

'And we had ice cream, even though it was freezing cold. And I ate mushy peas.'

'Mushy peas, huh.'

'Julian said they were a delicacy, but OMG, I nearly puked!' She started to laugh amidst the tears. 'I'll never forget that national dish of yours. I e-mailed my mom, and she told me to get home as soon as possible so she can make me a home-cooked meal. Julian laughed, y'know. Jeez, I made a new friend. And we clicked, y'know. It's miles to the track, and we walked together in the cold. It started to rain at some point. I, like, got myself soaked, and we hid under a tree and y'know, we never stopped talking. About books, and authors, and stuff. Roald Dahl, Salinger, Ira Levin, and writers he liked, y'know, Donna Tartt, Don De Lillo, all the

American greats. He's going to lend me Martin Amis's *Night Train.* I can't wait to read that! He, like, knows so much about writing and books. I learned so much that day. And y'know what? When it came to my turn to talk, he listened to every word. I've, like, got friends and stuff who never listen to me. They kinda wait their turn to talk, y'know, people like that.'

'I've met people like that, I agree,' I reply. Jo is getting it out of her system. I pray my pager stays silent.

'Julian listened. He listened to me. And I miss him already.'

'He was bad last night, Jo. He was horrible.'

'I *so* realise that,' she says. 'He is so *dead* when I see him again…'

Realising what she said, and its accidental inappropriate nature, she burst into tears, and this time, I sit down and put my arm around her.

We talk a little more, and she talks a little more, and she starts to get tired, and I leave her be, telling her that I am downstairs if she needs me. Julian told me that Jo Marron Saint is going to be a major star. All I know is I cannot remember meeting a more angelic person.

Later, Amy calls down. I had reached the point where I knew what she wanted before she said anything. Sixsmith had been dismissive of me when I went in for the drinks and the olives.

No.

Dismissive isn't the word.

He'd passed that point and had actively started to despise me. I could see it in his eyes. But he's not family. He's not a friend. He's a workmate, and they come and go, and as long as we stay out of the way of each other, life goes on as normal. He could try and skank me in many different ways, but he is the only person in the hotel with a problem, so, like Frank with the coppers, Cat is going to be all over him like lichen on a paving slab.

I realised over the weekend how much I looked forward to Amy's nightly call, and tonight was no exception. I *could* have filled the mini-bar myself, well in advance. I wonder whether she would *still* call, on some pretext. A stuck window. New shower accoutrements. Another pillow or a fresh quilt. A midnight snack. I liked to think she would, but I was clever enough not to test my hypothesis. I was surprised at my excitement once more – I am usually cool on guests, but there was something about Amy...

'How are you feeling?' I ask

'Shocked, love. Shocked.' She is sitting on her writing desk with a laptop open. A sleeveless black blouse with jeans today – she has a tattoo on her shoulder of a tree, with some writing underneath it, some Celtic thing – accompanied by hair freshly dyed burgundy. She dyed her hair daily – at least I think it was dye, but it might be something else. I know about porting, not ladies hair! She is barefoot, and I can scarcely take my eyes off her feet. Perfectly curvilinear, with no imperfections, divots or grooves, pale skinned, with black nail polish and a silver toe ring, they made me go all funny every time I saw them, and I swiftly pulled myself together. 'Been out today?'

She shook her head. 'Told off by Mary Beth. Given our orders. Can't go out even if we want to. We're on a strict regime now until Saturday. We've been naughty.'

'Well, you haven't. Julian –'

'Remember School?' She replies.

'Not really, no.'

'Remember when someone's naughty and the whole class gets detention?'

'I do, yes.'

'Same deal here. Mary Beth looks after Julian, so we're *all* in the doghouse.'

'But –' I reply, aware of the unfairness of it, but she went straight through my concerns.

'So, I've been scribbling, sweetness. A new short story. I've been most inspired by recent events.'

'What's the story about?' I say, making her a gin and tonic.

She grinned. 'An Awards Ceremony and its participants.'

'You are joking?'

'No, love. Look…'

I walk over to where she is sitting and look over her shoulder. She zooms in on a paragraph.

Looked at me and I couldn't take my eyes off him. His handsome face was a pleasure to look at, and I longed for the moments when I could – legitimately, of course, away from my chaperone – meet with him. The Awards no longer mattered to me. All I could think about was him, and I wondered whether Nat felt the same way about me. I lay on my hotel bed. I looked over at the mini-bar and knew that I would have to call him. It had been a breathtaking week.

One kiss borrowed. One kiss stolen, I didn't care. He was my

'I might change this, so it isn't the finished article, but yes, it's been based – very loosely – on this past week.'

'Really? Am I in it?'

She laughs. 'You're the *star,* love. None of this happens without you. Do you know what a Panopticon is?'

'I don't, no, Amy.'

'I remember it from Uni. Some French guy – it might have been Lacan, or Derrida, one of those lovely French authors – talked about it – the All-Seeing Eye. That's what it stands for.'

'The All-Seeing Eye?'

While she spoke, she had been rolling a cigarette. I usually abhor smokers, but there was something about Amy's smell. Tobacco, smoke, perfume, deodorant, hair dye. Intoxicating. It was like the smell of tobacco was the glue that kept all the component parts together.

'I'm going for a fag. You won't tell, will you?'

She looked at me, as she always did. 'Of course not.'

She stands, walks over to me, and touches my cheek with her fingertips. Her lips are full and red. There isn't an ounce of fat on her. I have no idea how old she is. Her smell, up close and personal, is pungent. She smells like she has been in bed all day with a rampant lover.

'Good lad,' she says, and a very childish part of me says *I am never going to wash my face again.*

I stand at the doorway to her bathroom. She sits on the toilet seat in that quirky, punky way of hers, with her feet pointing inward to each other and her arms semi-folded. 'So, the Panopticon?'

'Oh, yes,' she says. 'That's you, that is. The Panopticon. The All-seeing Eye. He who sees everything there is to see. He who is always there. The omnipresent.'

'Me?'

'You. Ever thought you might be featured in a book?'

'No.' I felt uncomfortable with it, but surprisingly flattered. I watched her take a deep draw of her cigarette and then remove a shred of tobacco from her teeth.

'Well, you might be. Good, innit?'

As I was about to reply, there's a knock on the door.

'That'll be Frank,' Amy says, putting her cigarette dextrously into the toilet bowl. 'Thanks for the gin, petal. I'll keep you posted on the story. You might become a star. I can see it now…**The Night Porter!**' She makes a sweeping gesture, implying my name in lights. Walks up to me and kisses me on the cheek as she passes.

'There is already such a film, Amy.'

'Yes, there is. But this one will be *a proper* romance, and you might be the star,' she says, letting Frank in.

His stare tells me he had returned to normal, staring daggers at me and mentally telling me to get lost. I say hello (and goodbye) and walk down the corridor, hearing the door shut behind me, unable to fully comprehend the thrust of her argument and the miasma of the mixed-messages I had just experienced.

Nothing matching anything like that experience happened for the rest of the night and for some of it, I watched Wheatley Fields come under attack from a typhoon of rain, hail, sleet and wind. Stones a centimetre in circumference pelted the walls. I watched a couple run like blazes from the Kings to their car. Dry one minute, utterly saturated the next. There was a storm coming, worse than the one that had already been, both in the hotel and out, and I was glad I was watching it happen through two sheets of reinforced double glazing.

Taylor and Morston

On Wednesday night, when I arrive at work, at six (unpaid overtime now almost an essential part of my life), before I even had time to remove my sodden raincoat, I am approached at the reception. It is the Police. I have expected this, but expecting something, as opposed to being surprised, doesn't stop a man's heart from racing as a consequence. I am still nervous.

'I'm D.I Taylor,' the man says. 'This is Detective Sgt. Morston. Can we go somewhere? We'd like a chat.'

'Will it be a long chat?' I ask.

'Just routine. Not keep you a minute.'

'Can we not speak here?' I reply. 'It's quiet, and I'm on my own. This is my work station.'

'If you're okay with that,' he says, with an overpowering sense of the non-committal. He wants to go home, I can tell. He's probably miffed that it's all hush hush. Under orders to keep it low profile.[50][51]

---

[50] I'm still surprised at the lengths that Arkwright Trust went to in order to keep the incident from spoiling the ceremony. I didn't think it were possible. Something about it

Taylor is short, stocky, about fifty, with unkempt grey hair and a moustache. I notice steel blue eyes. He wears a very pale green car coat straight out of an eighties cop show. His tie is askew, and his face is big for his collar. An air of weariness, though he's been interviewing all day, and he's been waiting for me to come to work. I hope the agency cook prepared them something to eat.

His colleague is blonde and looks a bit like Cat. She's wearing a black half-length raincoat over her suit, and she is much smarter than he is. New school, obviously. I'm impressed. She nods at me, but says nothing, and I do the same back to her. It's clear she's there to listen. There is a faint smell of perfume, a nice one, but it's completely unobtrusive.

'Okay, what happened on Monday night? In your own words.'

I tell him what I saw in the bar and afterwards. I tell him how I helped Julian to bed. I tell him how everyone

---

bugged me. Julian may have behaved like an arse, but I am absolutely convinced he has problems now and needs help, not censure. He's a substance abuser and a deeply troubled man. He has rights and needs protection. Just because he's unknown shouldn't make Arkwright's behaviour acceptable, and it doesn't make it right. Also, speculating selfishly, I'd hate that I would be as expendable in his position. Would The Saladin prevent the investigation of my assault? I wonder – especially now the Trust are co-owners and thus, my employers.

[51]It occurred to me this afternoon as I was lying in bed that I could be a suspect. Why not? The thought came to me in the middle of a nice dream about Jo. I won't reveal the nature of the dream, and I certainly won't be telling her. I remember thinking that she must be a suspect and then, out of the blue, and you may be surprised to know it was the first time I thought this, that if she is a suspect, then so am I. After all, I was there. I was there all along, at my night porter desk.

else in the bar was in a hurry to get to bed themselves. I tell him that I was the only member of staff in the building by two. I tell him I heard nothing. I tell him that it was only by chance that at 5am, I noticed Julian's door was open while I was going to serve another guest who required a porting task. I tell him that I looked inside and saw Julian on the floor, his head underneath the dressing table. I tell him that on inspection, I thought he was dead. I alerted an ambulance on 999. Fortunately, paramedics took just ten minutes to arrive. Everyone in the hotel was asleep and remained so. I tell Taylor that it was only when the paramedics arrived did I get confirmation Julian was unconscious and still alive. I thought he was dead up till that point.

'Any blood?' Taylor asks?

'His nose was bleeding. His body was at such a funny angle, I knew he hadn't just fainted. I knew it was an emergency situation.'

'Did you know he had been hit?'

'Not at that point. I suspected it.'

'You asked the paramedics whether he'd been hit.' Taylor consulted his notes. The detective had already enjoyed a "chat" with that team.

'I did, yes. It just occurred to me. Foul play, that is. Just a hunch as they were taking him away. One of the paramedics said more than likely. That's what I told the powers-that-be in phone calls afterwards.'

'Why did you think so? He liked a drink, didn't he?'

'It was just instinct. The nosebleed. And the paramedics confirmed it.'

Morston had not taken her eyes off me for a second. She was looking behind my eyes, not at them.

'You said to Catriona, your manager, and to Mary Beth that he had been hit on the head.' Taylor persevered.

'I did, yes.'

'Do you think you jumped the gun a little?'

'Possibly.'

'Bit dramatic? He could have fainted.'

'I've seen fainting, Detective Inspector Taylor. That wasn't fainting. I formed the opinion someone had hit him. And one of the paramedics, the one with the longer hair, confirmed that it was likely someone had hit him with a blunt object.'

They took notes, the detectives. 'The paramedic confirms saying that to you. Why did you call 999?'

'What? I thought he was dead!'

'Have you had first aid training?' Morston asks.

Her accent was South Welsh and would have been lustrous in another context.

'Of course.'

'Did you still think he was dead after you tested his breathing?'

'I was too busy calling 999 to think.'

'Did you touch the body?'

'Absolutely not.' I say, shocked. 'Should I have?'

'What about trying to resuscitate him.'

'I'm not allowed to,' I say.

'I beg your pardon,' Taylor asks.

'Speak to my boss. I'm not allowed to. I followed procedure.' This is true, all of it. 'But, truth be told, I was certain he was dead.'

'What did you do after you called the ambulance?'

'I shut the door to Julian's room and waited at the reception.'

Morston had grabbed hold of the bit and wasn't letting go. 'You didn't try to resuscitate him?'

'I thought he was long gone. I thought there was nothing I could do.'

Taylor put his notes down and leaned on the reception. He changed tack. 'What time was the fight between the authors?'

'It wasn't a fight,' I say. 'Julian said some harsh things. Frank punched him. He was temporarily unconscious and woke up a few minutes later. Julian didn't hit anyone.'

'Okay. When did this happen?' Taylor asks.

'About 1.30.'

'Who was there?'

I went through the list. 'Martin Sixsmith. Amy Cook. Jo Marron-Saint. Frank Duke. Gavin ... some other drinkers.'

'And you, of course.' Taylor nodded toward me.

'What?'

'You were there.'

'Much of the time, yes.'

'Not manning the desk?'

He was impugning my professionalism, and this, rather than the obvious fact he was putting me firmly in the suspect category, peed me off no end.

'I was doing my job. I don't just sit behind my desk, Detective Inspector.'

'But you were there? You saw it all?' He says, ignoring me while Morston watches on.

'Yes. I saw it all.'

'And after?'

'Everyone, bar Sixsmith, went to bed.'

'Sixsmith?'

'The barman, guv.' Morston interjects.

'Course, him. What time does he get to work?' He asks his colleague.

'He's called in sick. Flu.'

Taylor doesn't respond. 'You got his address?'

'Yes, guv.' Morston responds.

'We'll go round and see him. So –' He turns back to me. '– after?'

'Jo and I helped Julian upstairs.'

'I hear you've done that a lot,' Morston says.

'I like Julian,' I say. 'He needs help.'

Blank faces. 'So that night, you did what?'

'Jo and I took him upstairs. He needed assistance, not just through the amount of drinking he had undertaken. Frank packs one hell of a punch.'

I describe the fight in detail to him, and they ask me to show the fight scene, in the bar, even though they had probably already seen it five or six times. I suspect they are keen to see my reaction.

They follow me inside. The bar is full of drinkers, and I feel awkward, and embarrassed for no other reason that I am the centre of attention, and I do not like that. They look around, ask me some questions about the fight. They ask about Sixsmith's role. Taylor notes what I said. They seem satisfied.

I walk them back to the reception desk, and I lean on it, without going behind. I am nervous and jittery. I have only once been questioned by Police before this, and it vexes me. I want to get on with my job, and I want this to stop. It isn't going to: Taylor continues.

'In his room. When you took him up after the punch, how was he?'

'Groggy and incoherent. He was very weak, and Jo and I had to balance him. When we got into his room, I laid him down on the bed, and that was it. He did a drunken thing and curled up in a ball. His head was supported by two pillows and came back downstairs. Jo went to her room.'

'Did you see anyone else?' Morston, getting more involved, asks directly. 'While you were up there? 'I saw Frank go into his room. That's it.'

'That would make it midnight?' Taylor says.

'About that. They all went to bed about that time. I went upstairs about 5am. I have a record of the call I received for assistance here on my computer. It was from Mr Singh of the Trust. He wanted me to bring him an extra pillow.'

'At 5am?'

'It's not an unusual request.'

'And you heard nothing between midnight and 5am?' Taylor asks, scratching his nose and checking his notes. Finally, I detect the "chat" is coming to an end.

'Mr Duke says he was with Amy Cook from 1am onward. They have both confirmed that today. Can you corroborate their statements?' Morston asks me.

'I'm sorry, I can't. I saw Frank go into *his* room, and that's the end of it. I have no idea what either of them did afterwards.' I say, my stomach engaging in its familiar jealous churn.

'Who else has hotel room keys, by the way?' Taylor adds.

'Of the night staff, just me and Martin Sixsmith.' I reply, and every time he asks a question like this, I feel massively vulnerable. Taylor writes something down in his notebook.

'Where are the keys stored?'

I point to the pigeon holes on the side of the reception. It is an easily accessible storage space, and I can see what they are thinking, but their thinking is redundant, old school. The keys – a modern card system installed two years ago – are activated by computer and a bar code reader. Of the night staff, Kerry, and Gavin have no access to passwords. I have a major issue with Sixsmith having access. He is the type of person who would give rooms away free to his pals – a bunk-up, a weekend jolly, free ale in the bar. He's never done it on my watch, but Gavin told me once that it was common practice under the previous night porter. That's theft in my book. I didn't tell Cat though. The reason Sixsmith has access is that Cat requires a backup in case I am not at work through sickness. It is pointless telling her that I never get sick. I suppose this is why she's a manager.

'So, after putting Julian to bed, you came here and stayed here till 5am?' Morston puts the pieces together.

'I never moved.'

'Must be a bit boring at times,' she says.

'It wasn't boring the other night. Aside from my usual monitoring tasks, some security and observations, I had to fill in an Incident Report. Here it is…' I hand the

Incident Book to Morston, and she reads it, hands it back. 'I also had lots of thinking to do.'

'What about?' Asks Morston.

'Julian and the things he said. He was cutting.'

'Amy Cook said he was threatening to her, and Frank protected her, is that right. A Sir Galahad thing,' Taylor says, and they were starting to come from both sides.

'Julian called him The Black Knight,' I say. 'It's been like that between him and Amy all week. I was told to keep them apart, but I was dealing with a guest when it all kicked off. I feel a bit incompetent, to be honest, as if I took my eye off the ball. But what could I do?'

Again, they look blankly at me and do not comment. There is an awkward silence, which I fill. 'Julian insulted Frank. That kicked Frank off. It wasn't just about Amy.'

'Yes, I have notes on that,' Taylor says.

'He gave him some about Vietnam and his role in it.'

Taylor reaches for his notebook. *'...not good, is it, a nation with your resources being battered by little rake-carrying blokes who wear their slippers outdoors.'*

'Something on those lines. He followed that up with something about him lying about his war service.'

'We checked records,' Taylor says. 'Duke was definitely in Vietnam.'

'Common knowledge. I am surprised Julian used that as a brick to beat him with,' Morston adds.

'He'd been at Frank all week, on the QT. No love lost between them. Little niggles. Little digs...'

'About what?' Taylor asks.

'About Frank being a terrible author.'

'I've read one of his books on holiday in Tenerife,' the DI says. 'He's not bad. Enjoyed it.'

I don't comment, and the silence following his comment is again an awkward one. Morston breaks it. 'What about Miss Marron-Saint?'

'Jo? She sat watching the whole thing. Cried. Said nothing else,' I say and that seems to satisfy them.

'Did Julian have a pop at her? Taylor interjects.

'He loves Jo. They're friends.'

'And Amy Cook?' Morston comes back in.

'What about her?'

'What did he say about her? Do you remember?'

I tell her what I can remember. I also tell them about Julian's secret obsession that Amy has a dark secret, or at least a secret only the two of them share. I am desperate to share my opinion that they are ex-lovers, but I don't, even though they probably have ways of finding out. 'As I say, I can't remember much. Caught the fag end of it. '

'Was the barman anywhere around?' Morston continues.

'He went home after the fight.'

'Frank says Julian had a pop at the barman.'

'He was rude, yes.' I tell them what he said, and I have to suppress a grin, spawned in a dislike of the man.

'How did the barman react?'

I shrug my shoulders. 'A lot less violently than Frank Duke. Bitter. He's too pro to get seriously involved,' I say, ignoring the stamp on the leg.

Morston nods her head and writes down what I said, like a journalist.

'Okay. That will do,' says Taylor, putting away his green pocket notebook. 'You've been a help. Jennifer, let's go and have a chat with this barman, see what he knows.' He turns to me once more. 'Thanks for your help. If we need to ask you any more questions, we'll be in touch. We probably will.'

'You're welcome, Detective Inspector.'

'There's an element of Agatha Christie in this,' Taylor says, with the barest hint of a smirk on his face. 'All these creative types. All these authors.'

Jennifer Morston says nothing and the two of them walk slowly across the carpet out into the rain.

All these authors.

And night porters, I think to myself, relieved that they had gone and the questions, for now, were over.

Later, That Night

Later that night, I go to see Jo. As usual, she is in her Kimono and as usual, she is beautiful, all cream and pastes and natural ointments. Her hair is in a bun, and she is watching TV. I know the programme she is watching – *Holby City,* a programme about the lives and loves of doctors and nurses in a hospital down South. I have taken up flowers, drinks and chocolates, compliments of Arkwright, via Mary Beth. She reaches immediately for a chocolate and offers me one. I decline, exaggeratedly patting my waist-coated belly. I tell her about Julian. That there is no news. I also tell her I have been interviewed by the Police. She tells me Taylor had been to see her, but they never took any notes.

'Been out today?' I ask as I place the chocolates next to the TV.

'No way! Mary Beth would so have my butt. I think the three of us are going out tomorrow, though.'

'Where?'

'The Cinema. *Man of Steel* on IMAX. Special feature. IMAX is so cool. I love it. I didn't know you have IMAX cinemas over here.'

'We have quite a few cool things over here, Jo,' I say.

'Lucky for us. Love superheroes, especially Superman!'

'I'm more of a Batman man, myself.'

She laughs. I love the way she laughs, so free, and clear, and real.

'Amy called Mary Beth and got permission. I'm going crazy in here,' she says. 'Frank says it's called stir-crazy, so we called to see if we could go out, and stuff.'

I set the flowers in water and place them on the windowsill. 'Uh, huh. What have you been up to while going stir-crazy?'

'Some writing. Nothing much.'

'Really? What about?'

She sits up on the bed.

'About a haunted hotel in England. That's going to be Sonia's next adventure. Isn't that cool!'

'It certainly is,' I say. 'Would it be fair to say The Saladin will feature?'

She affects my English accent. 'It certainly would, Jeeves. Only in the book, the hotel is going to be called The Saracen's Head.'

'Oh, yes?'

'Because, like, Saladin was a Saracen. I looked it up on the Internet. It was amazing, all the Crusades and stuff. And, like, the sign outside has his head on it. Isn't that super awesome!'

'It is, yes. Very awesome, indeed.'

'Hey...' she looks at me, coquettishly. 'I've, like, written you into the book.'

'You have?' I say, flattered once more, puffing out the flowers.

'Do you like that?'

'It depends on the part. Am I a goody or a baddy?'

'Definitely a goody. Do you want to hear what I wrote about you?' Jo says, reaching for her notebook.

'Go on,' I said.

Sonia shook his hand and thanked him for saving her from the Geckos. 'That was so great. Thank you. I thought I was, like, done for there.'

'No problem,' John says in his cool English accent. 'Always glad to help a damsel in distress.'

'Those geckos are real bad. They've been after me for a long, long time,' said Sonia.

'Will they be back today?' John asked, his blue eyes boring into her, making her stomach do a back flip and forward roll all at the same time.

'I don't think so.'

'Then, why not come back to the Hotel for tea?'

'As long as I can, like, have Scones with Jam and Clot cream.'

He smiled. 'That's clotted cream, and yes, we can have some of those.'

OMG, I've just gone and died, and am in heaven. The Geckos got me after all.

I was embarrassed. 'Is that me? John?'

'Sorta. He's, like, a bit younger and looks a bit more like Joshua Nesbit, but he's got your *accent,* which I totally *adore.* And he's cool, like you. And smart.'

I am flattered, but my embarrassment is boiling like water in a pressure cooker. 'Is Julian in there?'

'OMG, yes. He's supercool, but also a bit of an ass. Everyone's in Sonia's new book. Frank's a vampire slayer, like Blade. Amy's a fortune teller. And Martin's a giant troll…'

Laughter, though I tried to curtail it, came easy. 'Great characterisation, Jo.'

'Thought you'd like that. I cannot wait to get home and, like, get to work on it. It's going to be awesome!'

'I shall definitely buy a copy.' I say. 'Well done.'

'Can I have another chocolate?' Jo asks, ostentatiously fluttering her eyelids. I bring over the whole tray. We talk for a little while longer, and my pager goes, and I say goodnight.

Strangers

Being a night porter means living among strangers. I live their unique experiences, opinions and madness. I watch them eat, drink, talk. They seek me out at my work station, and they communicate with me. It is a rare night I spend without conversation with a stranger. Some strangers interest me greatly – like the authors. I like listening to the problems people have. I sometimes think I should have carried on with my studies because I am a natural listener, I think. I relish the personal, and I can listen for hours if need be without offering advice or intervening. Some strangers bore me – the sportsmen, particularly rugby men and golfers – especially *golfers; the* barroom politicians, Tories, racists and those who talk for hours about their work. The professional element of my job means I have to treat the interesting and the dull in identical fashion, though I must confess to praying for the rescuing ring of the guest room telephone connection on occasion, when confronted with someone spectacularly tedious.

Usually Tory slash UKIP voting slash rugby-playing slash golfers high on the whisky.

But not always.

Some strangers are drunk and lonely, away from home. Others are drunk and ecstatic, away from home. I am of the opinion you can be addicted to the hotel life. I have met many men who, when given the option of a nine-to-five existence ten minutes from family, home and hearth, choose the hotel life a million miles away.[52]

For the hotel dwellers I meet every night of the week, their other home – the partner, the kids, the bills, the repetition, the comfort of the familiar – is a prison, and the thought of it inspires feelings of being utterly, absolutely, trapped.[53]

I know this is true because they tell me this –the heating contractors, the electricians, the industrial plumbers, the fitters, the joiners, the ducting engineers, the ventilation experts, the air conditioners, the sales reps, the demonstrators, the travelling beauticians, the

---

[52] Like war, the horror of it, those addicted volunteers who sign up for a second shift in hell; and a third, a fourth, until they reach a point where they no longer consider coming home at all. War is their home. They can never go back.

[53] Some travellers cannot sleep at home and when they do, they dream badly, a dark world of anxiety, nightmares and horrorscapes. On the road? Babies don't sleep as comfortably.

machine makers, the inventors, the photocopier sales teams, the managers, the training professionals, the social fund consultants, the company directors, the IT crowd, the social enterprise gurus, the government apparatchiks, the ubiquitous presenters, the freelancers, the authors, the educational inspectors, the network panjandra and the goblins and gremlins of community interest companies, the country far and wide – they tell me that the road is their home, and they can't handle the other part of it for long. They confess this to me when drunk. I meet drunks every night of the week, seven nights of drunks.

Julian.

Amy.

I know alcoholic night porters, and I wonder how they can cope with the dark mirrors that appear at 1am as the bars quieten and the notion of the night porter's work station seduces and enthrals.

Those dark mirrors.

The authors have become less than friends, but more than strangers. I feel connected to them in some way, though I am afraid this comes across as conceited, possibly narcissistic. Their fortunes, their travails, their quirks, their successes, their failures. I feel we are a tribe, and I have contributed in some small way to making us so, here, at The Saladin. The hotel has become our HQ and the ceremony will be our battleground.

I wanted Julian to win his two awards, but that's not possible.

I want Jo to win Best YA novel.

Though Frank and I have never really spoken, and he is more like a stranger than the others, I want him to win Best Thriller.

And I want Amy to be Best Writer.

The Queen of the crop. The special award.

I tell her this later, when I take up drinks and olives.

'Do you really, love? Is that what you really want?'

'I do, yes.'

'These kind of things can really do you in,' she says. I suspect that, despite Mary Beth's intervention, Amy has enjoyed plenty of gin today. She slurs slightly, and her eyes flicker when she speaks. She's still remarkably alluring to me. It's just jeans and a tee shirt tonight, and she's wearing lime-green socks, which slightly deflates. She has truly astonishingly *pristine* feet. 'Every novel I have ever written, I have wanted to win awards. I think they're like my babies. I want them to do ever so well. I don't like being criticised, and I can get pretty wound up about it if I let it.'

I want to ask her about Julian again. The impulse assails me, the curiosity like an itch. *Why does he hate you? Why? Tell me. We're friends now? We talk. Why? Unravel this conundrum for me: If you cannot take criticism, how come you let Julian take the liberties he does? Is there blackmail going on, Amy? You can tell me. I'm the All-seeing Eye. You told me this, but I am snow blind here: my eyes are blind, and I cannot see. Help me out, Amy. Please don't tell me he's an ex-lover, Amy! Please no? I'm struggling enough knowing you are bonking Frank. Not Julian! He's so scruffy and downright downmarket. Is he your ex-lover? Is he?*

But I say nothing. It is not my place.

'Come and sit next to me, love. Are you allowed to do that? Can you? I'm so lonely tonight.' She shifts over slightly on her bed.

If Cat caught me now, I could be sacked, and part of me gets ready to lacerate myself, because this is SO unprofessional, but I cannot help it, her query lingering in my consciousness like an echo, *Come and sit next to me, love, Come and sit next to me, love, Come and sit next to me, love, Come and sit next to me, love, Come and sit next to me, love,* my stomach rolling up and down in and out, up and down, in and out, and I am having thoughts, bad thoughts, dangerous thoughts, *six years, six years unemployment, an exemplary record super night porter, the silver night porter, the ultimate professional night porter, the world's greatest night porter, universal night porter, cosmic night porter, awards ceremony night porter, I can SEE EVERYTHING night porter reputation, Cat, Cat, Cat, Cat, NO, Panopticon, Panopticon, Panopticon,* and the physical reaction you might expect happens to me, and I am nearly sick with anxiety, but I do, I sit next to her.

'That's nice of you, petal. I feel as if I can trust you. I feel as if I can tell you everything…'

I feel as if I can tell you everything, I feel as if I can tell you everything, I feel as if I can tell you everything, I feel as if I can tell you everything, I feel as if I can tell you everything, I feel as if I can tell you everything, I feel as if I can tell you everything.

'Do you? That's nice,' I say.

She leans over, and I can smell her, and I know that she hasn't showered from last night. Everything is squared, cubed. My stomach is transported to an interstellar galaxy via a black hole, which tips it upside down a thousand times.

'Do you trust me, sweetness?'

'I do, yes.'

Amy sits back on her pillow and takes another sip of her gin, lays the glass on the ridge of her breasts.

'Not everyone likes your stuff – you have to understand that. You know your *work*. You would think family and friends would be the first to read your book, but they often don't. You would think they would. Your wife, your husband, even your kids. So when a jury stands in judgement, you can't predict what's going to happen. The bookies fancy me, you say, but I'm taking nothing for granted. It's lovely, it really is, that you fancy me for the prize. That means more to me than the bookie's opinion.'

I want to ask her to take her socks off. I want to kiss her. I want to…I want to…*I want…*

I know what I want.

I know.
Now
Now
Now

Tell me, Amy. Are you sleeping with Frank Duke? Or is it an optical illusion? Tell me about your marriage? Tell me about Kenya? Tell me about the dark side. Tell me about Julian again. Tell me one more time. Did I tell you it's been six years? Did I? Six years. Not a kiss, Amy. Not a peck on the cheek under the mistletoe at the hotel New Year party. Did I tell you that?

I want you, Amy. I want you.
Who do You *want, Amy?*
Major Benson.
Frank.
Julian. (No, please, please)
The Night Porter?
Who do You *want, Amy?*
Who do You *want, Amy?*
Who do You *want, Amy?*

'But you *do* want to win it?' I ask, looking for assurance, saying something Amy-centred to calm me, to calm the raging torrent.

'Yes, petal, I do. It means more to me than anything at the moment. *Amelia* is my child, and I want her to do the best she can. I want to be recognised for that. Is that vain? Narcissistic? No. I simply want to be recognised as a *writer*, not just an *author*. You heard what Julian said.'

'He said many things, Amy.'

'*Author*, love. He calls me an *author*, never a *writer*. I want to be recognised as a *writer* of substantial work. Of great work. Not just an *author* of stories,' she says, taking a sip of her gin. She puts down her glass and starts to roll a cigarette. I feel the urge to do the dirty on Julian.

'He calls you The Novelist, sometimes. As if that's a bad thing.'

She grins, licks the gum on her cigarette paper. 'Only *writers* will do for Julian. The rest of us can go whistle. Authors, storytellers, novelists, scribes. Not on his radar.'

'It's bizarre; he's written a novel. Doesn't that make him a Novelist?'

'With a small *n*, sweetness. A novelist. Julian Green is a *writer,* and the rest of us are…well…the *rest.*'

'I see. I think.'

She leans over on her left side and looks at me. 'Winning the Arkwright for Best Writer would be a vindication, wouldn't it, love? Of a sort.'

'It would, yes.'

We sit in silence for a few minutes, all the time I am expecting the knock on the door. I am still full of thoughts, full of mad thoughts, and desires, and longings, and surreal, disconnected feelings, but I am impressed with my control. She smells gorgeous. I wonder whether others notice this, the fragrance of her. The emission, like she's the most popular member of the Harem, in hourly demand by the Sultan. I have never encountered anything like it. The world's strongest perfume couldn't mask this.

Has anyone ever commented, Amy? Or is it just my madness? Does Frank know? Can Frank…

'Is Frank coming to see you tonight?'

'Frank?' Amy replies, a quizzical look on her face.

'Yes. He often comes over.'

'Does he? No, he's not coming tonight. It's just you and I.'

Amy gestures me to the toilet, this time not asking me for permission, where once again, I stand by the doorway and watch her smoke. She says nothing, deep in thought or deeply drunk.

And when the smoking is done, she says she is tired and wants to go to sleep, and I take that as my cue with a mixture of

(Relief?)

(Rage?)
(Disappointment?)
(Sadness?)

and I say goodnight, and she kisses me on the cheek, a soft kiss, the embrace of the tip of the wings of a butterfly flickering.

Like gossamer in a strong wind, she is gone, and I am standing in the corridor, bewildered and slightly dazed.

Questions I Might Ask Of A Suspect

It might surprise you to know that when I am at home, I loaf. I have my favourite clothes. My current favourite is a simple monkish black hoodie and a black *Avengers Assemble* tee shirt. Most of the time, I wear my favourite clothing until it stands up on its own, regularly changing only my socks and boxers. But I'm not sociable as you know – I don't need to be, not with my career – so in a sense, I could wear a pink boiler suit and ballet shoes at home and no one would ever know. I don't think about clothes in the daylight hours. Jeans and tee shirt and that will do me nicely.

Different matter at work, as I've said, for very good reason. Clothes – suits, shoes etc. – in a work context are a tool, a Yankee screwdriver or a battery drill. Stylish dressing has an adaptive function, and it is worth the investment. It enables a man to do his job to the best of his ability, to project an image of confidence and security to management, colleagues and customers.

Taking it a step further, investing in decent clobber for work enables a man to be the best. That's important. That's *key*. I always think that being well groomed at work is a critical instrument of the evolutionary process. It has to be, doesn't it? Otherwise, a customer would be confronted with hairy cavemen carrying a big rock club each time a service – as in my case, an overnight stay in a full service hotel – is required. A smart suit and a pair of

English-made shoes separates a man from his evolutionary history in the animal kingdom and redefines his place in modern culture. The next stage – *homo superior*, if you like. Any schoolchild will tell you that the fundamental driver of human development is the competitive instinct. And I want to be the best night porter possible, and so far, I think I'm doing a decent job in achieving that goal.

Earlier today, after five and a half fitful hours of sleep, and a colossal attempt to pull myself together over Amy (I know I am beginning to get a bit silly over her. I have been silly over women before, and I don't like it, don't like the loss of control at all). I slipped on my comfort clothes, without showering and shaving, accompanied by jeans and trainers of no particular brand, and began to think about the events of the last couple of days. The visit of the Detectives inspired the thought train, and once it started, it didn't stop. The thought train was a runaway train and its gathering momentum became, eventually, relentless.

I started, first of all, to think about questions.

If I were Detectives Taylor and Morston, what questions would I be asking of the people surrounding the attempted murder of Julian Green?[54] And what questions would I ask myself? I started off with first principles, kept it to the basics. Who. Where. How. What and most importantly, Why. Who was in the hotel that night? Who could have carried out the crime in practice?

Who could have attempted the murder *theoretically?* Who was around? Who was in the vicinity? Who had the motive? Who had the opportunity? Where did the crime take place? Where is the weapon? How did the attempted

---

[54] If, indeed, Attempted Murder was the true nature of the crime.

murderer get into the bedroom? Who are the probable suspects?[55] Did Julian let him/her in? It looks that way. How did they get to the room and back without being spotted? Unless they were spotted? How did they dispose of the weapon? Did they dispose of it? What did the attempted murderer have to gain? What was the motive? Why? Why bash Julian on the head? Why not poison him? Why not wait until the ceremony was over? Why not do it somewhere else – somewhere out of the spotlight?

Why Julian, anyway? Was he the *real* target?

Other questions occurred to me.

Was the attempted murder experienced or was this a random thing, an explosion, an unplanned, disorganised act? Did it occur as a response to something Julian said upstairs? Or was it all related to the things he said in the bar? In the week leading to the event. On the Internet. Was it something unrelated? Did the assailant plan this? Firstly, for no reason other than I could, and it seemed logical to do so bearing in mind the people I had been mixing with for over a week, more or less non-stop, I began to think of Julian's assault and the events leading up to it as a novel. A story. Something that emerged entirely naturally from the banality of existence into drama. Here we are at The Saladin Hotel, Wheatley Fields, an ancient full service hotel. There are four authors among the guests. The staff. An award ceremony. There is a powerful sponsor in the background.[56] There are powerful people whose interests, in the end, we all

---

[55] What did Holmes say in those old Basil Rathbone Nigel Bruce classics? Eliminate the impossible and whatever remains, however improbable, must be the truth.

[56] How much influence did the Arkwright Trust have over everything that went on? Some. All. None? And there are notions of celebrity and fame and glory.

serve. There is an attempted murder, which took place in the dead of night. There are Police. There are suspects, of which, the authors form the rump.[57] The other players – the day staff, the passing hotel guests, the drinkers of Wheatley Fields who drink in the bar, the diners of the town who eat in the Jerusalem restaurant – exist in the background, outside the focus – but they do exist –

– and because I thought of those people who exist as the backdrop, the organic wallpaper, the actors in the shadows, in the wings, it began to occur to me for the first time just how difficult it must be to write a novel like this.

---

[57]The hotel was full that night as it has been every night bar one since the writers arrived. In total, there were twenty six people upstairs who – theoretically speaking – could have carried out the assault on Julian Green. In descending order of importance, and giving the full title of the rooms, here are the potential suspects. Suite of Kings – Mary Beth Burnell, New York. Suite of Queens – Stuart Staples, The City. Chancellor Suite – Mr and Mrs Helmut Koch, Hamburg. King Charles Suite – Mr and Mrs Hubert Bream, London. Queen Anne Suite – Mr and Mrs Nils Pilsudski, Oslo. Cavalier Suite – Mr and Mrs Melvyn Paxton, Birmingham. Saracen Suite – Charles Matrix, Florida. Racecourse Suite – Stewart Simpson, Glasgow. Rooms 1 – 6 (First Floor). Maureen Phillips, Giles and Toby Clough (Textiles and Design), Maida Vale, Mr and Mrs Kenneth Pickles, Worksop, Mr and Mrs S Wainwright, Belper, Carrie Buck, San Diego, Mme Jean Duvalier, Dieppe and finally, Rooms 7-12 (Second Floor), Amy Cook, Frank Duke, Jo Marron-Saint, Mr and Mrs Eden Cadbury, Carlisle and Bob Lund (Fittings), Vermont. The one name missing, of course, is the unfortunate Julian Green. Then there are the night staff, of which Martin Sixsmith, chef Gavin Fremantle, Commis Chef Kerry Manor and, yes, my very good self would be the prime suspects. There is the possibility of a random attacker who had secreted him/herself in a corner while the bar was open and waited for three hours in the toilets, a cupboard, or the shadows. I wouldn't rule that out.

Julian's cynicism had worn off on me in the short time I had known him, and, yes, the word processor *had* made it simple to write one word after the other, one sentence after another, one paragraph after another, and one chapter after another, until *et voila*, you had a novel on your hard drive, but when I thought about it, on my giant armchair – more a balloon than a piece of furniture, so big it envelops me, so voluminous I can pull my legs underneath me and disappear into it – it isn't easy at all.

If I tried to write this, where would I start?

How would I start the novel?

What did Julian say? The three main perspectives a novice author can take are First Person (I), Second Person (You) and Third (Character). So, whose point of view should I take? Who is the story about? Is it about Julian? Is it about Jo? Who? Is it about Arkwright and the shadowy trust who function in his name? Or is it about The Saladin Hotel itself? Is it about the attempted murder? The ceremony? The histories of the authors? The relationships? What?

How does it all fit together? What's important and what isn't? WHO is important? What do I include and what do I leave out? How do I demonstrate my thought processes? Those of Frank's? Those of Jo's? How do I demonstrate the interaction and growing relationships between the people in the hotel? And what are the key dimensions? What is the criticality? And how do I isolate the crucial reader variables? How do I move from one part to the other? How much detail do I give and how much do I take away. There is the technical stuff: How does one sentence relate to the other? How does one *chapter* progress into another? What perspective should I use –

– the more I thought about it, the more I realised that writing a book was not easy at all.

Julian was wrong and had been wrong all the time.

Even if Amy and Frank were basic in the way they wrote stories, the way they moved from one sentence to another. Even if they were students of the Plain English/Plain and Simple/Once Upon A Time movement, with their stories having a beginning, middle and an end. Even if they were Popular Novelists appealing to the beach reader, the poolside enthusiast, the bus peruser, the train line lingerer, the bedtime somnambulist, the Sunday afternoon sofa dipper – even if these were their uncritical constituency, they still had to *construct* their stories. They still had to build them. And toughest of all, I would imagine, was the ability to keep the reader interested.

Whoosh.

Writing's hard. Even thinking about writing was difficult for me. At least, if I was given the task of writing all this time, I would have the names of the characters. I wouldn't have to invent them. I'm not sure I could do that, inventing names.

The Troll

The next night, the Thursday, two days to go to the ceremony, at about 10, Sixsmith marches over to see me.

I've seen him earlier: He's been grumpy all night. Quiet and uncommunicative with everyone – but particularly me. I suspect it's something to do with the Police. Our bar manager wouldn't be impressed with their attention. He's one of those men – a small town gangster, one step up from a minor criminal – who dislike the Police as a matter of form, rather than thought. It is inevitable, really. I don't know why he is behaving like this. Interrogation is routine. They interviewed me and Gavin, and it was incumbent upon them, in turn, to interview him.

There is no point him wandering about like a bear with a sore head as he has been doing.

It is a becalmed hotel tonight, with few drinkers in the bar and few covers in the Jerusalem. Possibly because it is the November before Christmas, and the locals are saving their pennies. All the guests are in bed.

It's a cold and rainy night in November, and Sixsmith is about to make it much colder for me, I can tell. He's wearing a black shirt for once. Usually, he wears a standard polyester white underneath an American style Boston Barbershop apron, but tonight he's all in black. I suspect I know why.

Standing directly in front of me, he shakes his head as if he is disappointed about something.

'You grassing...' he sneers in a whisper, almost. Follows it up by calling me something unrepeatable.

'What's that in aid of?' I reply.

He speaks slowly, and he moves close to my face. We are almost nose-to-nose. I can smell his vodka breath with a hint of onion. His piggy eyes have dilated and expanded, and I know his snake brain is in control. I suspect he wants to hit me.

'You grassed me to them coppers.'

'I did not.'

'Yes, you did. You said I didn't like that Julian. You said I was part of that night. That's why they came to see me.'

'They are seeing everyone. It's just routine. They've interviewed me, Gav ' –

'– you told the coppers he had a pop at me. That's not routine. That's *grassing*.'

I stand firm and straight. Say nothing. This annoys him.

'You lying, grassing...' he repeats.

It's time to steel my spine. I straighten up and slightly puff out my chest, like a viper.

'It's not a lie. I told them the truth.'

'I'm just the bar manager. I was behind the bar. No part of this. Them coppers now think I'm part of it. Thanks to you, night porter soppy bollocks, they have as good as accused me of attempting to kill the bloke. That's down to you. Arsehole.'

'You saw the altercation, Martin. Julian had words with you as well as Frank.'

'*They* weren't words. *I'll* show you f'in words.'

'Martin – '

He leans over and grabs my shirt. 'Let me stress something to you. Let me stress something to you loud and clear. I. Saw. Nothing. Do you understand? I am no part of this. I left the hotel by the time he got banjaxed and my Stephanie can confirm that.'

'You were ther –'

'– I SAW NOTHING,' he loses it for the first time, angry and frustrated. 'Do you understand?' He's tugging at me, and I'm waiting for the punch.

'I'm sorry, but you could have…'

'I don't want them COPPERS in my life. Do you understand?' His face is contorted with rage, and his fists are clenched. 'Why did you say I was involved? Why did you tell them that? Why didn't you mind your own f'in business?'

'I told Taylor you were part of it, as I was.'

'I'M THE BAR MANAGER. I WAS NOTHING TO DO WITH IT,' he shouts. Lucky for me, Gavin hears all this, comes out of the kitchen and ambles over. He's a witness now, and I felt protected, but Sixsmith continues to rant. 'AND you TOLD the coppers I don't LIKE Julian Green, you GRASS…'

Gavin tries to stop the barman, 'Martin, calm down…' but he is thrust out of the way, and I know now he's going to hit me.

'THEY THINK I'M A SUSPECT. BECAUSE OF YOU, YOU GRASS…'

'But Martin, I told them the truth. That's all I told them. The truth. One. I told them that you were behind the bar. Two, I told them Julian had words with you. Three, I told them that you don't like him. You tell everyone you come across you don't like him. The Police knew this, Martin. I wasn't presenting them with a revelation. I wasn't giving them a sermon on the mount. I only confirmed what they already knew about you.'

'You should have shut your cakehole.'

'Why, Martin? You watched the whole thing. What was I supposed to do? Pretend you were nowhere about? Pretend you don't have access to the hotel? And the keys? Pretend you actually *liked* Julian? You wouldn't serve him unless you were told to. You'd bar him if it were left to you! You told the entire public bar your feelings. You told EVERY author this. The Police needed to know your feelings. It's the *truth*, Martin. It is the truth. A fact. Why are you behaving like this? I don't understand?'

Sixsmith pulls away from me slightly, but keeps hold of me. He begins to chuckle. Not laugh, precisely, but a deep throated chuckle.

'I'm behaving like this because I don't like you. I've never liked you. Not from minute one. I've been waiting for an opportunity to put it to you. You're an arsehole. A la-di-da arsehole. A goody two shoes creepy bloody night porter. A stupid night porter. A bag carrier, a bloody glorified waiter. And you think you're something special. If you were an ice lolly, you'd lick yourself to the stick in five minutes flat.'

'Er, well, sorry abo –'

'– and most of all, arsehole, I'm behaving like this because you informed on me. That makes you a *grass*. In my book, that's one up from a nonce. An f'in nonce. I'm going to make life difficult for you here,' he interrupts. 'I'll make sure you've left The Saladin by Christmas. You won't be able to stand the pressure. Everyone in this hotel will know what you did. Every one of the team will know you are a grass and that they can't trust you. No. Better, I'll tell everyone in the town. I know people. I was born here. I *know* the *right* people. You grassed me. I'll tell everyone I come across what you are.'

'Martin, I don't –'

He ignores me, but let's go of my shirt. It's ripped slightly. Underneath the collar. I know I'm going to need a new one. He points his gnarled finger in my face.

'Mate, I want to batter you so bad, I really do. I'm f'in aching to punch you.'

I'm surprised he hasn't. The big man is hyperventilating now and slowly beginning to control his rage. I have seen men like him before. I am glad Gavin is there, the essential witness. Martin cannot touch me.

He takes further steps back and finishes off his *grand guignol*. 'I'd watch your back. Out there. In the town. At night. I'd watch your back. You're brown. You. Are. *Brown.*'

Gavin and I watch him as he walks back to the bar chuntering. Gavin shrugs his shoulders, gives me a conspiratorial wink, as if to say he understands, as if to reassure me he has also had a beating like that from the mercurial barman in the past and that it is, in the end, nothing to worry about. I look at him blankly, and he walks off, back to his lair, leaving me to mine.

I sit back. I make a mental note to turn the heating down because I have a slight layer of perspiration on my forehead. I'm hungry. Stress always makes me nibbly, but I don't want to go into the bar, nor do I want to see Gavin again. The whole incident has made me feel weak and out of control of my environment. I find this disturbing, and I want it to pass. Time is a great healer and one day, Gavin will not deem it necessary to tell everyone on the day staff what he saw and that this will pass into the microfiber, the ether, of the history of The Saladin. Working with Sixsmith is going to be impossible from now on, I think, so I know, in order to protect myself on several fronts, that I will be putting an official grievance to Cat about him in the morning. It has to be done. There is no other choice. Grievances mean attention and spotlights, and I would do without those if I could, but what other choice have I? He abused me and threatened physical violence. It will cost him his job if I push it, and I don't care about that. It's good for The Saladin. He is an odious man. And his comments about night porters are unforgivable and need addressing by a higher authority. I don't care about what he says about me in his haunts. I'm not part of his small town, semi-criminal world, his constellation of local bullies, his pub thugs, his peculiar, warped, masculine sense of honour. I don't understand it. I never have done. I'm not part of that tribal thing, that enforced Omerta. I'm a lone wolf in the jungle and I stay quietly under the radar of people like his lot. I might report him – and his threats – to the Police, to cover my back. If I do get a whacking one morning on the way home, then Sixsmith is as guilty as if he hit me himself, assuming he gets a pal to do the dirty. Yes. That's another good plan. I shall do that tomorrow, after taking out the grievance.

Martin Sixsmith is a vile man who has no place in a smart hotel like this. I didn't inform on him. I know I didn't. It's all in his head. I told the Police nothing they didn't already know. Even if they didn't know, they would have found out from other sources. His explosion earlier was pure hatred, coming anyway, regardless of his dislike of helping the Police with their enquiries. I don't care that he doesn't like me. I knew that before his rant. He's a loser, small time, barman thug, trapped in Wheatley Fields forever. I can get another job whenever I want, wherever I want.

I have a contact and an old colleague in Montenegro who has written to me about a night porter position in a small and prestigious hotel called the *Casablanca*. I could pick up the phone and call Nick in Durham at *The Bison Arms*. That's an amazing gig. I could e-mail Gillian Parsley in Hove and become night porter in *The Cavendish* without an interview tomorrow night.

Sixsmith, when sacked from here, will be lucky to get a job behind the counter at the off-licence.

That will show him, what with his wife pregnant, and a landlord fond of putting the rent up every month.

He can threaten me all he likes, but he's the one who lives in a cage.

Then it occurs to me.

What if *he* did it?

Ah, ha! A eureka moment. Methinks he protesteth too much! What if he did come back through the kitchen? What if he hid in a cupboard, and waited for him to go to bed?

What if he knocked on the door?

Julian – drunk and disoriented, perhaps expecting someone else – could have invited him in. Buy why? Sixsmith may have invented some convincing pretext. A manly chat, perhaps. Julian was far more into that entire male bonding thing, that let's-sort-out-our-differences-in-the-car-park type diplomacy than I am. Julian agrees to the natter, turns round, Sixsmith produces a heavy object and wooosh, bang. Julian is horizontally carpetwise. The barman leaves him for dead (and, to an untrained eye like mine, Julian looked deader than a doornail. If he was breathing, it was through air pockets in his blood or something), makes sure no one is coming and leaves by the back way.

And he could have done it, let's be honest.

His protest makes it more likely.

Taylor and Morston clearly gave him a hard time, as they did with me for not resuscitating the victim. I wonder what happened in that inquisition? I'll bet he lost it. I'll bet he gave them loads back and got himself into trouble. I'll bet he put himself right bang in the picture. All it would take is the weapon with his chubby dabs all over it and The Saladin would be getting a new bar manager while Sixsmith festers in chokey for a ten.

The thought of this makes me reconsider the grievance and consider an alternative.

I don't need the spotlight a grievance entails, and I don't need the hassle. Grievances, unless sorted early, can take it out of a man and whether victim or aggressor, the process can leave a stain that's difficult to shift.

I have used the process once, in Llandudno, a sexual harassment thing, an over-active gay assistant manager, and luckily, it got sorted to my satisfaction before it reached anywhere *political*. Before the judges got involved. It was all smoothed over, and I got left to port in peace, which is all I wanted in the first place. I don't want a stain on my record. It affects mobility and my professionalism may, in certain circumstances, come into question. I don't like that. It occurs to me that the Police might do the job for me in three days' time, when it's all gone back to normal. They might think he did it. When the authors have gone home, awards or otherwise in tow, and The Saladin welcomes a new bunch of interesting hotel guests for me to port for. They could pick him up and roast him for 48 hours and make him confess. I don't need to get my hands dirty at all. I could just sit and wait.

Yes.

I like that plan even better.

And another one, a corker that has been fermenting like home brew for the past few days.

Thought processes, huh.

That's the great advantage of having a career like mine. Sometimes you have time to think, to contemplate.

Amy and I talk for an hour about books. We lay next to each other on her bed and this time, she is not wearing socks. I am transfixed by her black toenail polish, creamy skin and silver toe rings. Tonight, her hair is a purple colour, mixed with crimson streaks and it is spiky enough to leave trails in sand. She is wearing a short flowery skirt, which means I can see her legs, and they are wonderful and shapely. Her essence assails me from all sides. It envelops me, it ambushes me. I am in a kind of heaven and feel stupefied, unable to think coherently. We touch on Julian's health (stable), and we touch on the Awards. I want to talk about Sixsmith, to unburden my sense of angst and injustice on someone else, but I don't. She shows me her ceremony dress. It is black and backless. Her shoes are hand-made and exquisite, also black. I do not have the vocabulary to describe them. She reads to me from *Amelia.* It is beautiful. It is the first time anyone has read to me since my late mother. Amy has a beautiful voice, and I am transfixed.

After half an hour or so of her reading, with her head balanced on my shoulder, there is a knock on the door. It is Frank. I take it as my cue to leave when he glares at me like some kind of burglar. Amy takes a cigarette into the toilet and Frank adopts my position in the doorway as I skulk off to my workstation, still slightly drugged and now more jealous than ever.[58]

---

[58]After Amy, it had been a long night, the longest I'd experienced for some time. A night of anguish and discontentment. A night of contemplation. I realised that the vibe had changed in the hotel since Julian's attack. For a week, it had been upbeat and fun, and full of intrigue. Now, everyone seemed subdued and distracted. Obviously, this happened for a reason. Maybe, too, it was the ceremony's impact. I'd like to cheer everyone up, but I can't actually be *proactive* in this. I can't actually turn up outside Jo's room with a party pack of lager and a dozen blowouts. A night porter is like a vampire – we have to be *invited* into a space. We can't just enter. I can't force the guests to talk to me. If they want to actually *sleep* in an evening, well, that's that! So, after seeing Amy, the night had been long and restless for one reason or another, I took no comfort from standing on the porch in the night's darkness. Sometimes that works, but last night, the silence of the night functioned only to make me maudlin and unsettled. The Saladin seemed impossibly large, like a mausoleum full of dark spirits. The Blue Lady was about last night, I was sure. I was in the right mood to meet her. But what would I have said? All in

The next morning, I didn't hang around to wait for Cat. Hayley came to take over bright and early and I slipped off quietly, glad to leave for once.

Ceremonial Dress

Cat is waiting for me when I get back to work. I'm not in the best of moods. I don't particularly want to be at work, which is unusual for me. It's clearly some ripple from last night's Sixsmith earthquake. She is actually sitting on my chair at my PC, though she gets up when she sees me coming.

'Hiya.'

'Hello, Cat.'

'I hear there was trouble last night?' Cat asks, and I am surprised. Only three people could possibly have said anything. I haven't, so that leaves two. I can't see Sixsmith saying anything, so it must be Gavin. I had made up my mind to say little.

'It was nothing, Cat, honestly.'

She leans in close to me and puts her hand on my arm. 'Mate, what did Martin say to you? Gavin said he had a right pop.'

'It's all about the coppers...' I say, and tell her what it was about. She listens intently. I don't deviate from the truth, though I fail to tell her about Martin's threats, and I don't mention him grabbing me. I've downplayed this from a Hurricane to a Cyclone, or maybe less, a passing storm. She looks at me as if she knows what I've done. 'Do you want to start a grievance procedure?'

---

all, I was glad to get home and once I'd showered and hung up my clothes, I boiled water for a hot water bottle, put on my Bose noise cancellers, tucked myself up under three massive quilts and slept for just over nine hours.

'Absolutely not, Cat,' I say. 'And if you want to help this incident pass into history, don't say anything to Martin, either. Just let it go. No damage done.'

'I can't do that…'

I am firm with her. I use my age and experience to outweigh my position relative to her in the hierarchy. 'Yes, you can, Cat. If you give Martin a dressing down, he'll only make it worse for me.'

'Did he threaten you?' Cat asks. 'Honestly, I'm not having my staff fighting. I'm not having it. Tell me.'

'No, he didn't threaten me,' I lie. 'It was just an argument. A silly thing. You know what Gavin is like…he's a drama queen. It's nothing, seriously. Can I start work now? Please?'

'I'm going to get Martin's side of the story tonight. I'll see what he says. I trust you. I don't need any fuss when I'm not here. I want a nice, tidy, clean ship –' she says, coining an ancient vernacular, '– we've already had a big wave hit us side-on.'

'– and our argument was just a ripple from that, Cat. Honest, it's back to normal tonight. Don't worry. The ship is going to be nicer, tidier and cleaner than ever. I'll make sure of that.'

She smiles a little. 'Thanks. Oh – I've got this for you. I nearly forgot.'

Cat reaches into her document wallet and pulls out an envelope. 'This is from Mary Beth. I've already said yes…see you tomorrow.' Cat says and walks off toward the bar to wait for Martin.

I take a seat, open a drawer and remove a gold-coloured letter opener I keep just in case. The long, thin envelope is Vellum, grey marble coloured, with turquoise impressions, real quality, with my name written in ornate blue handwriting on the front. It is scented, old-fashioned, and on the back, the flap is sealed with an elaborate A. It seems a shame to deface this piece of art by opening it, but I do so, and open it.

Inside, in an identical grey marble colour, but embossed with gold leaf is an invitation to the ceremony on Saturday night. I am stunned and have to double take.

My name is there.

Wow.

That's all I find it in me to say. *Wow.*

I have never been to anything like this in my life, and I never thought I would. Although, on occasions, I have held court on the prospect of a Night Porter Awards Night, I am certain they do not exist, and as I am not especially creative, until I held this invitation in my hand, Award Nights and I seemed inexorably to be travelling in different directions. I notice a Post-It has fallen to the reception desk from inside the envelope. I pick it up. It's handwritten in blue ink, feminine and informal.

...and don't worry about your shift. I'll take it myself. Cat xx

I smile. She knows exactly what I am thinking. I feel like following her and handing it all back. The Post-It inspires a thought cascade and I stare at the grandfather clock. Bad thoughts assail me quickly before I can prevent their intrusion. *Should not be going. Why am I even considering this? Why? Why? I am the night porter! I don't want time off. I don't want a holiday. I don't like Christmas, or Easter, or Bank Holiday. I don't like surprises. I'm not comfortable with leaving my post. Down with the ship. I certainly don't want management doing my job. Why is Cat pretending to be me? Why would she want to? What will she wear? Why? What does she mean by this! Who is CAT? What do those kisses on the Post-It mean? Does she WANT me? What! Why? How? CatCatCatCat. Why am I going? Why am I even considering the act! Why am I even considering this? I AM the NIGHT PORTER – not one of the writers. I am THE Porter at NIGHT. Le port de nuit! Le NUIT! I have no business there, and I need to be at work. NIGHT*

PORTER. NIGHT PORTER. NIGHT PORTER. N.I.G.H.T P.O.R.T.E.R. A definition as well as a vocation. A state of mind. AGGGH. I am PAID to port at night, not swan about in a POSH ceremony. Duty. Duty. Duty. Down with the SHIP. Oh, NO. I NEED to PORT! Is Cat pitying me? I wonder whether she is trying to ease me out. Is she? Is she? I must check the computer, I must...I must...

Cascading like sentient squash balls bouncing around the court hundreds and hundreds, but it only lasts ten seconds or so, and I realise that I am being silly, and I go back to feeling flattered, gracious, and absolutely delighted that I am invited to the ceremony. By the time Amy asks me to fill up her mini-bar again, I am already planning my wardrobe for the evening.

The Night Before The Ceremony

The night before the ceremony, I stood and watched a spectral, fearsome storm from a window on the first floor. Two o' clock in the morning. Lightning blitzed across the sky, leaving after-images like shrouds, which were almost as bright as the strikes themselves. Thunderclaps cracked like bullwhips over the town. A chaotic, howling wind powered the torrential rain up and down, in and out, lashing the window with violent, unnatural force. Weather like this was once considered a portent of doom, a vanguard for the apocalypse. I could see why. Watching and listening to the weather outside, I almost believed it myself. Torrents of dead rain flowed down past Dorothy's place like wild, rocky rapids, inexorably flowing towards the theatre where the ceremony would take place. Idly, I considered the prospect of cancellation, of abandonment. Weather gurus on every media from the BBC to Old Ned's Yew Branch.com had predicted the weather would continue like this for the whole weekend and beyond. TV news had predicted imminent flood warnings for the area, and

Police had warned the public not to travel unless in emergency. Yet, weighing things up, balancing the pros and cons, as a good night porter should do, I doubted the organisers would postpone. In the end, there would be too much to lose.

Mary Beth had showed me a logistics breakdown earlier, and I pondered what I saw as the rain came down in biblical fashion. The statistics were impressive for an independently financed enterprise. She told me that the Arkwrights had taken over a year and a half to organise – which is partly why the ceremony is biannual. Nothing had been left to chance.

She said it was the most minutely micro-managed ceremony of all time: Fine toothcombs miss more minutiae than the organisers of this year's ceremony.

The logistics were considerable when contemplated as a whole. Every hotel, Inn, Public House, Boarding House, Guest House, Lodgings and spare room for miles around had been booked for months. The Saladin was rammed solid. It was obvious that they were coming from all over to go to the Arkwrights, and they talked about it non-stop. They had ate, drank and slept books this weekend, so cancellation would disappoint far too many people, and I knew that Mary Beth and the Arkwright Trust would move heaven and earth to make sure the ceremony proceeded.

At the front of the auditorium, twenty dining tables of eight. Three hundred seats encircling the amphitheatre from above in grand, *la belle époque* style. Around five hundred people would attend the ceremony. Seated would be a diverse mixture of literary pundits, journalists and critics; writers there to present awards (some big names, some serious players, some giants of literature and popular fiction), and, of course, the forty nominees themselves. On top of that, forty specially invited Arkwright members, trustees, panjandra, apparatchiks and associates, including seven direct descendants of Joshua Arkwright. A host of roving reporters and TV crews, including a team of eight from **Brilliant Books,** televising the entire ceremony live to their subscribers on satellite TV. For the BBC, MC Pietro Armstrong-Holmes had come from London with a team of four researchers to prepare a half hour highlight show. The Trust had engaged the City Symphony Orchestra in the pit – last ranked the nineteenth best orchestra in the world – to provide suitable accompaniment. The orchestra alone is sixty three people strong.

Of course, an event like this needs its spectators. Three hundred members of the reading public had been invited to sit and watch in The Gods above. Last, but not least, consider the people who make it all work. The engine room. The superstructure. The hamsters, the nuts and the bolts. The culinary expertise of four expensive world-class chefs and their associated support staff; event managers, ceremony consultants, conference organisers, table layout team, the professional exhibitioners, location supervisors, the soundmen, the lighting team, which, Mary Beth again tells me, were last seen presenting the light show at the Donington Monsters of Rock festival.

There are the ushers, security; ticketeers, cloakroom attendants and the valets. An economic multiplier effect a hundred and eighty strong; an entire temporary workforce recruited, trained, prepared and paid for eighteen hours minimum (whether they worked it or not), to ensure the finest service of all time, for the greatest literary ceremony of all time, the Arkwrights doing for books and writers what the Oscars did for films and actors. In all, the Trust had spent millions of pounds in setting this up, plus the price of the theatre itself, which, some said – when considering the environmentally advanced materials – English, sustainable, non-intrusive, protective of natural resources and wildlife; built by local tradesmen and designed by newly qualified City architects – the attention to minute detail, its comfortable size, its avowed mission statement to supply affordable tickets to its audiences, and its eccentric location (in a small town a hundred miles north of the capital city) – would take a thousand years to recoup its costs.

There was the ego and the prestige.
The Arkwrights were a family, which fed on prestige. Failure and abandonment was not an option. They would protect the theatre with imperial purple tarpaulins, and they'd build an Ark to get the punters there if they had to.
Of course, there is also the story to consider.[59]
And where there are writers, there is always a story.

I hear a sound, and it is Amy. She stands next to me by the window.
'How can people sleep through something as beautiful as this,' she says.
'I know. It's astonishing.'
'I have always loved the lightning. My books are full of lightning storms. They make for great devices.'
'And metaphors, no doubt.' I say, realising that I had definitely soaked up the literary atmosphere.
'Absolutely. Nothing better than a good storm to provide a meaningful metaphor.'
'Looking forward to tomorrow?' I ask.
'Do you think I'll win?' She says, partially ignoring what I just said. 'The big one, I mean?'
'Yes, I do. You know that.'
'I'm lonely. I just wanted you to say it again. You know everything that goes on in here.'
'Only at night,' I retort gently.

---

[59] What would cancellation do to the story? No award? What an anti-climax that would be! The narrative of the past fortnight would be redundant. If they cancelled the ceremony because of the storm, what would it have all been for? No. A tale like this, with characters like this, the Julians, the Amys, the Franks, the Jos, the Mary Beths, and the hotel itself *needs* a big technicolour climax in order to exist.

'Just wondered whether you knew how the story turns out,' she says. She's drunk, but the only way I can tell is how slowly she speaks, and her eyelids flicker more than usual. The lightning flashes once more, and she is illuminated, like a ghost. I notice her hair tonight is dyed jet black, and it suits her more than any other colour she has sampled.

'I'm just the night porter. I don't know much at all.'

She doesn't look at me, but after a few seconds, perhaps contemplating what I have just said, she picks up my hand. I am shocked and slightly uncomfortable, but I allow it to happen. The usual thoughts hit me and the usual feelings. She holds my hand, like a lover might do. The touch of her excites me – she has soft, author's hands – and I want her.

I want her.
I want Amy Cook.

I shouldn't want her. It's unprofessional. Last night was unprofessional. The night before was…it's bad. It's everything I hate. Night porters should not feel like I feel now, nonononononono, but I am aroused nonetheless, and I allow her both to touch my hand, and to rest her head against my chest. Amy is shorter than me, and the gesture is natural. Up close, she smells strongly of underarm deodorant, booze, last night's pepperoni pizza, Old Holborn, expensive moisturiser, hair dye and the expected hormonal, underarm odours resulting from a long and arduous afternoon of love.

I have never met anyone in my entire life who smells like Amy Cook.

I have noticed in the recent past, though I shouldn't have, that Amy has hair on her armpits, which I find, personally, probably unforgivably, arousing. It's an animal thing. I wonder once again, what she is like in bed. I feel sick and disoriented all of a sudden, but I am frozen in place. If Cat walks in on this unprofessional horror, I am history at The Saladin Hotel, but I dare not move, I dare not, the weight of her face on my shirt is sublime and I NEVER want the experience to end.

I want to kiss Amy softly. I want to hold her, to take her to bed for a week. I want to tell her I love her. I want to marry her, even though that would be illegal, impossible and insane. I want her.

My head spins. She rests her cheek on my chest and strokes the palm of my hand with her finger. I suspect her eyes are shut.

This is it. This is it. This is it.
This is it. This is it. This is it.
This is it. This is it. This is it.
This is it. This is it. This is it.
This is it. This is it. This is it.
This is it. This is it. This is it.

As fast as it happens, this brief and magnificent moment of intimacy – thunder, like a thermonuclear explosion rocks the sky – and she pulls away.
'Thought you knew everything,' she says, and ambles back toward her room without so much as a backward glance.
I say nothing.
I wonder whether the rain is slowing down. I walk back down the stairs to my desk, and I don't say or think anything for a long, long time.

Part 4

Enter The Ceremony

Uptown, Saturday Night

'It all leads to the Gold Award for Best Writer,' Amy says.

The Arkwright Memorial Theatre is a grand building, even more so when alive with people as it is tonight. It is glorious and arrogant. If a building can be the master of everything it surveys, this fulfils that definition. I have never been before, but already, I intend to come again. I'm sitting right in front of the giant stage on a circular table the size of a galleon's wheel on a ship of giants. There are similar circular dining tables everywhere – a constellation of interlocking wheels like the inside of a grand Swiss watch. The atmosphere is excited and anticipatory, but because of Mary Beth's work, it is less than combustible. I doubt a fight will break out tonight on her watch.

The environment is cool, almost chilled, tables full of beautiful people in beautiful lounge suits and beautiful dresses made from every shade of every colour of the rainbow.[60] Hundreds of people[61] are watching us eat from their places in The Gods. It feels uncanny being watched. It feels mad being here. I am out of place amongst all

---

[60] The ladies throughout the theatre had done themselves proud tonight. They looked magnificent. Not just Jo, and Amy, and Mary Beth, but all of them – a superb effort. I have never been in the company of such splendidly dressed women. For the record, Mary Beth was suitably regal in an imperial purple evening dress with lace edgings and pearl earrings. Jo wore a plain but stunning rose pink dress and her hair up. Her jewellery, gold and onyx. Amy, if it were possible, topped her younger co-nominee for beauty and style. A simple black dress, with diamante spiders and impossibly steep high-heel shoes.

[61] 'Grockles', Julian called them when we discussed the Ceremony one night. Invited spectators, readers, bloggers and interested parties who won their tickets in media competitions.

these creators and beautiful people. I am seated next to Mary Beth on my right, Jo to my left. Amy is next to her and Frank.

'I'm just happy to be here, y'know,' Jo replies. 'It's just awesome. The theatre – Wow, oh, Wow – and the food. I'll never forget this as long as I live.'

'It's damned good,' Frank says. 'I have never eaten steak like that in my life. I am definitely coming back to England. And they told me you guys couldn't cook. They told me to bring lots of Hershey Bars!'

'And did you?' Amy asks coquettishly.

'Nope. I took my chances.

'I think you can win yours, sweetness,' Amy says, leaning towards Jo, picking up her hand and squeezing it tightly. 'Imagine the write-up on the front cover of your book! **Arkwright Award Winner 2013.** That'll send sales into orbit.'

It had surprised me during the past fortnight that despite Amy, Jo and Frank already selling sea-going container loads full of paperback books, they all talked sales. That was the barometer for them. Not quality, or pushing the boundaries, or writing the perfect novel,[62] it was sales. The bottom line.

Jo looks fleetingly uncomfortable at Amy's comment, inspired as it is by a bottle of very expensive claret and a large aperitif gin and tonic.

'It's such a privilege to be here, I can't allow myself to think like that, Amy. I'll just cheer for you when you get the big one,' Jo says, typically modest.

---

[62] After a jugful of Big Jack, Frank, in a rare moment of candour (at least with me), revealed his philosophy one night: 'Man, who wants to write the freakin Great American Novel? The critics and the academics don't put bread on the table. Give me the Great American Bestselling Blockbuster any day of the freaking week…and that, my friend, is a fact!'

Amy gives Jo a peck on the cheek. 'You're so gorgeous! Thank you.'

The two women hug each other as Frank looks on. Young waiters periodically fill our glasses. I am pleasantly stuffed. We are waiting for the awards to start, the real main course. Around us, packed tables eat, drink and make merry. Men in uniform penguin suits and black patent shoes, like mine, and black bow ties. Only the shirts differ, a mix of snow white, jet black, blood red and imperial purple, as far as I could see.

The atmosphere is infused with the scents of strong perfume and after-shave, mixed with the meats, and the fishes, and the sauces we'd just devoured – all overlaid with the hormonal ferment of sex and attraction, the type of anticipation this kind of gathering spawns, and the excitement of the awards to come. You could feel that. You could see it in the faces – not just of the writers. Critics and pundits would have bet like crazy people, because the only way (and I knew this) to back up a judgement and a strong opinion, an opinion worth fighting for, an opinion worth risking derision for, is to back it with money. Proper money.[63] The orchestra beneath the shadow of the brightly lit stage – a majestically empty space, made even more grandiose by

---

[63] For what it is worth, my betting portfolio on the event with the local Ladbrokes is this. I had one hundred and fifty pounds on Amy to win Best Writer at 13/8. Because I had bet such an amount, I left her alone for Best Romance – she was 1/3 for that, so I wasn't losing anything. I backed Jo to win Best YA at 2/1 to the tune of one hundred pounds. I really fancied my chances with that one. I had backed Julian to win Best Contemporary Fiction at 50/1, but I got my money back on that, sadly. Outside our little group, I backed Scotland's Ngaire Elder to win Best Children's Author (on Mary Beth's recommendation, a sneaky one made after too much gin), at 10/1 for fifty pounds. Her book is apparently something else. I didn't back Frank to win. I'll leave you to work out why.

the placement of a single podium in the shape of an Arkwright at the centre – plays a mixture of classics from the masters and stuff I recognized from films – Zimmer, Vangelis, mostly – and I realised that tonight's musical accompaniment had to be from the world of films because there is no musical accompaniment to a book, though, Julian told me ninety percent of the world's novels are written to music. He mentioned Bukowski's poems written by moonlight to the sound of Brahms and Beethoven. With the tables cleared, the lights start to go down and though what is about to happen is not announced, everyone in the room, as if compelled by a silent command, puts down cutlery and glasses. Waiters slowly disappear to the margins almost unnoticed. The spectators above put down their programmes.

It is about to begin.

I am excited.

'Is this it?' Jo asks me.

I aver that it is so.

'Oh, My God. This is so much *fun*.'

I smile. 'Yes, it is.'

Mary Beth stops talking to a Trust apparatchik and turns to me. 'You're going to enjoy this. And I'm sure there will be surprises along the way.'

'Mary Beth, you've done a magnificent job. This is wonderful,' I say.

'Thank you, kind sir,' she says, confidently. 'But the night is young.'

A man I recognise walks onto the stage. A giant of a man with a red beard of genuine character and a belly to match. I smile inside. I look at Amy, and she recognises him. It is TV's *Brian Bolus*, Shakespearean actor, bon viveur, raconteur and mountaineer. Our MC. His voice booms, scarcely needing a microphone.

'That's Brian Bolus,' I say to Jo under my breath. 'Famous over here.'

'He looks fun,' Jo says.

'Great choice for MC,' I say, excited.

He tells a few jokes and gets everyone warmed up in that profundo basso voice of his, and he says, without further ado and with a broad sweep of his hand, as if he was playing King Lear on the boards at The Globe, he asks us to **Let The Awards Begin.**

'Brian is the Master of Ceremonies,' Mary Beth says. 'Each award is separately administered by a famous author who reads the nominations…'

'Just like the Oscars?'

'You're catching on…' she says, grinning. 'First one is Crime Fiction.'

A Swede and an American woman whose names I don't know, and therefore ignore, walk onto the stage and begin to read the nominations for Best Crime Fiction. I have no interest in this so I allow myself to wander a little in my head. Jo is enraptured and claps like a dervish. All three of the authors next to me have, at one time or other, asked my opinion of their chances of a win, but Jo genuinely doesn't seem to care. She could be a brilliant actress, but I believe her.

As a man named *Mike Edwards* is greeted enthusiastically by the throng as Best Crime Fiction Author and walks up to collect his award, I watch her applaud as if it is a member of her family up there instead of a middle-aged man in a lounge suit.

Yet, I expect her to win.

If the world is a just one, she will triumph. In two weeks with us, she hasn't said a single word of criticism about anyone. I have never met anyone so saintly.

There are undertakers named Coffin, carpenters named Plane, weather presenters named Rain, and politicians named Power. Jo lives up to her name. Most beautiful women in my book are dark-hearted, but not her. Beautiful and *nice* – **a deadly combination.**

Yes, I think. *My money is safe.*

Best Fantasy, Comedy and Historical Fiction come and go.

The fantasy winner, **Matthew Posner,** from New York, is rapturously received in The Gods for his *School of the Ages: Book of Magic*. He gives a funny speech, which I listen to as I examine Amy, sipping red wine, occasionally applauding what she sees, occasionally whispering to Frank and occasionally nodding at whatever Frank says.

As the awards continue, Amy is visibly tensing.

Her face tightens, and she sips more wine, attracting the attention of Mary Beth. During Historical Fiction, she sips wine like she is reloading a gun with the enemy banging on the door. Frank puts his meaty hand on hers and seems to tell her to calm down. She squeezes his and nods imperceptibly. Of course, she can't smoke in here, and this might be sending her into orbit. She's wearing patches and has an emergency supply of NicQuit in her clasp bag, but it's not helping her tension.

Of the quartet, Amy wants this the most.

She really wants it.

Romance is seventh in line, but that's not what she wants. She's been there. It's the big one she covets, but Best Romance will be a good guide to the thought processes of the Judges.

I remember her conversation on the night after Julian went down.[64] It haunted me, and I haven't forgot what she said.

---

[64]'Do you think I can win it?' She asked, lying on her bed.

'Yes, I do. You can win this, Amy.'

Quiet again. I looked at her and knew I had a significant crush on her, one of those crushes that masquerade as love from time-to-time, especially when she goes all philosophical and dreamy like this, and I can see her feet, with that toe ring, those legs...her hair, tonight dyed pink and peach. Eventually, after a couple of minutes or so, she turned away from me and leaned on her elbow, reached for her tobacco pouch and papers.

'I don't deserve it. Even if I did win, I don't deserve it.'

'Why?' I asked.

Historical Fiction ends with polite applause and Amy leans over.

'Here comes Dolly Swinbank.'

'Dolly who?' Frank asks.

'Romance. Big buddy of mine. Wish me luck.'

Dolly, in a dark blue dress, with silver-grey hair, stands at the podium and in a Southern American accent, makes a mild comment about her being more nervous than anyone in the theatre and wished everyone well. She opens the golden envelope and begins to read the nominations. I look at Amy. She is alert and on tenterhooks. Jo squeezes her arm when her name is mentioned – accompanied by an enthusiastic ripple of applause from the crowd. Mary Beth claps loudly. Even Frank gives her a playful pat on the shoulder. Though it is dark, I suspect Amy has blushed under her rouge, and I feel proud of her. Dolly reads the last two nominations.

'And the winner of Best Romance is...' she says, pulling out another smaller golden envelope. She drops it, to laughter from the audience. 'My God, I've not been so embarrassed since my husband dropped the *ring* at the altar,' she says, and the audience laughs again. Everyone except Amy, who is wired and ready to go.

She is holding Jo's hand and has grabbed Frank's arm. Her eyes are those of a zealot about to receive the word of the Lord. I have not seen this side of her.

She wants this.

She *wants* this.

Quietly, as if revealing a secret she shouldn't, she replied, 'Because I'm lousy, love. I'm a bloody horrible person.'

'Amy...'

She laid on her pillow and somehow managed to roll a cigarette, all shoulders and arms, the shag tobacco sprinkling the hotel pillows. Then she turned to me as if nothing had ever been said. 'Can I smoke this in the bog? Too cold outside...' and I knew the conversation was over.

'Second time, everyone,' Dolly says, as she retrieves the smaller envelope. 'And the winner is….'
She wants this.
She's going to –
'…my great friend **Amy Cook**, writing as **Madeline France** for *Amelia*.'

The audience goes wild, a hot favourite going in, and a much loved author getting her just desserts: It is true what Julian said – Romance is hot. The spectators in The Gods, many of them women, scream and shout their wild affirmations. Amy pats me on the shoulder as she walks past, in floods of tears (which I also didn't expect), toward the stage. Jo is in tears and standing now, clapping like a performing seal. I notice Frank is on his feet, and I join in. A man with a TV camera suddenly points the thing in my face, and I sit down again, slightly worried about not belonging. Frank smiles for the camera and Jo hugs Frank.

'Don't worry, 'Mary Beth says. 'They'll edit you out! GO AMY!" she hollers, standing as Amy hugs Dolly, the pair of them in tears.

There isn't a dry eye in the house and after the relatively calm proceedings so far, the ceremony takes on the character of a concert. Amy bows to the audience, says a few words of thanks, and, to rapturous applause, returns to her seat where she is hugged by everyone at the table, including me.

'I don't know what to say. I *didn't* know what to say. I'm always like this. It's like the first time every time…' she says. Frank gives her a huge bear hug she responds to. I am jealous, but I smile along with everyone else.

The next category is **Best Children's Author.** Of everyone at the table, I am the most interested in the outcome of this award. I stand to win a cheeky little sum. This is my first bet of the night, as I didn't indulge in Amy's short odds victory. Jo, Frank and Amy whisper and discuss the "Alf" standing proudly on the table in front of her. I listen intently to Children's Author *Eunice Jones* read out the nominations. I feel the familiar anticipation I experience on a Saturday afternoon watching Newmarket, Sandown and Ascot on the telly. I only recognise one name in the field, and there's only one I *desire* to recognise. There is a silence just before she reveals the winner, and I have to suppress my excitement in victory when, against the odds, and to the surprise of many, small press Scottish author **Ngaire Elder** wins the award for quest novel, *Dragon's Star*.

The hall erupts, and I am similarly ambitious with my applause as she walks up to claim her prize. I don't stand – I want to, but I don't. I turn to Mary Beth and she winks at me. She has no part of the judging, but she clearly hears things, the right things, and I wonder whether this was a thank you gift of some sort. I don't ask her; just smile and mouth the words thank and you.

Ngaire walks up to the stage. Of all the authors so far, she looks the most bashful and embarrassed by the fuss. Her dress is stunning though, and she is dutifully polite in her thanks to the audience and to those involved.

Frank leans over and tells me, 'I had my dough on her,' he winks, and I smile back – though this bashes a hole in my theory that I am somehow, special to Mary Beth. Winnings will ease the pain in my ego.

There is a Special Award for Fiction, which is won by a nonagenarian from Wales called *Alwyn Jolly*, who (so Brian Bolus recounts), wrote many fictional pastorals featuring a simple shepherd called Nathaniel solving life's problems amidst a world of outstanding natural beauty. Genuine warmth glows, and there is a rest break, (and some of the *saucier*'s more extravagant concoctions will undoubtedly mean queues for the cabinets).

'My category is on next,' Jo says to me, not moving, as Mary Beth and Amy head for the ladies. 'I'm so excited. Do I stand a chance?' I've, like, not really thought about this.'

'I've backed you.'

'What?'

'I've put money on you, Jo. I think you will win.'

'OMG, you have? With that bookie you were talking about? What if I don't win?'

'I will lose,' I say, shrugging my shoulders. 'But you won't lose. I know it. And therefore, neither will I!'

'I love it when people have confidence in me. I don't, really. I always think I'm a bit of a, like, freak. I don't know why people like Sonia. I'm like, say what, when they tell me my books sell. I'm just Lil' Jo, you know?'

'I do. Yes. I do know.'

She gives me a nice cuddle and pulls away swiftly.

'Wish Julian was here.'

'Yes.'

'He was always nice to me. Oh, My God, he should stay totally away from the booze.'

'He should,' *But he won't, Jo. I've met many blokes like Julian before. The booze defines them.*

'And he should stop bitching about other authors,' she continues. 'It's only *books*. I mean, hey, it's not like it's real *life*.'

'No,' I agree.

'And all that stuff he says about Amy...she's *awesome*.'

'She is,' I agree once more, this time feeling it. 'Truly awesome.'

'I miss him, though. He's my friend. I love his kind side and the way he listens.'

Listens? 'Yes. Listens.'

'We're going to keep in touch, and he's going to come visit, he says. That would be, like, totally great. My parents would love to meet him – but he'd have to stay away from the booze. My mom doesn't even take a glass of wine with her dinner.'

I laughed. 'Things could get awkward around the dinner table.'

'Kinda. How is he, do you know?'

'Not heard for a couple of days.'

Jo's eyes moisten, but I interrupt, passing a napkin.

'Come on, you. You've got to look your best for the cameras when you win. Julian would want that.'

Pulling herself together, she kisses me on the cheek. 'Oh, God, yes. He'd want that. Y'know, I'm going to miss you when I fly home.'

'Me?'

'Yes, you, wise guy!' She says, pinching me. 'You've been awesome. You've been there for me. Man, oh, Man, you English guys are totally amazing.'

'Thanks, Jo.' I want to kiss her on *her* cheek, but something stops me and then, the gang return.

'Miss anything?' Frank says. 'You gone win this thing or what?' He says to Jo.

She goes shy. 'I'm not here for…'

Amy puts her arms on her shoulders as if she is resting. 'She'll win, Frank. I can feel it in my water.' And Mary Beth nods, which is encouraging.

And when Jo *does* win the Award for Best YA Fiction, we go mad and if anything, it's even louder than when Amy won.

Jo returns from the podium – after giving the assembled throng a masterpiece of a performance full of youthful exuberance, genuine humility, magnanimity to the losing nominees,[65] embarrassment and boundless joy – and describes it as the best day of her life,[66] and she

---

[65]Particularly, Renee Padwick, expected to win, but who applauds enthusiastically along with the rest of us.

[66]Come to think of it, it's not far off my best day ever either. I'm starting to think I ought to have had a Lucky Fifteen

dispenses hugs and cuddles like a reformed alcoholic at her last AA meeting.

It's another Special Award next, for Contributions to Publishing, an industry award and after that, it's Best Thriller. I have no idea what Frank thinks of this. He and I don't mix, and he seldom talks, apart from that one night. I have no idea whether he could win or what he thinks about it. He is a blank slate to me. He could be the world's biggest narcissist or its biggest joker. He could take this with all the seriousness of an arctic explorer or all the frivolity of a tourist off to the beach for the day. I just don't know. Saying that, it's a tough division.[67] The Thriller award contains the biggest price favourite and the shortest price outsider. Anyone could win. Frank is a massive price for Best Writer, but a value one for this.

There were quite a few Afro-Caribbean/Afro-American connections nominated and attending, but none quite so imposing. Yet, his bulk hid everything else about him. I wondered if Amy knew anything. She probably

bet, but that would have been greedy, and when my father and I got on, he gave me some excellent advice – never bet on anything that talks.

[67] I can't call Best Thriller,' wrote Paul Nash of the Telegraph. 'Each time I look, I come up with a different result. To an extent, that's part of a thriller's nature. They have a beginning, a middle and an end, and all four of these books, and all four of these writers, are conformists. There are explosions, death, murder. There are beautiful heroes, and heroines, and dastardly villains. There is death. There is threat. There is the implied menace of the coming apocalypse, and there is sex. Frank Duke, of all the writers, manages to include all the core elements of a thriller and adds a rare element of diversity. Plus, his hero is called Mungo, and he talks to his dog. I'll back him at 11/2 but keep the stakes small because this is a tough old race indeed.'

did, but she treated me as if Frank did not exist, and the two of them had never met for Big Jack every night. She never mentioned him to me. He was a huge McGuffin[68] in our interaction. He just existed in her life and her life only. I didn't know what she felt about him (or he for her), or what they talked about. *Were they having sex?* Frank hardly showed any interest in Jo. Lucy made just the one appearance, and she didn't stay the night. Yet, he was often with Amy after dark. He sometimes stayed the night with her, but does that mean they were intimate?

If it walks like a duck, quacks like a duck, and has webbed feet like a duck, is it a duck?

Amy is a talker, and Amy is married. Julian was convinced they were at it, but I wasn't sure. Maybe I was just denying, saving myself some pain because of my crush, which – when I saw her dressed up tonight, with jet black hair, her face made up professionally, in that simple plain black dress, and gold jewellery, and those high-heel shoes – felt much closer to lovesickness than a simple crush. As a night porter, I should be objective. It's a golden rule. Treat everyone the same. Everyone.

Be a professional.

I tried to say to myself that I didn't back Frank for Best Thriller because he might not win, it was a tough division, and I had bet enough, but the truth is (and I hated to say it), I kept my powder dry because I am jealous of his relationship with Amy. I look at him now, as **Jack Peterson**, the world's biggest selling Thriller author approaches the podium. Cool as a cucumber, tall, silver haired, tortoiseshell spectacles, in a black polo neck and a black suit, classically American, Senator or Serial Killer, he could be reading a newspaper on a park bench in Louisville for all the emotion he showed.

---

[68]Another Julian introduction I now use in regular conversation. Buying bacon from the butcher on the High Street takes a bit longer than it used to.

Amy held his hand with her right and had the first two fingers of her left crossed. Jo stood and ruffled his shoulder. I leaned over and offered my hand, and he took it, saying cheers, with the faintest of smiles on his face.

And when Frank won the award for Best Thriller, for *Shakedown in Chicago,* he wandered up to the stage, with the applause of the crowd ringing in his ears, still looking as cool as ever.

The two thriller authors met amidst the stage lights, and the adoration, and it was an immediate, almost gladiatorial clash of coolness up there. Julian would have had something to say, I'm sure. I was cursing now, missing an eleven-to-two quote for the sake of a childhood crush and an attitude problem, which may just have been miscommunication.

Blokes!

Tough working those out.

Still, I applauded.

Next to me, Amy and Jo were going mad – for a win for one was a win for all by now, and Mary Beth applauded wildly. That was three for three from our table, an amazing result. TV cameras were everywhere – three Alfs in a row on the table – and I remembered when Julian got hammered at that press conference. Julian, a racing man, should have known he was in a tough division. The press were bound to concentrate on the front runners. He shouldn't have been so hard on himself, but that's clearly just him.

Three Arkwright Award winners.

Three Alfs.

The prospect of one of them winning Best Writer had just improved.

The atmosphere flattened a little, thanks to a Horror author. Best Horror went to a woman from Minnesota called *Shandy Unuk*, who wrote (so the presenter said), an extremely scary novel of demonic possession in a middle class Minnesota suburb. A fifty-to-one shot in the betting, the massive outside of four. Shandy didn't cry, looked bitter, sourer than week-old milk, was clearly bored by it all, and didn't thank anyone at the podium. ('She doesn't like people much, obviously', Jo says, a little embarrassed at her compatriot's antics.)

Mary Beth is not pleased. I can tell.

Something tells me Shandy won't be defending her title in two years' time.

There is another special award and another break. 'Three awards left,' Mary Beth says, taking a sip of her wine. 'Contemporary Fiction, Best Publisher and the Golden Arkwright for Best Writer.'

'Contemporary was Julian's, right?'

'Not strictly. They had their own special award – Best Independent – but Julian was double nominated in Contemporary. He was *that* respected by the Judges. Did you get to read any *Notes?*'

'Mary Beth, I haven't read any of their books. I've been –'

'– forget the rest,' she interrupted. 'Read *Notes.* It's epic. If the worst happens, I'll nominate him for a Special Award in two years' time. If he survives, I'm going to bust his ass until he writes something else. And he can stay off the computer bitching,' she says, with that determined look. 'Damned fool gets on everyone's nerves every time he opens his mouth. I'm going for a rest break. Keep an eye on my vino – this is sublime! Think I'm going to have a hell of a head in the morning.'

Julian.

I'm sitting on a table with authors and rich apparatchiks for a Trust worth billions and tomorrow, they are all going to be under the spotlight with the coppers. It's easy to forget that someone bashed a nominee named Julian Green on the noggin with a blunt object. Four of the potential bashers sit around this table. If you include me, five. It's a slightly jarring thought, though obviously not as jarring as Julian being hit on the bonce. Someone around this table could be an attempted murderer.[69] Six people have been protected from interrogation by the organisers of this ceremony and tomorrow, the cops will be all over The Saladin like vultures on a corpse.

That's the deal.

I *know* Jo didn't do it and so do the cops, but it's not impossible that she *did*. I just can't see the motive. Why? There is no *why* there.

I look over at Amy who has gone quiet again, with Best Writer coming up. Did she do it? She has the motive. She had the opportunity. She has the strength, and I have been told of her legendary temper. She stares at the stage. The orchestra playing something from *Gladiator* as everyone chats. Brian Bolus is being interviewed, and he laughs heartily. Watching Bolus operate is like watching a presentational genius at work, and Amy seems to be watching him. *What is she thinking*? I picture her hitting Julian on the head and it doesn't ring true, it doesn't fill my eye. I can't have Amy in the frame, but it isn't impossible. I am biased, anyway. I have seen her soft side. I have felt it up close.

I have experienced her pale tenderness. No. Not Amy. *Surely,* not Amy.

Frank's already laid Julian right out. The waspish writer had slaughtered one of his best friends, Irish thriller hack, Seamus Deegan. He had been ridiculed in front of Jo and Amy. He's a big fella, a military vet. He had the motive. He had the opportunity, and he had the strength. But did he *hate* Julian? Did he? He's just

---

[69]The other is tonight serving cocktails and pints of *Bishop's Mitre* back at The Saladin.

too…too…*cool* to hate an English geek with a fat mouth like Julian, and he certainly isn't jealous of his work. Frank's in it for the cash. Julian is in it for the glory – there's no clash there. Why would Frank do it? I don't see it.

Then there's me.

Did I do it?
I had the opportunity.
I have the strength and direct, non-invitational access to the room.
But I **love** Julian.
I've got no motive.
Hang on, I'll bet you are thinking, yeh, but **you love Amy** also, don't you, and Julian said some hideous things to her that night after dinner.
Some unforgivable things.
He wouldn't shut up. I remember feeling bad about the things he was saying, but did I *really* want to kill him for it? He deserved a slap. He deserved a kicking, but he didn't deserve what he got.
I've seen death up close on three occasions, and Julian did not deserve to die, and whoever hit him wanted to kill him, and thought he was dead. I've no background in bashing people. But neither, I'm prepared to bet, have Amy, Frank and Jo.
This was the work of a virgin headbanger.
Then there's Sixsmith.
Martin Sixsmith –
'– what are you deep in thought about,' Jo says, interrupting my train of thought and lightly stroking my shoulder on her way back to the seat. I tingle at her touch.
'Was I?'
'You were so away with the fairies.'
'Thanks, Jo. Must be the wine.'

'I've been on camera,' she says. 'BBC Newsnight and *Brilliant Books*...my God, this is totally awesome.'

'How did it go?'

'I so talked *drivel* and giggled,' Jo laughed. 'But I guess I got away with it.'

'I'm sure you did. Can't wait to see that, Jo.'

'I'll download it and show my folks. They'll love I was on British TV.'

'Two good shows ...'

We stop for a bit. Mary Beth comes back with her two Trust colleagues. She appears to be watching Amy who is on her third bottle of wine. The Best Romance winner has not said a word for a while and is deep in thought. Frank talks to Lee Delgado of the Trust on his right and the two appear to be in serious mode.

Jo leans into me. 'Think Amy will win Best Writer?'

I am non-committal. 'It's too close to call. I really don't know, Jo. Do you?'

'I totally hope so. We're on one lucky table tonight,' she replies. 'It would top off a wild evening.'

'Let's hope our luck holds.'

She turns round and gives Amy a hug. The older author leans into Jo's shoulder, and the two cuddle. Will Amy win Best Writer? She has one serious opponent, Susan Limehaus. Her opponent is expected to win (four-to-seven last show with Ladbrokes[70]), so I hope Amy

---

[70]'The two cornered fight,' writes Jez Petrescu, of the TLS, 'for that is what it is, between Amy Cook and Susan Limehaus – not even a balanced one. It's a mismatch. Limehaus, with *Sonny Fargo, House of Ashes, My United Kingdom* and *Peace and Love,* has proved time and time again that she is amongst the world's best fiction writers. Amy Cook, whose *Amelia* is the first attempt at something serious, something outside her champagne and chocolate reveries, has neither the track record nor the pedigree to win the Golden Arkwright. Get theeself down to the bank, withdraw £700 and back Limehaus today. Call it finding £400 in the street. Call it your lucky day.'

braces herself for the worst, the applause for the enemy as the camera behind us closes in for the look of defeat.

Yet, Jo is right. Everything has gone well for us tonight. We're a lucky table. I stand up, move behind the girls and bob down. Amy is drunk, I see that now, and she involves me in the deep cuddle, and she kisses me on the cheek, and I feel her hot breath on my neck. She strokes my cheek, and neck, and comments on my aftershave. Up close, she is beautiful, and exotic, and sexy, and flawed and...

...I pull away slightly.

'Just want to wish you the best of luck, Amy.'

'Thanks, love. Do you think I'll win?' She slurs.

'Course, you will,' I say.

'Your friend keeps looking at me,' she gestures over toward Mary Beth. 'Thinks I'm sauced.'

'You've never been sauced, Amy. Never met anyone who can hold it like you.'

'Will you come to my room tonight,' she asks, out of the blue, a left hook, and I am stunned. 'I like you. I will miss you when I am home.'

'What about Frank?'

She laughed.

'Haha. I have been waiting for you to make a pass at me for a week. So that's why you've been holding off. Frank? He's a love. And he's...'

She giggles a little and takes a sip of her wine.

'...what?' I say.

'Married,' she adds quickly, though I suspect that wasn't what she was going to say at all. What she was going to say was none of my business, and it was the drink talking. 'So am I, married, married, but he's *proper* married, married, *married.* He's still with Harty. Still with her, you know.'

'And you're not?' I ask.

'With Harty, love?'

I laugh. 'Of course not. The Major?'

'Hah. The Major. The good Major. Major Benson. Sweetness, the Major and I lead separate lives and have done for many years. Everyone knows this, even the press. He's probably tucked up with his personal assistant as we speak. We haven't been intimate for many years, love. And do you know what?'

'What.'

'We both love each other, and he'll be proud of me tonight. We stay together for the good of our careers – it's bloody good for a Romance author to refer to "her husband" in every interview; it provides comfort to her readers on so many different levels. It's also good for a Major of a British Army Regiment to have a respectable wife! Every now and again, we go to functions together as a couple. He really is the most excellent company. I love him to pieces, and both of us have sworn to be very, very discreet about our love lives.'

'You are a dark horse, Amy.'

'Apparently, I am, petal. Now enough of this tomfoolery. Do you think I'll win? I really want to, you know. I really want that award.'

I was hoping she would continue the *come back to my place* theme, but she has this habit of throwing that subject in and withdrawing it, and once again, she showed no sign of stopping. I don't know whether it was the two glasses of claret I had sipped, or whether it was the highly charged atmosphere in the theatre,[71] but I decide to push, for the first time ever as a night porter.

---

[71] Men, women, status, media, politics, money – loads of it, positively oodles of it – the promise of parties, the art of parties, the TV cameras, the sense of importance, the sense of being somewhere important, somewhere differences are made, the movers, the moved, the shakers and shaken, the spectators in The Gods feeding the mad narcissism they see below them. Art, arrogance, right brain, left brain, total professionalism, lust, the snake brain, cerebellum, cortex, creativity, pride, grandiosity, expectation, competition, winners, losers,

'Tonight. Can I come back to see you?'

'Would you like that?' She says. 'You can come and watch me smoke on the toilet again.'

'Amy –'

'You're not working, are you? It wouldn't be unprofessional for you to come see me?'

'It would probably be grossly unprofessional, but I...I...'

The lights above started to dim. It was about to begin. The final lap.

I'd missed the moment.

Drat.

Bout one. Contemporary Fiction.

Bout two. Best Publisher.

Bout three. Best Writer.

And all I want to experience is Amy's kiss. Her perfumed, lip-sticked, dyed, faggy, boozy, saucy, sumptuous kiss.

But she's gone now, back into Best Writer-In-Waiting Mode, and I return to my seat feeling queasy, and ecstatic, and despairing all at the same time.

Without Julian, I am uninterested in Contemporary Fiction and the recipient, *Beecham Mills*, a London-based novelist, who wrote a book about an office worker who sells his soul to become leader of the Tory Party and subsequently, inflicts a living hell on the British people, takes his award to polite applause. There is none of the football-style thunder and lightning that accompanied

---

presenters, masterpieces, anticipation, gambling, drink, pheromones, hormones, adrenalin, enkephalins all mixed, all of it. It creates a sex atmosphere like nothing else. Nightclubs and discos have nothing on a ceremony, a ritual, like this.

Amy's win in Romance. Even the orchestra seems subdued.

'Maybe Contemporary Fiction isn't the draw it was,' Mary Beth leans over and says to me. 'It used to be such a hot ticket. Nowadays, it's genre, genre, genre! I'll drop this to the earlier segment in two years – leave it to the Booker and the Whitbread.'

I nod, watch Mills walk back with his award. The audience is now clearly waiting for the final countdown and Brian Bolus alludes to this as he introduces the Best Publisher presenter, a lady whose name I miss because of the general rumble. Behind us, a man guffaws rudely, just as Mills walks back past him. I am sure the two incidents are not connected. It's getting late. People are tired and have had a lot to drink. The audience is restless and await the climax. The whole point of any ceremony, of any tournament – of any game – is the *grand prix*. The top award, the Golden Arkwright, which some people call the Golden Calf, and maybe it's taken too long to get here. I make a note to mention this to Mary Beth, though she is so sharp, she must have already noticed. People are restless, and tense, and getting drunk.

On our table. I am restless and tense.

Mary Beth is staring at the screen, her fingers crossed.

Amy is restless, and tense, and looks as if she is plugged into the mains.

Jo is staring at the screen of her mobile phone.

Frank has stopped talking.

The final countdown is about to begin.

To my left, underneath the right hand Gods where the waiters had gathered, I happen to notice a security guard (like all of us in Tuxedo), pick up his mobile phone. I am more interested in this than the special award for publishers, and I watch his body language as he talks.

He's large, like Dolph Lundgren, and I suspect he's from one of the farming communities around Wheatley

Fields, a big bruising type, something of a strongman. Animated, without saying anything obtrusive, he gestures to one of his colleagues, and they walk around the side of the amphitheatre to the back. It could be an emergency, a random occurrence, a flaw in Mary Beth's grand plan. There is an element of drama in this, and it is more interesting than the fellow reading out the nominations for Best Publisher. I feel guilty for a second: I feel like one of those parents at a school Christmas concert who only want to see their child (dressed as a King, or Joseph, a key part), and the rest are incidental.

I watch three security guards disappear into the entrance hall. As I watched that, I hear the result of the Best Publisher Award. The winner is a small press from London who, apparently, according to the temporary MC, publishes militant, neo-lesbian fiction "of an occasionally fruity nature!"

Their representative, who, in a formal evening dress, looks radiant, ignores the comment and takes the award with great joy, to generous applause.

I notice Mary Beth reach into her handbag and pull out a small walkie-talkie.

A purple light on it flashes. I suspect it also vibrates.

She looks at me with a slightly concerned look on her face, and she clicks straight into gear, ever professional, gets out of her chair and walks quickly to the left double doors at the side, her movement and activity obscured by applause and the swirling symphony of the rumbustious orchestra, who have picked up the tempo for some odd reason. I feel like following her, but it's clearly her business. She floats over to the swing doors at the extreme right of the theatre and disappears inside.

'What do you think that is?' Jo asks me.

'Some commotion outside. I saw the guards...'

'Gatecrashers?'

'No. They wouldn't have needed Mary Beth. Something's proper cracking off outside.'

'OMG, just before Amy...'

Amy, who has been listening, leans over and in a subtly admonitory tone, which betrays her nerves, speaks directly to Jo.

'Don't tempt fate, love. Not won yet.'

'Gee, I'm so sorry, Amy.' Jo replies, and I feel like putting my arm around her.

I whisper to the YA author as Amy renews her pose, eyes on the stage.

'Hey, she's tense. I'm getting tense as well.'

'Uh, huh. Totally,' she says, putting her phone back in her black and gold clasp bag.

I wink at her and she puts her arm in mine and smiles.

It's noticeable that Jo and Frank, who theoretically could win the Award, are not in the slightest bit expectant. It's Amy, widely tipped, and thought of as deserving. She's wired. Second favourite. She *could do it.*[72] Her face is pinched, the joyful patina imbued by her earlier win faded. It's this one she wants. Mary Beth appears from the swing doors and walks around the side, a symmetrical mirror image of the security guards earlier,

---

[72]'Amy Cook's work has the advantage of popularity and accessibility,' writes Holly Fleet of the Times. 'Susan Limehaus has clout amongst the lumpen London literati and significantly resonant intellectual cadences. Her work, particularly, the stunning *House of Ashes,* is worthy of any award in the world. But she's a *writer's* writer, rather than a *reader's* writer. I've never had a bet in my life, but when my Editor told me Amy was 4/1 with the bookmakers, I went out and chanced a sneaky tenner with a William Hill's in Wood Green High Street. For the simple reason that Arkwright judges weight popularity in a way the Booker teams never do. Limehaus has a way with words that would make Tolstoy cry, but her books sell a quarter of Cook's alter-ego, Madeline France, and that could swing it. Best writer? Amy has no chance, despite *Amelia* being by far and away her best ever book. Best *Arkwright* writer? My editor thinks the bookies have made a big rick, whatever that is.'

hugging the wall as if she wanted it to swallow her. I noticed several diners watch her go, and there is a minute rumble as other diners twig something might be happening outside, but that rumble is smashed to smithereens by the darkening of the lights – not a fading, but a complete blackout.

There is a gasp as diners wonder if the electricity has failed due to the terrible weather we all endured to get here, but it's deliberate. One spotlight from The Gods illuminates a drummer who rolls his drum. Another beam, as if from the heavens, spotlights the enormous presence of Brian Bolus at the very front of the stage. With red beard and mighty arms, he looks like Odin, the master of all he surveys, staring across the Rainbow Bridge. He controls the audience to the extent you can hear a pin drop on thick carpet.

In his hands, he holds a **Golden Arkwright,** polished and sparkling, projecting and refracting the individual colours of the light stream back out into the crowd.

Streams of red, and blue, and yellow, circulate and dazzle. I wonder whether it is a special effect – the singular jets, emerging as if from an amplified, energized mirror ball, dazzling and entrancing the audience. As an effect goes, it is a magnificent one and provokes spontaneous applause, made more intense and passionate by the fact that it is the award itself, the focal point of the whole evening, now controlling the light show.

'And now,' he booms, scarcely in need of a microphone, 'the moment we have all been waiting for.'

The audience applaud as the lights, like imps, like fairies, dance around the tables. I see Jo covered in red, Amy in gold, and Frank in purple. It changes. Green. Orange. Pink. Purple. White. Blue. Nothing stays the same, the full chromatic scale diffused through the award itself. I realise that the statuette – in glass, in crystal, in gold – he holds is something special, something *scientific*

– a light diffuser, a fragmenter, a specially constructed lens. Science in the hub of the arts.

'I have been reading since I was six years old,' he booms. 'I have read ten thousand books. I have read the works of Shakespeare, of Trollope, of Bronte, of Wodehouse, of Byron, of Walpole, of Pound, of Updike – and of JK Rowling,' he says, the crowd-pleaser, to rapturous applause from the audience.

'And I will be READING a book on the day of my last breath,' Bolus says, and some in the audience stand and applaud. 'My famous last words will be the last words I ever read because BOOKS ARE LIFE ITSELF'

The crowd, every last one of them, on the floor and in The Gods, stand, to a man and to a woman, and they cheer and applaud as Bolus stands there, in the darkness, Odin himself. The applause lasts five minutes and there are tears. 'Had my gift been that of a Writer's Imagination, I would have written, but alas, that gift was given to someone else…a PITY…' he booms, startling the audience, '…because readers make magnificent writers, but without that gift of imagination, a writer can produce books, but they can never produce *wonder.* And tonight…' he says, the audience in the palm of his hand, '…we will welcome to the pantheon of celebrated literature, these marbled halls, a WONDERFUL writer to whom this' – he holds up the Golden Arkwright – 'will be fulsome and glorious tribute.'

There is more applause.
The lights slowly rise and Bolus returns to the podium in its midst.
Amy tenses.
There is utter silence in the hall as he puts on his spectacles and holds up the envelope.
'Herein lies glory,' he booms, theatrically. 'Herein, lies majesty. Herein, lies the name of the winner of the

Arkwright Gold Award for Best Writer. The Gold Standard by which you are all judged, the font of imagination, the repository of wonder and imagination.'

Amy tenses even more.
I wonder where Mary Beth is.
I hold Jo's hand.
Jo holds Amy's.
Amy holds Frank's.
We are together.

The excitement is electric, visceral. Bolus has manipulated a magnificent silence. Amy's tension morphs and transmits to us all. I wonder who Susan Limehaus is. I wonder where she is. I wonder what she looks like. I curse myself for not researching. Bolus makes us wait an age, milking the moment for all it is worth. He lifts the envelope, seemingly weighing it, assessing it, examining it. He takes a golden opener to the flap and slices it neatly. I hear a fork drop on the floor six tables away.
I hear Amy breathe and Jo squeezes my hand.
He takes out the sheet.
He holds it away from him at arm's length and examines it, almost academically.
We watch his every move.
And we hear him. He smiles, puts down the paper.
'And the winner'
Jo squeezes my hand even tighter.
'Of the 2013 Golden'
Amy closes her eyes and bows slightly.
'Arkwright Award'
Frank looks at Amy and also closes his eyes.
'For Best Writer is'
We all close our eyes, for this is purely aural now.
...
...
...

...
...
...
...
...
...
...
...
...
...
...
...
...
...
...
...
...
...
...
...
...
...
...
...
...
...
...

'Amy Cook writing as Madeline France,'

he booms

...
...
...
...

...
...
...
...
...
...
...
...
...
...
...
...
...
...
...
...
...
...
...
...
...

Pandemonium reigns.

...
...
...
...
...
...
...
...
...
...
...
...
...
...

...
...
...
...
...
...
...
...
...
...
...
...
...
...
...

It takes Amy an age to reach the stage because everyone wants to hug her, and kiss her, and I see why, now I see why the Arkwright Ceremony is so important as I applaud, and applaud, and applaud, and shout, and cheer along with the rest, everyone on their feet, the glorious tumult

It's not about brilliance in writing.
It's not about the way things are.
It's not about who can write and who can't.

As Amy struggled with her scrum, and the Orchestra played a suitably triumphal symphony, I remembered something Julian said to me when he first arrived.
The difference between the world's greatest writer and the world's greatest functional illiterate is about 1%, identical to the difference in DNA between a human and a chimpanzee.
It's not about pushing the boundaries of fiction.
It's not about publishers,
and/or self-publishing,
and elites,
and Tarzan,

and bookshops,
and slush piles,
and fame,
and money,
the lack of money,
the copiousness of money;
it's not about any of that, all their obsessions,
It's not about who's good and who's bad.

It's about people.
It's about reading.
It's about the joy of books.

It's about love.

As the applause rages, the orchestra plays something triumphant, a mountains-worth of multi-coloured ticker tape falls from the sky. We are covered in it, and the spotlights seemingly locate each and every one of the millions of tiny pieces or paper.

As the tears fall, I curse myself for not reading a book for twenty years. I make a note to visit Waterstones and buy as many books as I can, but I make the note mentally because I am roaring and clapping like a performing seal, tears pouring down my face, hugging Jo, watching Frank clap and smile – genuinely, warmly – now watching Amy hug this man, and that woman, and this man, and that man, the cameras following every footstep. A waiter, unable to control himself, runs over and hugs her, and kisses her, and Amy holds his arm up in the air as if he's the victor. Enormously popular, the Judges had made a shrewd choice. No one would forget the Arkwright Awards of 2013.

On stage, Bolus weeps, every inch the Odin of these ceremonies, and truly, there is not a dry eye in the house. Amy ascends the stage. She applauds her throng. A young girl in a white dress emerges from stage right with a sumptuous bouquet of yellow roses and hands it to her.

Brian Bolus embraces her with tears still in his eyes and Amy is weeping.

She places the bouquet on the table.

Picks up the Award from the podium as the applause continues, rapturously, lavish and boisterous.

Amy Cook holds her Award in the air.

And then, at that very moment, she looks into the distance.

The smile leaves her face.
Something is wrong.
I can see it.
I *know her.*

The freeze is momentary, but it has an impact. It has *had* an impact. She smiles once more, steps up to the podium and begins to speak as the applause for her achievement starts to fade into history. I turn round to look for the source of anxiety, the instigator of the lapse.

What bothered her?

Mary Beth?
Dolph?

I see it.
Near the swing doors at the back of the auditorium.

I see Mary Beth.
I see Dolph Lundgren.
I see someone else.

(Oh, Jesus.)

As if psychic, the connection between the four of us – created by our chain of hands – still active, still powerful, I notice Jo and Frank have also witnessed the scene unfolding at the entrance.

Amy speaks – wonderfully – but her eyes are fixed like a tractor beam onto the back of the theatre. To all intents and purposes, she looks like she's reading from a distant autocue.

There isn't one.

Her speech is strong, and warm, and fun, but if you know her, as I do, it's a wounded speech, an act.

I could see why.

I cast no blame.

'OMG, look who's here,' Jo says.
Frank says nothing.
Neither do I.

Julian Green stands there.

He is on crutches and stands in-between two giant security guards. His head is bandaged.

He stares at Amy on stage.

Mary Beth is on her walkie-talkie, and I guess she is arranging transport back to the hospital. Or the Police.

He shouldn't be here.
He shouldn't be out of bed.

Part of me is happy to see him.

Part of me feels he is intruding on Amy's Big Night.

(That's why he's here. He's a gambler. He knew she was going to win. He gave me all the betting ideas. He told me. There was no doubt. Of course, of course. He wouldn't miss this for the world.)

Amy thanks everyone and says this is the greatest night of her life. Julian stares at her, and she stares back as if no one else exists. As if the two of them are on an astral plane.

The applause rings out once more, and it looks to everyone else that Amy is basking in it, treasuring and savouring the moment.

But I know different.

She's staring back at Julian.

Mary Beth can see it.

Jo can see it.

Frank can see it.

I can see it.

(Why would he come? Why? Why?)

And in the midst of that stare, I knew.

Don't ask me how I knew.

Awful lot of psychic stuff going off around this table tonight.

But I knew.

(My God)

(My God)

I knew at that moment, right at that moment of Archimedean connection – the six of us, nodes, stretched and displaced, a hexagram, a distorted topographical circuit diagram powered by some psychic energy, some sixth sense generated in the ether – I knew why Julian Green hated Amy Cook.

Aftermath of a Famous Literary Victory

After the inevitable scrum, the interviews, the cameras, the darlings and the hugs, the loves and the tears, the salutations and the promises, eventually, Amy fights her way through the well-wishers and acolytes and meets us in the lobby.

Julian has joined us, and Jo is talking to him when Amy, accompanied by a stern looking Frank, walks over. She ignores the rest of us. She is flushed and glowing, but Julian's appearance has reduced the ecstasy, the top ten percent of the good feeling, and Amy will never forget that. Her eyes accuse.

'I knew you wouldn't miss this, 'Amy says to him. Around us, groups of delegates gather and await their lifts to the parties and gatherings all over the Fields. I see Brian Bolus holding court. You could imagine Brian Bolus holding court wherever he went.

The largest party is in the old Summer House behind the theatre and that is the hottest ticket in town. All of the award winners are invited, and I suppose I am, but no one has said anything.

Julian subtly bows. 'Of course not. I am pleased for you. Well done.'

Underneath the obviously borrowed lounge suit a size too big, is a *Black Sabbath Vol 4* tee shirt, the same one he was wearing when he was hit on the head. Ozzy Osbourne in full cry, a silhouette. Ditto the Adidas Forest Hills trainers with the three gold stripes. His bandage is fresh and clean. Turns out he left the hospital voluntarily and at the last minute. Totally spontaneously, he says.

'You don't mean that, Julian,' Amy says. 'You're the only person in this building who would wish my failure.'

He looked sheepish. 'I know why you would think that, but I do mean it, Amy. Well done.'

She laughs contemptuously. 'Okay, I'll accept what you say. NOT!'

'Hey, Amy. Let's go to the ball,' Frank says, unequivocally stating his position.

Jo does the opposite and links arms with Julian.

'No, Frank. I want to know why he's come. I mean, *really*.' Amy says, a little drunk, a little shocked at his appearance. 'You came to spoil things for me.'

'Sorry, Amy,' Julian says, quietly. 'I came to wish you well.'

'You came to ruin my speech, like you did.'

'He didn't really –' I interrupt.

'– you ruined my speech,' Amy said, ignoring me.

'You were very good,' Julian says, and he looks like he's telling the truth. Hospital and the impact of the blow may have knocked the swagger out of him. He's gaunt and thinner than he was, and the suit doesn't fit. Jo is treating him more like a frightened rabbit in the garden, some injured animal she discovered. Mary Beth is trying to reach the hospital, and Frank is staring daggers at him, as he would. 'Very professional. And you deserved it.'

'Such an arse,' she says. 'There's a nasty joke coming along any minute.'

'No jokes. I just came to say well done and now, like a will o'the wisp, I'm going to leave you to your party. Or Ball, as Frank says. By the way, Frank, I'm sorry about the other night. Way too much beer.'

Frank doesn't even look at him.

Frank doesn't even acknowledge him.

Frank looks at Amy and repeats what he said about going to the ball, as if Julian wasn't there.

Julian smiles thinly. 'Is my room still free?'

'Er, Mary Beth is taking you back to hospital.'

'I've discharged myself. There's already another nutter in that bed. There's nowhere for me to go. Socialised medicine and all that,' he grins at me and winked, and I couldn't help but grin in return. 'It will save Arkwright's a few quid on their posh doctors. No, I'm a free man. Good as new in a week.'

'Okay. Your room's made up for you, Julian,' I say. 'I'll take you back.'

'Good man,' he says. 'You can make me a hot toddy for my head. Amy, seriously –' he holds out his hand. 'Let's let bygones be bygones. I'm sorry for everything I've done. I've been an arse. A total arse. One hundred percent. Well done on a great award.'

Amy looks at him.

She looks as if she is considering his apology.

And she looks like something else is going on there. Her right eye, just for a moment, flickers.

There is silence among the group, and everyone has tuned out the hubbub and the jibba jabba around them.

We all look at Amy Cook.

We watch her shake her head.

'No. I'm sorry. I can't accept this. What you said was over the top, Julian. A campaign of terror. You were well over the top. I'm seeing solicitors. I'm sorry. I cannot have you say those things again. I can't forgive you this time. I'm sorry.' Without looking at any of us, she takes hold of Frank's hand and the two of them walk away.

Julian shrugs his shoulders.

'Can't say I blame her.'

'I guess I'll come back,' Jo says. 'I *so* cannot believe that.'

'Aren't you going to the Summer House?' I ask.

'Guess not,' she replies.

Julian props himself up on a crutch and strokes her shoulder. 'Hope you like hot toddy.'

'What's a hot toddy?'

'He'll show you,' he says, nodding at me and propping himself straight on his crutches, the two of them walked slowly to the door.

'Hey, hey...' Mary Beth shouts.

I walk over to her.

'It's alright. He's checked out. I'll look after him.'

'He's not *well*. He should be looked after by professionals.'

I give her a hug.

'Well that's alright, Mary Beth... I'm a professional.'

The Hook of Revelation

Cat was surprised to see us all, but Mary Beth called her and told her the full story. I make the toddies as we all sit in Julian's bedroom. Julian lay inside the bed still wearing his tee shirt, and Jo sits cross-legged on the bed in her beautiful dress. Whatever happens, these two will always be great friends. I don't think they could ever be more than that, because it would be a real beauty and the beast situation, and the press would rip her to pieces, like they did Julia Roberts that time, but in a different world – *in a different world...*

'Why do you think Amy refused to make up with you, Julian?' Jo asks. 'I was, like, Wow. How could she do that? She was so totally cold.'

Julian took a huge sip of his toddy and swallowed a couple more of his painkillers. I could see he was flagging. I planned to stay with him tonight on the sofa bed in his room and had already fetched a spare quilt. I was tired. I could do with a kip.

'Families, Jo,' he says. 'Almost impossible to rebuild family rifts once they occur. A bit like trying to seal the Grand Canyon with a plaster.'

Jo looked at me.

Then back at Julian.

'So, like, run that past me again,'

'He worked it out, I can tell.'

I nodded at Jo.

'Not long ago, actually. Right at the end.'

'Like, what did he work out?'

…
…
…
…
…
…
…
…
…
…
…
…
…
…
…
…
…
…
…
…
…
…

'Amy Cook is my mother, Jo.'

...
...
...
...
...
...
...
...
...
...
...
...
...
...
...
...
...

...biologically, at least. Once upon a time, when Amy was sixteen, she went and got herself pregnant by my dad. That was thirty six years ago. She was still in school and back then, that was a *big* deal. Nine months later, while living in my grandma's house in The City, and while still studying for her A' levels for as long as she could before it became physically impossible, she gave birth to little old me. Six months after that – and I don't know why, don't know the circumstances – she disappeared in the middle of the night and that was the last anyone in my family ever saw of her. Not a birthday card, Christmas card or postcard from her holidays. Dad was an apprentice plumber at the time and so I was bought up, more or less, by my grandma and granddad. They were only in their late thirties. Dad took a right bollocking for getting mum up the duff.

'Pregnant?' Jo asks, looking genuinely shocked by the whole thing.

'Yep. In the Family Way, Bun in the Oven. But there was never any question of a termination. They took me on, helped dad, and we were all one big happy family. Secretly, I suspect they were glad Amy had gone. My grandma was only thirty nine. She was like my mum until I was nine, until dad got married to Katrina, my stepmom. I never knew Amy. I can't remember her. Dad hardly mentioned her and even when I asked him outright when I was fifteen, having a crisis of confidence in myself, one of those teenage suicide and cigarette moments, he wouldn't talk about her.'

'What about your grandma and granddad?'

'They were dead loyal to dad and said nothing. My granddad took me to one side and told me to move on, that the past was another country. It's a long story, which I won't bore you with, but I kind of forgot her. Went to Uni, separated from family, became the healthy, well rounded personality you see before you, and moved on. You know, I didn't even feel a hole in my life. Katrina's lovely and though she and dad divorced two years ago, we still speak on the phone now and again. They never had kids. I'm the classic only child. Amy wasn't even part of my spirit.'

I thought about my own dad.

I knew him. I saw him. That was the hole I felt. I wonder whether Julian would have experienced the hole had his dad did to him what mine did to me. I guess he would. My mother died when I was ten. I knew her. That's two holes. My consciousness would leak like wine through a square of Edam cheese if I let it, but I plug the leak, a bit like Julian.

"So how did you find out?" I ask, still thinking of my own situation. Things like this being a trigger.

'I met Amy Cook on the Internet on the Tarzan forum. Quite by chance. And we got on. I mean, seriously. Don't know how it happened. She's got 350k followers on Twitter, the maximum 5k on Me.Com, and her threads on Tarzan about writing attract hundreds of replies. But over time, we started to talk. I mean, I f'in crucified bad authors, Goblin authors, eroticists, wannabes, and thriller authors, I was a total *enfant terrible*, always getting banned, always respawning, always trolling the needy and the greedy, always showing the narcissists the black mirror, but I liked Amy. We became good pals. I think she liked my frankness, and I know she liked *Notes*, the stuff I shared of it on my Blog. She commented on there. I mean, Jo, Jo, Jo, this is MADELINE FRANCE on my Blog! I couldn't believe it. It's unheard of. It made the rest of the Grockles on there even more envious of me. We started chatting on Me.Com's chat, and MSN, and all that stuff, and got close. You know where I'm going with this, don't you...'

Jo pulls a face of genuine pain. 'You didn't...'

'Oedipus very nearly came to dinner, yes, Jo. I invited her to see a football match with me down in London. I'm a Notts County man, and we were playing down there, and she follows Orient for some odd reason, so we arranged it. She booked me into a hotel, and I KNOW it was a double room,' he says, grinning, 'Sick, or what.'

'Now, that is so *totally* gross,' she concurs.

'Biblical. It's biblical, and it nearly came off – you ought to see the IMs! – were it not for my dad calling me on my mobile a year ago when I was at my PC.'

'What happened?' I ask, engrossed.

'I'm buzzing, right. Here's me, trying to be a writer, and I'm about to go on a f'in date with Amy Cook/Madeline France, one of the best in the world. Dad and I talk – we're more like best friends than anything else – and I was just about to tell him that the date was probably going to end up in a vigorous bout of horizontal pink action when he stops me dead. Tells me he's coming round. When he gets here, he brings a bottle of Laphroaig, and he tells me the f'in lot,' he says, animated now. 'The whole lot.'

'The works?' I say.

'The whole thing?' Jo says.

'The whole enchilada,' Julian says. 'My son, Amy Dot Cook Stroke Madeline Dot France Open Dash Bestselling Novelist Close Dash Is Your Mother.'

'OMG,' Jo says. 'I'd have been completely weirded out.'

'You're not kidding. I was furious. I smashed my PC and very, very, very nearly punched my dad.'

'Really?' I interject.

'Put a huge hole in the kitchen wall instead. Don't know my own strength at times, even though I'm a skinny git. Dad understood. He kept it from me because of what I'd do. See, I'm an angry person.'

'Is that a fact!' Jo laughs.

'*Quel surprise*,' I add.

'Oh, you've both noticed. Soz. He kept it from me for many reasons I won't bore you with, but that was the main one.'

'I assume the date was off?' I said.

'You assume correctly, sir. Ladies and Gentlemen, Oedipus has left the building. I didn't just kill the date, but the whole lot. I blanked her. Blanked her large. You don't do online stuff?'

'I don't, no.'

'Cutting someone off is not easy. You have to block, and leave and delete pages, and resign from groups. I was a big player on The Wizard's Court, but I left, pleading some lie or other. She sent me message, after message, after message, but not once did I reply. Night after night, I lay in bed, and the more I thought about it, the angrier I got. I tried to write letters. I tried to write letters arranging meetings. I tried to tell her what I knew. I so wanted to meet her, but I could not write a letter to that effect. The words would not come. I kept seeing one thing. A woman putting on her hat and coat, the rain outside, the moonlight shining through the front door, picking up her suitcase without a word to me, without a kiss goodbye, and leaving me behind. That's all I could see. Her leaving me behind. Only, in the picture, it was the Amy Cook you see today, not the sixteen year old girl; she must have been dressed up like a Bay City Roller or someone out of the Rubettes. And the more the image haunted me, the more I began to hate her. And that hate became literary. That hate expressed itself in the shape of Total Cyberwarfare on Amy Cook.'

'I've heard about that,' Jo says. 'Glad I didn't see it.'

'Do you blame me? I wasn't in charge of my emotions. Everywhere Amy went, I respawned. I rejoined groups. I retraced my steps. I hunted. I stalked. I sought. I found. I destroyed. I was the Ultimate Troll. I treated her with hate, derision, and contempt. Some of the things I said to her were so bad, I was threatened with the Police. When I couldn't flame her any more, I transferred the hate to every single Romance author there was, the entire genre, the entire body of work. The knowledge of Amy being my mother amplified my hatred of successful authors, and especially successful Romance authors, Eroticists, and Thrillermen. Ergo, the enfant terrible found himself banned, detested, scorned...'

'...but also the subject of a cult following,' I interjected.

'Yes, I am embarrassed to say. And the rest, you are aware of. Amy and I ended up at war from, well, you know. Ergo, we arrived here.'

She gave him a cuddle. 'I am so sorry you had to go through this, Julian.'

'Last Monday night changed me. The drink, the rage. I was well OTT, and I deserved the bang on the head.'

'Who did it, Julian?'

'No idea,' he replies. 'I had my back turned.'

'But the door?' I quiz. 'It was open.'

'You must have left it open when you dropped it off. Or it was someone with a key. I never answered it. I was leaning against the wall trying to avoid being sick. That wall is beautifully cold, the coldest part of the hotel room. I was lying in bed, and it was all spinning, all of it, the ceiling, the walls, the carpet and the only way I could keep the vomit in the vomit box was to rest my cheek against a cold spot. It was then I got whacked. Could have been anyone. Could have been that old bloke from next door complaining about the noise. Could have been *you*,' he points at me, laughing. 'You looked well peed off with me that Monday night.'

'I was. You were completely out of order.'

'I know, chap. I'm off the sauce and on the happy juice from now on. I shall be gathering at the river with all the other sadsacks at AA. I can't behave like that again.'

'Really?' Jo says, her eyes brightening.

'Nah, I'm just kidding. I'll stop drinking whisky. At lunchtime. In the week.'

'Julian, you –' I laugh.

'– sorry, just being facetious. You'll never see me like that again. I wanted to tell Amy that, I really did. I was an arsehole. Maybe one day I will get the chance.'

'Are you not angry with her?' Jo asks.

'What for?'

Exasperated, she throws up her hands. 'Julian, like, for *abandoning* you. I so would hate her for that.'

'She was sixteen, Jo. Five years younger than you. She was just a kid. She did what she thought was best. I was in a loving home. I wasn't abandoned in a bush. No. She was just a kid. You can't hate kids for not facing their responsibilities.'

'That's true,' I say.

'I didn't like that hate feeling. Not really. It tore me to bits. It was only when I was drinking I could get rid of it. And I couldn't. It's a waste of a life. I wonder whether I was angry because of her all along and finding out just made it worse.'

'As your granddad said –'

'– yeh, I know, Mr Therapist. I shall move on. Now if you two don't mind, I'd like to move into the land of Nod. My bonce is throbbing like I don't know what.'

'Can I stay here tonight, Julian? I'll be quiet,' Jo says.

'Are you going to read some of your stuff to me, Jo?'

'Is that what you want?' She asks

'Yeh. From your second book, please. That one with the pink cover.'

'I'll go fetch it,' she says. 'You like that one, huh?'

'Totally,' he replies, smiling. He winks at me, and I take that as my cue to leave.

There are so many questions unanswered here.

So many questions I want to ask, but I think I know the answers to most of them, so I don't ask him. At least right now, with his head hurting and the company of a beautiful young girl reading him to sleep. Lucky man! There was only one person who could categorically answer the questions I wanted answering so I walk back down the stairs and sit next to Cat. She is tired – and in my night porter's seat – but she wants to know everything about the ceremony so I sit, and I tell her everything I know, while I wait for the one person to come home who can answer the questions I need answering.

I don't have to wait long.

Mommy, Dearest

In her room.

'Of course, I knew he was my son,' she says.

I am consistently in awe of her ability to drink and retain in control. You would scarcely know she'd been on the bottle since seven in the evening, and it was now close to four in the morning. With a tired Cat porting downstairs, it left me free to complete the puzzle. Not that it mattered. I have always been curious.

This tryst had been planned, but now, this wasn't why I was here. I felt asexual toward her, even though she looked stunning as she lay on the bed, still in her black dress and sheer stockings, though the magnificent high heels she had been wearing earlier were now discarded, along with her gold earrings and accoutrements.

'But I didn't know until about a couple of months after he'd thrown a wobbler on me.'

'How did you find out?'

'Paul contacted me through my agent. Paul. That's his dad.'

'Okay.'

'We met up at Covent Garden and had tea. Ironic isn't it. I was going to meet my own son in the same place for an embarrassingly different purpose, and I end up meeting his father instead, a man I had not seen for thirty seven years.'

'Julian told me that you were…'

She interrupted me. 'Embarrassing, isn't it. Did you know that most incest cases involve members of the same family who don't know they are related? Many of those incidents are accidents.'

'I can imagine.'

'Fathers and daughters. Mothers and sons. Brothers and sisters. Estrangement. Dysfunctional family histories. Reunions. Very emotional things.'

'You two didn't seem very emotional these past two weeks.'

'I was. I was emotional. Think I drink like this all the time? Julian just hates me. Or hated me.'

I remembered Cat's memo. Much of it turned out to be right. Some of it turned out to be wrong. I don't say anything to her. 'He was pretty drunk most of it. Maybe he was feeling it.'

'It's a clinical case, isn't it. People deal with things like this in so many different ways. Julian has been foul. I guess he beat the emotion out of me.'

'You're both very similar.'

'Sorry?'

'Body shape. Facial shape. Eye colour. I missed it because of the dye.'

'Think so?'

'Lots of similarities. Intelligence. Wit. Social networking on the PC. You're both *writers*. And you both like a drink.'

'You should have worked it out earlier in that case.'

'I thought you and he were ex-lovers.'

Amy laughed. Started to roll up a cigarette. 'Nice one, Sherlock.'

'I'm just a night porter,' I say, laughing. 'I never considered the incest stats. That's interesting.'

'I must have considered the implications, at least subconsciously. I wrote about it in *Amelia.*'

'Yes, you did. Julian told me last week.'

'He called me a pervert online. It was only a subplot and no, the separated characters don't shag.'

'Anger. Julian was full of it.'

'And I don't blame him. I never have done.'

'He's not angry now. It's left him.'

'I can tell. Must have been the bang on the head,' she says, bitterly.

'Why do you think Paul told you about Julian?'

'To avoid confusion in the future, I think. Also because Julian blanked me and started the abuse. The author's circles we mix in are concentric and tight. Also, I think he wanted me to know. He wanted me to know who my son was. Thirty six years later.'

I am stirring sugar into my coffee and listening avidly. It would be four hours before the sun rose above Wheatley Fields, but outside, cars travelled to and fro, and stray revellers from various Ceremony parties wandered about in the bitter cold. It was still raining, off and on, but nothing like the time when she touched my hand the other night on the first floor. She lights her cigarette and this time, she doesn't go to the bathroom and starts putting the ash into a saucer. After all, she's leaving tomorrow.

'Was the meeting civil?'

'Cordial is a better word,' she replies, taking a deep draw on her cigarette. Clouds of silvered smoke circulate like the souls of ghosts above us. 'I went to school with Paul all the way from Primary to Secondary. He was my best friend, and he was my first love. I was scared to meet him, I was literally scared out of my wits – all the emotions, all the old stuff – but when we met, there was nothing there this time. I ought to have known better. I wrote about childhood sweethearts in a book called *Two Roses* a few years ago. A lot of river passes under the bridge. It was like talking to a stranger, which I guess, he was. There was no spark. We went walking along the Thames, and he told me about his life – Julian' life, that is. And, do you know, I cried.'

'That's understandable.'

'I cried my eyes out. I did, yes.' I hear her voice begin to tremble and it crumbles into dust.

She buries her head in her hands.

I am prepared, like the professional I am, and pass her paper serviettes I had brought with me from the bar. She wipes her nose.

'Will you hold me?'

Her brown eyes glisten. I am myself tonight. I am me and not a night porter, so I walk around the other side of the bed and lie next to her and hold her tight. She lays her head on my chest, and cries and cries onto my pristine white dress shirt, which is going to be ruined and discarded – mascara, the lightest of shadows, rouge – as it would take an industrial chemical cleaning option to eliminate the stains.

I don't care.

I stroke her shoulders and listen to her unburden.

'After Paul returned to the train station, I returned to Egham and began to compose a letter to my son. Paul didn't mind me doing so. There was no hatred there. I wouldn't have blamed him for hating me, but in the end, I was the one who lost a son and lost out on an entire life. Paul's much brighter than Julian and I put together – he knew I had lost things that I can never recover. I never had kids. Did you know that?'

'I didn't, no.'

'It was too painful. I devoted my life to writing novels. They're my kids, my displaced surrogate kids.'

I hold her a little tighter. She rests her stockinged leg on my thigh. 'How many people know about this?' I ask.

'Very few. You. Julian. Paul – Paul's family – and me. I assume you told Jo. I told Frank the other night. The Major doesn't know. None of my fans or readers, not that *that* matters. Just six or seven people.'

'Julian could have made a massive scene tonight.'

Amy lifts up her head. 'No publisher in the world would have used it, love.'

'I'm sorry?'

'If I submitted a gr*and guignol J'accuse* ending like that – you know, YOU ARE MY MOTHER type thing, at the moment of my great triumph, with Victorian villains and hard-done-to orphans, my publisher would have kicked me off the contract. It's so *old.* Julian is as sharp as a razor. He probably wanted to out me. He probably wrote an outing ending in his head, but, in the end, petal, he writes *contemporary* fiction. He writes about the way people are. He writes about the way we behave. No fantasy –'

'– no talking goblins.'

'You got it. Julian taught you well. Outing me in the amphitheatre would have made him look something of a nana, wouldn't it.'

I think about it for a bit. I remember seeing Julian staring at the back of the ceremony. How would I have ended it, there, in the heat and the anticipation.[73] In the end, I would have done what he did. It was human. It was entirely logical.

'Yes, it would. So why did you turn down his peace offer?'

Turning round, she reaches for an olive and now I know she's playing at being a writer. She takes two. One she holds above my lips. I take it. It tastes meaty and bitter. I watch her eat hers, and the way she eats is erotic, rolling her lips and tongue over the green orb before consuming it. 'You ought to have seen the things he said about me online. You *heard* what he said about me on Monday night. I am STILL furious with him for THAT...'

'He's apologetic.'

'He can stew for a bit longer, the lad. I'm only human. He HURT me. Don't you know that? Can't you see it? Can you imagine how I felt? I know I shouldn't have abandoned him, but he didn't *suffer.* I didn't *beat* him. I didn't *abuse* him. And some things he said...my, oh, my...'

Amy starts to cry again and this time turns away from me. I prop myself on my elbow and stroke her bare back.

'He was angry, like I said...'

'There are limits, sweetness. Limits,' Amy says, amidst the snuffles. 'To anyone's endurance.

When it came to the written insult, Julian was Satan, so I understood why she walked away. I let her cry and sniffle for a bit, and she lets me spoon her.

'I thought of something tonight.'

'That must have made your brain hurt,' she replies, humour amidst the tears.

---

[73] He could have pulled out a sniper rifle. He could have held the entire ceremony at gunpoint. He could have run up to the stage and kidnapped Brian Bolus and announced the presence of a bomb. How would you have ended it?

'Did you pay for Julian to stay here for the extra two weeks?'

'Clever boy.'

'Why – if you don't mind me asking, that is.'

She turns round. 'Hasn't he told you?'

'No.'

'No. I don't suppose he would. How I did it is a secret – and bloody complicated! – not so much the paying for it, but hiding my involvement. That was the tricky part. He would have laughed in my face if I offered.'

'I don't understand. Arkwright paid for two weeks, even yours.'

'It was nothing to do with the ceremony,' she says, quietly, not looking at me. 'I paid for him to stay an extra two weeks because he's homeless...'

'What?'

'Bloke can't look after himself at all. Got behind in his rent, and they served an eviction notice on him six weeks ago. We all pee in the same pot, us authors, and purely by chance. I got to hear about it. Julian told a buddy of mine on the net – a vampire writer named Emma Edwards – one night after a session on the ale, and she told me in strict confidence.'

'Strict confidence?'

'You know what us women are like, sweetness.'

I grinned. 'Yep, I do.'

'If a woman sleeps with a new bloke, her bestie knows within the hour. In strict confidence, of course.'

'But of course.'

'I was told this shortly after he accused me of plagiarism. Apparently, there is an Indie author who wrote a book very similar to *Amelia* a year before mine. Julian wrote a long post on The Wizard's Court.'

'The author's group? He mentioned that.'

She nods. 'In the post, he called me a cheat and a liar as well as the world's worst author ever. He said I made Barbara Cartland look like Muriel Spark.'

I suppress a mild snigger and turn it into the blankest of faces. 'That's harsh.'

'*Amy Cook has to plagiarise vulnerable, low-selling Independent authors in order to write a novel worthy of attention, because she isn't capable of anything else. She is nothing more than an illiterate thief. Illiterate Estonian book pirates have a stronger moral framework when it comes to writing.*'

'Ouch.'

'It was possibly the worst attack ever. The group – about thirty, forty members – went mad. It was horrible. One bloke, a good friend of mine who writes historical fiction thrillers, bless him, offered to fight Julian anywhere in the country.'

'Who says the spirit of gallantry is dead.'

'I calmed it down, but no one will ever speak to Julian again. The accusation is utter nonsense – luckily our group is inaccessible to the general reader, and my lawyers hit him hard almost immediately. So he shut up and withdrew his post. Of course, members of the group spread the word, but it became all just trolling and rumours, so no damage was done. Even the author of the Indie book, Kandice Du Tourney, contacted me, and said the accusation was unfounded. That kind of tittle-tattle is fatal for a writer and a massive taboo. *You just do not say things like that*. Even though it was my son, and he didn't know that I knew of our relationship, I was furious. The Moderators of The Court asked if I wanted to have him banned – again, I might add – and I said I'd think about it. He was *persona non grata* by the end of the day, anyway. He'd gone, had Julian. His hatred of me, his detestation of any author apart from himself, any *successful* author, his colossal drinking and his relative failure, it all combined. Then, I found out he was about to be made homeless…'

'You must have been conflicted.'

'Not really. He's my son. I got to work.'

'They banned him still?'

She laughed. 'He could be my son from a distance. I didn't have to be anywhere *near* him. But I could do something motherly.'

'And he doesn't know?'

'Absolutely not.'

'What does he do tomorrow. His stay ends.'

'I've just paid for another two weeks. Can't see my kid homeless. I just can't.'

I lay back on the pillow. 'This is complex. This is *really* complex.'

'Not anymore,' she says. 'I'm sure it'll get much simpler from now on.'

Isn't it funny how, like a crossword puzzle, once one clue is solved, another opens and is quickly solved. Before you know it, the puzzle is complete. A *gestalt*.

We lay there for a bit. It might look sexual, it might look as if the scene had emotional content, but it isn't. It's all about comfort – though I do say having her stockinged thigh draped over my crotch appeals to something *base* deep inside me – a side I quickly suppress. There seemed nothing left to say – except one thing, which occurred to me, another piece of the puzzle.

'You sent his book to *The Guardian*?'

'Gosh, you're clever. If you ever fancy leaving your job here, I'm always looking for a good PA. You can help me construct my plots.'

'Thanks.'

'I might try my hand at a Detective novel. Just like JK did.'

'Nothing like diversity.'

'Not with my readers, sweetness. *Amelia* sold half of my usual. I'm glad I won that –' she points to the glittering trophy on the sideboard '– as it will put a smile on my publisher's face again. And a few quid in his pocket, I don't doubt for a second.'

'Julian doesn't know, does he?'

'About *Amelia*'s sales?'

'No,' I grin, 'The Guardian. You.'

She leans over me. I sense something change. Her body softens and her leg travels higher, up to my belly. Eyes shine. Lips redden. Her fingertips touch my face. 'And you're not going to tell him. Now, that's enough talk. Kiss me.'

I do so.

For the first time tonight, her essence rises…

Departure

'You ever seen a film called *Welcome to Blood City*?' Julian says to me.

9pm. Tuesday night. The hotel is quiet. Three locals discuss real ale in the bar. Gavin has closed the restaurant and gone home for the night. Most of the hotel guests had gone home, including all the authors and Mary Beth. Julian sits with me on the big armchair.[74]

'No, I must have missed that one,' I reply. 'Any good?'

The authors were allowed to go home on Sunday because Julian had decided not to press charges. The Police threatened to go ahead with it themselves, but in the end, as far as they were concerned, the case was closed. The Crown Prosecution Service had no objections, perhaps because of the labyrinthine mysteries inherent in it. They couldn't agree to a charge. Was it attempted murder? Was it aggravated burglary? Assault? What was it? Julian refused to have anything to do with it, and they lost the lot. I suspect they would have wanted to pull Frank in, but I still don't think he did it.[75] [76]

'It's brilliant. It really is. It's a clever Western, a Canadian film. You know what them nutters are like when it comes to films. Madmen, the lot of them.'

---

[74]Somehow, he had managed to get out of going back to hospital. 'I come from a family of stubborn people with thick heads,' he says. 'Some beer and a family-sized tube of Tramadol, and I'll be sound.'

[75]Can't be bolloxed,' he said. Besides, I deserve it. I was an arsehole that night.'

[76]What about you? Who did it? Answers on a postcard, please.

'I've not seen many Canadian films,' I say. 'At least nothing conspicuously Canadian.'

'Cronenburg.'

'Yes?'

'He's Canadian.'

'Did he direct *Blood City*?'

'No, he didn't,' he says, with a hint of irritation. 'He directed *Shivers* and *The Fly*.'

Once the ceremony was over, there was no reason for any of them to stay. Trains, planes and automobiles were ready and waiting for them, as were families and loved ones. Their own beds. Two weeks on a hotel bed, even ones as good as ours, can be tough work. Still, I would have loved them to stay for one more night. I had grown fond of them, and I had never experienced a psychic connection before, like last night, just before Amy won Best Writer.

'So what's it about?' I ask.

'It's about fantasy and reality,' Julian replies. 'The supremacy of one over the other.'

'Sounds good,' I say, fiddling with a pen.

Jo's plane left Heathrow for LA at midnight. Frank's plane left for Chicago from Manchester and Mary Beth, who was the first to go, was staying in London for three nights reporting to the Trust on the event, which had been, so far, universally hailed a success.

Typically, she remained at the Theatre until very late and supervised the early stages of the clearance. She visited the Trust party for a cocktail and returned to The Saladin. Cat told me later that she was still on the phone at 5am in the morning, chivvying, reporting, administering, doing her thing. She never stopped, and I guess she never will. She lived to work, just like I did, a million years ago.

'Did you enjoy yourself last night?' She asked, as her cases were being carried to the door by her driver, an employee of the security company she had hired last night, at the last minute, for an obviously tidy sum.

'I've enjoyed the whole fortnight,' I replied. For once, she was casual, wearing blue jeans and an *I Love NY* tee shirt. A woman like Mary Beth could never carry off the casual look though – in her hand, her organiser and iPhone, and I knew they were both going to get plenty of bash on the M1 down to London.

'You've been immense,' she said, leaning over to give me a hug. 'I covet the way you relate to people. You've looked after the gang unbelievably well. If you ever need anything...'she passed me her business card, '...or ever find yourself in New York looking for a job, look me up.'

'Thank you, ma'am. I appreciate that.'

'You're a real professional. World needs those. Take care and if not before, I might see you in two years.'

'Yes. You might just, at that.'

I watched the Range Rover drive away down Eastgate and I felt sad.

'Jack Palance is in it.'

'Is he?'

'The gunfighter from *Shane*.'

'Not seen that either,' I say.

'*Pick up the Gun.* You know.' He feigns the hard dark accent, and points his finger at me as if he is about to shoot an imaginary pistol. '*Pick. Up. The. Gun.* Classic moment in cinema.'

'Must have missed that.'

'Yeh, he's in *Blood City*. He's the big bad gunfighter. He got typecast, in the end.' Julian says, sipping his energy drink. 'Sad. Great actor.'

Frank Duke left without saying goodbye to me. I didn't expect any tears or emotion from him, nor did I expect a handshake. He was just passing through. Jo was nice to him, and Hayley shed a tear for him – apparently the two got on really well in passing on the daytime shift. He and Amy embraced on the front entrance as the taxi came, and I felt a little pang of jealousy. After what she told me last night, I wasn't as envious as I usually was, when I had seen them together. Frank looked every inch the English gentleman in his pinstripe suit and the raincoat. He seemed happier now he was going home and more contented. Lucy from the Benbow came over to say goodbye to him and have her books signed, something he was glad to do. He waved goodbye, an ostentatious salute, not just to the people gathering in the hotel, but to the *hotel* itself, looking up at the magnificent sign outside, of Wise Old Saladin, with his Wise Old Eyes. Into the back of a Hansom Cab called from The City, the Chicagoan Thriller Author was gone. In many ways, her news wasn't a surprise, but I am sworn to secrecy, and I am a man who believes in the strictest confidence, in the dictionary definition of the word.

Naturally, Frank never said goodbye to Julian.

Did Frank try to kill him that night? I didn't think so, but I can see how others did. We will never know. Even if Julian does – and I suspect he knows more, *much* more than he is letting on – he would never say. One thing's for sure: I don't think the two of them will be swapping Christmas e-cards.

'So what is it about?' I ask, curious.

He's reading a paper and acting the goat again, messing me about. 'I've just told you.'

'No, Julian. What is it *about?* i.e. What happens in it?'

'It's great. A geezer finds himself in a western town with only a pistol and a pair of long johns. The town is full of gunfighters, and it becomes apparent, after he's shot at, that the town is a big game where you get ranking points for killing other gunfighters. Our Hero, this geezer with the long johns, after working out what he has to do, proves pretty good at the game and works his way up the rankings by shooting everyone in sight. He becomes a top gunslinger, bar room brawler, Sheriff, etc. He bonks the best looking women in the saloon and eventually, it comes to pass, that he has to fight The Bad Guy. Jack Palance. Gunfight in *Blood City*.'

'A bit like *Westworld*?'

'Have you seen that?' He looks at me quizzically.

'I have, yes.'

He laughed. 'Yes, Mr Porter, it is indeed a bit like *Westworld*. Only more so…'

I took Jo's many bags to the waiting taxi and came back. She hugged me, and I think I will remember her hug forever. The brief moment where our cheeks met. Her perfume, her sheer American freshness.

'I'm so going to miss you,' she said. 'I've had amazing fun.'

'It's been great, hasn't it?'

'You're welcome anytime over at my place,' she said, dabbing a tear, which moistened her brown eyes.

'I'm sure your mum and dad will love that,' I replied.

'Hey! I'm moving out when I get home. God, it's about time.'

'I'll sleep on your sofa.'

'You and Julian can share it,' she said, laughing. 'I'll buy a large.'

'Sleeping bag in my suitcase,' I said.

'You're such fun.'

We exchanged contact details, and I left her to Julian, who was standing awkwardly by the door.

Their parting was sorrowful. Julian went upstairs, and I didn't see him until several hours later and, by that point, he was very, very subdued.

'Spoiler alert.'
'What is?'
'Do you want to know the ending?'
'Of *Blood City*?'
'No, of bloody *East Enders*!' He said, frustrated.
'Sorry, I'm far away.'
He looked away and picked up his phone. 'I won't tell you.'
'Oh, don't be so mardy, Julian. Tell me the ending.'

I said goodbye to Amy in her room, but there were few words. We had said everything that needed to be said early Sunday morning in bed.

Later, there weren't many words we could say to each other amidst the tears (hers, I must say, though I was close). A night porter should be impervious to anything and have a heart of steel, but I nearly went, right at the end, but we did arrange to meet in Covent Garden in three weeks, so that was okay.

That took the edge off. [77]

I didn't know where all this would go and I certainly didn't plan to tell Julian any time soon. It was probably going to be one of those holiday romances.

Yet. There is a *lot* of chemistry between us. It's too close to call. What would Ladbrokes say? How can I ask my betting advisor? The liaison between Amy and I was an unpredictable event, but we just clicked. It just occurred. I didn't know it was going to happen between us. I didn't predict it, or manipulate it. It just came into being and if I do eventually, in a parallel world, in a parallel universe, become Julian's stepdad, I'll cross that bridge when I come to it.

---

[77] Typical writer. She'd only suggested a meeting at the same place she was planning to meet Julian and where she met Paul, Julian's dad.

Besides, how *would* he feel?

How?

Hey.

Something like that is the subject of another story, isn't it. Not this one.

'I won't tell you precisely. You might want to see it, though the DVD is impossible to find. In the end, the hero has a final choice to make. To return to grim reality or to stay trapped in an ephemeral fantasy world that isn't real in any shape or form, but is *way* more exciting. I love the film, Mr Porter. It is indeed magnificent.'

Oh.

And Amy visited Julian in his room before she left. Neither discussed the emotional *content* of the reunion. But she did shake his hand, and they've arranged to meet up, but that's all I know. Julian isn't saying. He's gone all Trappist Monk on me on that subject.

I remember Sunday, about four. I watched her get into her taxi. She wore jeans and a dark blue puffa jacket. Underneath her Inuit hunting cap, her hair had been dyed once more – this time jet black with flashes of burgundy in horizontal strips. I don't know where she found the time to do that on leaving day. She waved to me and later, when I was back at work, I got an e-mail from her, sent from The Chocolate and Coffee Company at St Pancras Station. It was lovely and it made my stomach go a bit topsy-turvy, something which, as a professional night porter, I had to suppress.

I also decided to help Julian with his issue.

His slight issue. You know the one.

His slight issue with *accommodation*.

He's far too proud to take extended charity from his estranged mother, so the way I saw it, he had two weeks.

We had two weeks.

It was time for The Night Porter to go into action.

I know he had been an arse. A complete arse and I can understand you wondering why I don't just let him rot, but he became a friend. I don't have many. Night porters don't, you know. You can't choose your friends any more than you can choose your family: It's a myth. And he's fun. He sat in the armchair with four cans of Mad Bull and not a drop of alcohol in sight, and do you know what? He never mentioned to me that he was homeless and had nowhere to go. He would have just left and disappeared into the ether. I couldn't let that happen. I decided to kill two birds with one stone.

So, on the Monday afternoon, yesterday, the day after the authors left, I went to the bank and withdrew £220, which was most of what I had remaining until I picked up my winnings from the bookmakers at the weekend, Wheatley Fields being a complete bookie-free zone. I put the money in my pocket and went back to the hotel. I waited for Martin Sixsmith to come to work, which he did. I greeted him warmly, and tried to be nice. As expected, he completely ignored me. I chatted to him in the staff room about Ian Poulter, Jose Mourinho and Gina Faulconbridge (the latest *Zoo* sensation) until he changed and disappeared to his bar. He always hung his parka on the hook behind the staff room door (The King Of The Pride), and tonight was no different. When he had left the room, I swiftly slid the money into the inside pocket of his parka and zipped it up. An hour or so later, using a spare key Cat entrusted me with, I entered her office and located the float in the (open) top drawer of her filing cabinet. I knew it was there, because, before a formal invoice arrangement with the off-licence had been agreed, I used to pay for the things we needed in emergency from that float. Again, I had a spare key to the tin – I am the night porter, and I may need actual cash in emergencies, and I may not have sufficient on me. Essentially, I am the night *manager,* and Cat recognised that. She trusted me. I knew precisely how much money was in the float because I had checked the night Sixsmith laid into me, straight after, my plan fermenting and bubbling even then, as I mentioned, and unless Cat had spent any in the interim, I knew there were eleven purple notes in there, cashpoint stiff.

Wearing surgical gloves, I opened the float and lo and behold, the notes were present. I removed them, carefully placing them inside a sheet of 100gm A4 paper, then inside an envelope I had typed earlier, addressed to Nick in Durham, at *The Bison*.

I left everything (except the money) as I found it. Luckily for me, Sixsmith and Gavin were nattering like fishwives and the hotel was virtually empty. No one saw me leave the hotel and post the letter in the Post Office box fifty metres up the road. It took no more than thirty seconds and in the gathering gloom, I was a ghost.

Later, when the Monday night guests began to book in, I disabled the desk PC, making a big fuss of it, a loud fuss. It was simple to wipe out the PC, a simple trick. There was no reviving it that night. It would need IT support from head office, and guests needed to be booked in. Stressed and upset, I called Martin and said I needed the physical room booking sheets, which were in Cat's office. The bar was empty and there was a queue at my workstation: As much as he wanted to, he could not turn me down for assistance when I gave him the spare key to her office, and asked him to bring me those sheets.

So he did.

Ten people saw him go in there, including Gavin, but I was even luckier – he shut the door.

I know Martin Sixsmith.

I know him of old. Not only would he want to upset me, make me even more stressed, he would want a good root round. Curiosity would get the better of him, and he'd have a good ruffle through Cat's drawers. So he spent five minutes in there and when he returned, he threw the booking printouts on the desk along with the key with utter contempt.

I left them there, careful not to touch them.

When the hotel became quieter, I went back inside Cat's office and removed the float tin. Put it on top of the filing cabinet. I didn't open it. Left it there, as if someone had forgotten to put it away by accident, in a hurry.

I returned to my desk and contacted Julian, asked him to come downstairs. That phone of his. I asked him whether I could borrow it for five minutes.

Willingly, he said.

I disappeared to the loo and sent a text to Cat.

Hello. I think there's sumut cracking off in t'hotel, Catriona. Someone is abaht to ey a shit in the top drawer of your office and it ain't a 'Cat', as it were. Luv, your 'ansom admirer.

I cleared the message from his cache, or at least thought I had done, and handed back the phone. I got a call on the hotel line within the minute. Cat. She asked whether someone had been in her office. I said yes, Martin. She asked why. I told her why. She put the phone down quickly, and I knew she would be here in ten minutes.

When she arrived, in her red tracksuit and white trainers, her hair in a bun again, a gym look, a bit "glowy", she ignored me and went straight into her office...

I knew the procedure from there.
Of *course,* I did.

She immediately called the Police.
Management are entitled – legally – to search coats and lockers.

Cat did so, with a witness.

Which just happened to be me.

She searched me. Raincoat. Locker. I emptied my pockets. Told her what I saw, and confirmed I would write a statement.

She called Gavin. Asked the right questions. Asked for permission for a search. Searched his coat, his bag, and his locker. Asked him to empty his pockets.

He did so, without fuss.

He would do, wouldn't he.

Kerry. No fuss at all.

Then Martin.

He happily granted permission for everything with a big grin on his chubby rural cheeks, his Countryside Alliance beam.

No fuss at all.

If he was an ice cream cornet, Martin would have licked himself to the wafer in five seconds flat.

Course, you can, Cat.
I've got nowt to hide, ducky.
Nowt at all.

You should have seen Martin's face when Cat discovered the £220 in crisp purple notes in his parka pocket.

Really, you should have seen it.

A face, which became even more comical, even more *understandable,* with the Police coming through the door at the same time as he lunged at me, with very real intent to kill...

After, in her office, Cat, stressed, harassed, worried, head in hands, upset, sat opposite me and wondered where she was going to get a Bar Manager from. *She* couldn't do it. She was harassed, and overworked, and had personal issues. Kerry was young. The agency only dealt with chefs, and it would take three or four days for them to find a replacement. Then there was the money, *the float, the planning, the rotas, the stock, trust, the weddings booked for next week, the, the, the...*

Luckily, I had a suggestion.

A clever suggestion.

One which she listened to, at first with a face full of cynicism, then full of outright laughter, then total rejection. And then, after I had finished, that elfin face had a thoughtful look upon it.

And that's how the now teetotal Julian Green came to be the temporary[78] live-in Bar Manager[79] [80] of The Saladin Inn, Wheatley Fields.

And me?

Well...

---

[78]'I'll help you out, mate', he said. 'But I'm a writer. That's my main job. That's my life! This would be just temporary, right?'

[79]Martin avoided prison on condition he never came within a hundred metres of The Saladin or any of its staff. His sentence was suspended for a year. I even predicted that, too, what, with Stephanie and the new baby to look after, though I heard on the grapevine she kicked him out and went to live in Charlestown with a bloke who works at the Post Office. I think Martin is unemployed at the moment, unfortunately.

[80]He must have seen the text in his Outbox, but he never said anything to me. I think he was grateful.

...let's face it, everyone's writing a book these days, aren't they?[81]

---

[81]'You're not going to finish with an epilogue, are you?'
'Why not?'
'It's out of fashion. You may as well go out and buy flares.'
'Who says it's out of fashion?'
'The GURUS?'
'Who?'
'The people who teach creative writing. Internet critique group leaders. Goodreads commentators.'
'There are people who teach creative writing? *Really?*'
'One can study a Masters in the subject.'
'Woosh.'
'Can you imagine Charles Bukowski studying for a degree in Creative Writing? He wouldn't even *speak* to other writers. He was horrible, truly horrible, to other poets.'
'Like someone else I know.'
'That's the old Julian. I've turned over a new leaf. I'm a nice guy now. Oh, and go through your MS and get rid of any adverbs.'
'What?'
'Seriously unfashionable.'
'Adverbs?'
'Slowly. Gingerly. Rapidly. Enjoyably. Kill them all. Go on, use your find and replace function and destroy.'
'Who says?'
'Same people. Creative Writing Gurus. I blame Palahniuk.'
'Who?'
'Where have you been living? Under a stone? Writer of *Fight Club*. Popularised all the above and also Kitchen Critique Groups.'
'Which is?'
'You write a paragraph, page or chapter – or theoretically even a line – and put it forward to your group happily awaiting your work around the kitchen table.'
'That sounds like writing by consensus?'
'It does, doesn't it.'
'What about singular authorial vision? The writer as *auteur*. What about the inner voice. You keep going on about those.'
'Seriously unfashionable. I mean, jeez. Bell bottom trousers are trendier than the singular authorial vision.'
'I don't want to show this to anyone except you.'

'Then don't, Mr Porter. That's the wonderful thing about Independent writing.'

'What is?'

'With a Spark and Tarzan, you can do what the crispy duck you wish, chap, and let the devil takes the hindmost.'

'Does he?'

'Does he what?'

'Take the hindmost?'

'Generally, so I'm told.'

'What about the tense switches? Will they confuse the reader?'

'Love them. Mr Porter, I think you've got real talent.'

'Really?'

'Well. Apart from your relationship with my mother…'

'We've discussed this, Julian.'

'It ain't over yet. Discussions are continuing.'

'Julian, it's –'

'– and you get Frank all wrong. He's a *badass.*'

'But he's…'

'Careful. Solicitors…'

'Okay. What about all the footnotes?'

'You kidding? You ever read '*House of Leaves*'? David Foster Wallace? Cutting edge, chap. Parallel narratives, monologue displacement, additional information, which doesn't interrupt the flow of the narrative. You're on a winner, meowd.'

'I think it's odd.'

'Just give me the manuscript now. You're getting nervous.'

'Am I?'

'Spend an excessive amount of time looking at a novel you've written, and you think it's a pile of dross. It's a psychological condition, which can only be cured by an editor, i.e. me.'

'Oh. Thanks. I think.'

'When I've got rid of the punctuation errors, the spelling disasters, the tense complications, the occasional blasts of self-indulgent purple prose –'

'– but I like purple prose.'

'Fashionable as fondue. The modern reader likes it *dry*.'

'Not purple?'

'Apparently not. I'll send it to my cover designer in Arizona. I *love* Arizona. After all the rain, I'd be off next week, if –'

'– Julian, no exposition. *Seriously* unfashionable.'

'Exactly! Winklepickers and Brylcreem, Mr Night Porter.'

About The Author

Mark Barry is the author of many works of fiction including the cult football hooligan novel, *Ultra Violence,* the seriously reviewed, dark and harrowing romance, *Carla,* and the feel-good thriller, *Hollywood Shakedown.*

He lives in Nottinghamshire and has one son, Matthew, who, so far, shows no sign of following in his father's literary footsteps – though he does fanatically support Notts County (which is a *much* more important trait).

Mark is also the proprietor of Green Wizard Publishing, a company dedicated to publishing cutting-edge, innovative, and accessible fiction firmly based in reality.

The majority of his books are set in either Southwell ("Wheatley Fields") or Nottingham ("The City"). It is a proud boast that local people who have read his novels can follow the trail of the quirky characters they encounter inside the jacket covers.

Printed in Great Britain
by Amazon